TWELVE ALIVE

by
R. Stanley

authorHOUSE®

AuthorHouse™
1663 Liberty Drive, Suite 200
Bloomington, IN 47403
www.authorhouse.com
Phone: 1-800-839-8640

First published by AuthorHouse 4/21/2009

ISBN: 978-1-4343-0622-7 (sc)

Printed in the United States of America
Bloomington, Indiana

This book is printed on acid-free paper.

SYNOPSIS OF TWELVE ALIVE

This story is a collection of things that I've experienced within my lifetime, such as Vietnam, racial indifference, the removal of "amen" at the end of the pledge of allegiance, the return of POWs from Vietnam, and the persecution of Americans all about this world.

This story is a collection of my daydreams, bits and pieces of stories I've read, and movies I've seen such as the use of a PT boat, from the movie PT 109 about President John F. Kennedy. In fact, I mention President Kennedy and his PT boat in this story.

The idea of these POWs is derived From W.W. II and the Vietnam Era. The search aircraft and search patterns are based in part on the movie *Mid-Way.* I used an aircraft carrier for two reasons. One reason is due to its great versatility. The second reason is that my story in part takes place in Vietnam and the carrier I named actually had a duty station off the coast of Vietnam.

The Russian is from the cold war, as they can be merciless and uncaring or they can be warm and friendly. You will learn about a naive young man, who had two of his biggest dreams come true through the efforts of the one he loves and assistance from family members. One of his dreams is to marry his childhood sweetheart. The other is to attend the navel academy, Annapolis.

Religion is from my childhood having grown up in a religious Pentecostal home. As a rule I don't use foul language and I don't appreciate others using it around me. In this story you will see JW and James asking others not to use God's name in vain and to refrain from the use of foul language.

You will come to know man's inhumanity to man, and the struggles of the final twelve. You will see men die to save another, the ultimate gift of one man to another. With the help of God, you will see one man communicate with his wife as she ends up with a piece of tattered cloth from the rags he's wearing when she's more than 3,000 miles away.

You will learn that no matter how long a mother is separated from her child, she and she alone will recognize the child of her flesh.

I'm sure you will find this story interesting. As well, I hope you find it entertaining. With very few exceptions, this story is totally fictional.

CREDITS

Patricia A. Stanley
Sergeant; Galvan J. with the Department of Corrections
Anita J. Boulware; my mother in-law
Kathryn B. Stanley; my wife
Carol A Patton; my daughter
Chaplain Richard Baldwin
COII Rodriguez
Linda Patterson
Fanstory.com

My wife Patricia, now deceased, will always hold a very special place in my heart. She encouraged my writing and encouraged the purchasing of my first computer.

My daughter, Carol A. Patton, assisted in my early work in writing this novel. She helped me with spelling and grammar. This was in the very early years of writing this novel. I love you daughter!

Sergeant Galvan, as my shift commander, could see that I was struggling with my bad grammar and spelling. He decided to assist me in my dream. He took on the monumental task without hesitation. Sergeant Galvan accepted this as his personal challenge. Sergeant Galvan, I thank you for all your help.

My mother in-law, Anita, has been a long time inspiration. I have known her since I was 15 years old. Between Anita and her now late husband, I was encouraged to pursue other avenues of interest, such as the navy. Through Anita's love of gospel music along with her love of country music, I found a whole new world of meaning in music. Anita and her husband also had something I could never get out of my mind. They had a thirteen-year-old daughter (Kathryn Boulware), someone who never left my mind.

Kathryn B. Stanley (Boulware, Berg, Stamper) is now my wife for only three years. She sat many long hours alone in the living room watching her soaps while I sat in front of my computer writing and then re-writing *Twelve Alive*. Honey, I love you for all you're patience and understanding.

Chaplain R. Baldwin is a man I have known for about seven years. I've seen this man come into the prison to consol an inmate or inform them of something bad occurring in their family. Chaplain Baldwin was also a corrections officer for eight and a half years. As a corrections officer, I'm not allowed to inform an inmate of any family matters. This is left up to the Chaplin. This man has come in with a bad cold and a runny nose; he has come in on Christmas day more than once. Chaplin Baldwin assisted me with the prayer used in this short novel and approved my final entry.

COII Rodriguez is a fellow corrections officer I've worked with for five or so years. Rodriguez is called Rod by most all officers who know him and is quite the artist. He has multiple drawings of other officers and sergeants proudly displayed in the complex sergeant's office for all to view. While Rod and I were posted in complex medical, we were discussing my book. As I described the condition of the survivors, Rod drew the picture of James West that appears in this book.

Linda Patterson, a family member and teacher, assisted in the editing of the story. Linda has been teaching for over twenty years. She taught writing for eight years. She entered the picture in editing this novel just recently and quite by accident. I was talking to her son, my wife's cousin, and happened to mention I was looking for someone to edit my novel. He talked with his mother and then told me that she would consider editing. I sent her a copy of my novel, and she agreed to be my editor.

Fanstory.com: I found this site quite by accident while looking for a possible writing contest in which to test my writing skills. For a small fee, anyone can join. You can write short or long stories, and then post them on Fanstory.com for other members to view while giving their opinions.

Table of Contents

Chapter One
The Spring of 1967

It was still a bit too cool in the mornings, but by midday the weather was perfect. It was the time of the year when everyone could take off those heavy winter cloths. All the young men and women were able to see the changes that had taken place to each other over the long cold winter.

It was the time of year that trees started to bud and bloom, the flowers and grass in the yards started to grow, the birds started to sing, and the bees started to buzz. Other kinds of bird and bee activities started to happen, too. School was almost out and life started anew, much like the life cycle of a butterfly.

For some young men and women, this was a short break before college. For others, this was a brief break before starting some job where they would work for the rest of their lives. One young man from this small town would attend the academy in the state of Maryland on the Chesapeake Bay—Annapolis Naval Academy.

It was early Saturday morning and JW was putting the final touches on his mother's car after washing his own '49 Chevy pickup. Let's face it, if you washed your mom's car without being asked, it could help out in the favor department, and JW was looking for a favor!

While JW was washing the car, some of his friends came by. They were talking about what they had in mind for the day. Some of them were going to see a movie with their girlfriends while others were going to see friends. Two of his friends were preparing to start their summer jobs. It seemed none of the usual group was going to the rope, the favorite hang out spot of the town. JW thought this was strange because the weather was perfect for the rope.

JW, John Fredrick Walker to everyone but his friends who knew him best, told his friends he had completed his yard work the night before. Washing the car was the last thing he needed to do before going to the rope unless his dad had something else for him to do. His dad did that sometimes.

After his friends all left and he finished washing his mom's car, JW put away the hose, the bucket, and washrags. It was time to go in the house to test drive his favor.

JW entered the kitchen where he was sure his mother would be. On the table sat a picnic basket. His mother was at the kitchen counter making sandwiches and putting other picnic foods in small containers.

JW started to ask his mom about the basket. Before he could get a word out, she spoke up, "JW, go get in the shower while I finish the rest of this basket!"

"Thanks, Mom," JW replied, as he turned to go take his shower. On the way to his room to get his clothes and bath towel, JW marveled at the way his mother always seemed to know what he wanted without a word between them.

While taking his shower, JW was thinking about where he would be spending the day. In his mind he was thinking about a ten-foot deep pool that was overcast by a very large oak tree. From this tree grew a thick branch that shot out over the pool, and from this large branch hung a long rope. The rope was about one inch thick.

In the heat of the summer this was said to be one of the coolest places in the state. Some local folks said the governor stopped here sometimes late at night. Others said the governor's life started here some fifty plus years ago on a warm summer night.

Well, this was where JW wanted to go on this day, and he didn't want to go alone. He had in mind a fine young lady. This wasn't just any young lady. To JW, she was God-sent. If she wasn't God-sent, then someone was in a very good mood when she was made. As far as JW was concerned, this young lady had everything in the right places-- places no man's hands had ever been. JW hoped that in time a small ring of gold would change that for him!

JW finished his shower, got dressed, and headed for the kitchen one more time. As he approached the kitchen, JW could hear his mom and dad. They were talking and laughing softly. Something about the sound made JW realize he really was not sure what to expect. When he entered the kitchen he saw his mother putting the food and refreshments in the basket. His dad was sitting at the table watching the action.

JW sat down at the table next to his dad. He noticed his dad hadn't looked at or spoken to him. This gave JW reason to think that maybe his dad had something for him to do. He had done things like that before. JW recalled one time his dad waited until JW had showered and then told him to change back into his work clothes. After changing once again, his dad started laughing and said,

"I've changed my mind, Boy! Put your glad rags back on, Son, I'm sure I can do the work my damn-self."

JW's dad turned to his wife and said, "You remember when you and I used to go to the rope? Damn, we had some good times then didn't we." He got up from his chair and moved behind his wife, putting his arms around her waist.

JW's mom replied, "We sure did, as you remember." She turned around in her husband's arms.

He whispered, "I love you, Woman."

She whispered back, "I love you, too. Oh, if only we were young again."

JW's dad picked up the basket with his left hand and tossed it to the table. He turned to his son and boomed, "Be gone, Boy, your mother and I have things to do."

JW decided not to give his dad the chance to change his mind. He took the basket and went out the door to his truck. As JW started up the '49 Chevy pickup, he looked back at his mom and dad's bedroom window. Seeing the blinds being pulled down, a big smile came to his face. JW's memory flashed back to when this would happen years ago. Nine months later a little brother arrived. Another episode brought a little sister into the world.

As JW drove down the street, he passed Mrs. West's house. She was the grandmother of a very good friend of his. James West was a clod-kicking dirt farmer who lived on the west side of the state. They had been friends as long as JW could remember.

JW looked towards the house as he drove by. He could see Mrs. West in the driveway and thought it looked as though she might have been crying as she was getting into her car. Although JW wondered about it, he had other things on his mind and continued driving down the street.

Turning onto Fairmont Street, his thoughts were all about a redhead he would be spending the day with and one day hoped to marry. As he turned into the drive of 1621 W. Fairmont, he could see a young boy, who was Karen's little brother. JW and he had gone fishing many times and always had a good time, but this time her brother ran into the house as soon as he saw JW's truck. This seemed odd to JW because Karen's little brother always asked to drive or at least sit in JW's truck.

JW parked, got out of his truck, and walked up to the front door where he rang the doorbell. He stood there for a long moment, thinking just how odd it seemed about Karen's little brother. Then the door opened.

The doorway was filled from top to bottom and from side to side with Karen's father. Now keep in mind that JW was not a small man, but Karen's father was one big Irishman. He had big hands, a grip like a steel vise, and a booming voice that could be heard all over town.

Mr. McIntosh bellowed, "What do you want?"

JW had a surprised look on his face because Mr. McIntosh knew JW was coming over to pick up Karen. JW and Mr. McIntosh had talked about this just the day before.

JW spoke up nervously, "Sir, I'm here to pick up Karen to have a picnic at the rope. Mr. McIntosh, don't you remember, Sir, we spoke about this yesterday?"

"Yes, I do remember, but just what are your intentions with my daughter? I damn sure don't want any little governor floating around my house. Get on in here! You and I got some talking to do!"

5

With a huge right hand well placed on JW's left shoulder, Mr. McIntosh effortlessly hauled JW into the house. JW could feel the power in Mr. McIntosh's hand but was completely dumfounded as to what was going on.

When they walked past the sitting room, JW could see Karen sitting there. All Karen could do was shrug her shoulders as if to say, "I don't know."

Passing through the house and entering into the kitchen, JW could see Mrs. McIntosh. There was a picnic basket sitting on the table, but JW was directed on out the back door to the porch without a chance to speak to Mrs. McIntosh.

Now this porch was something JW knew quite well, as he had helped build it. It was a covered porch with a built in barbeque that served the family and friends well on many evenings. JW was told to sit across from Mr. McIntosh, who sat with his back to the door. Mr. McIntosh bellowed, "Now tell me just what your intentions are with my daughter and mind you, they better be damn good or I might do something ugly to you, Boy!"

"Well, speak up! Or does the squirrel got your tongue?"

JW spoke up with confusion, "You mean does the cat got your tongue. That's how you're supposed to say it."

The expression on Mr. McIntosh's face changed from merely commanding to stern. As he squinted, his eyes that seemed to burn right through JW.

JW thought, "I've never before feared Mr. McIntosh and I don't fear him now. Well not much any way… However, I am concerned for his well being and maybe a little for mine!"

"Boy, you know what I'm talking about! You wanting to take my daughter to the rope, now you know the governor got his start there and he's a damn republican!" He slammed his hand down hard on the table, "I don't tolerate republicans in my house and I'll be dammed if I will have any little people running around my house that their mom and dad aren't married."

Now in a little higher voice than normal, JW again spoke up, "What about the sheriff, he's a republican? And he comes to your house all the time!"

Mr. McIntosh shouted, "You leave him out this! Besides he's married to my dim-witted sister! And I'll be dammed if I'm going to have any little people running around my house!"

JW was beginning to tire of the talk about babies. Taking on a very stern face of his own, JW told Mr. McIntosh, "You've no reason to speak of Karen and me like that! I've never done anything that would give you reason to even think like that! Now just what the hell is your problem?"

Mr. McIntosh placed both hands flat on the table with force and stood so quickly his chair slid back about two feet. As he leaned toward JW, the veins on his forehead bulged and his face turned red.

JW mirrored the actions and the expression but told himself, "Here comes the ass whipping I always never wanted." Like two raging bulls they stood facing each other, poised for battle. At no time did they lose eye contact.

Mr. McIntosh spoke between clenched teeth, "I'm about two shakes of a rabbit's butt from doing something ugly to you!"

JW took a deep breath and said, "I believe, **Sir!** The saying is 'two shakes of a lamb's tail'!" JW could see that statement didn't help, as he watched the anger welling up inside Mr. McIntosh.

Just then the back door opened. Without turning to look, Mr. McIntosh demanded, "Mary-Beth! Bring two beers and not that pussy ass light beer you drink, either!"

JW's view of the door was blocked by the sheer size of this big Irishman standing before him. The only way JW knew who was there, was a quick glimpse from around the edges of Mr. McIntosh. Mrs. McIntosh left and returned quickly with two beers, full power buds already opened. She set them down on the table and returned to the house without a word.

Mr. McIntosh ordered JW to sit down before he needed help to get off the ground and calmly said, "The beer will help settle your nerves. A young pup like you doesn't need or want to take on an old war horse like me!"

JW settled back in his chair and thought of what his dad had told him how a barking dog couldn't bite. JW's nerves started to settle but not before he reached for the beer. JW could see his hand shake a little and was sure Mr. McIntosh saw it as well. The taste of the beer in JW's mouth was bitter.

The back door opened again. JW couldn't see her face but could see the red hair and knew it was Karen.

Mr. McIntosh stated, "Karen, there's two men out here talking. Get your ass back in the house."

JW wanted so much to tell Karen to join him, but she was still Mr. McIntosh's daughter and always would be. It was right that she respect her father's wishes. Besides

JW hadn't yet asked her to marry him so it wasn't his place to tell her what to do. JW thought about the $60 he still owed on the ring set. Until the rings were paid for, he couldn't take liberties as though he and Karen were already engaged. As he sat talking with Mr. McIntosh, JW wasn't sure if he wanted to ask Karen to join him just to show he could control her or if it was to show he wasn't a man to trifle with. The longer the two men talked, the more relaxed JW became and realized his need for Karen to join them became less and less important.

After awhile Mr. McIntosh asked for two more beers. JW expressed that he thought the beer had such a bitter taste so early in the morning, and he wasn't used to drinking beer any way. Mr. McIntosh bowed to JW's wishes by closing his eyes and tilting his head slightly forward and to the left then reordering just one beer. JW felt the mood shift between himself and this intense older man.

After a few more minutes, JW turned to Mr. McIntosh and spoke honestly, "Sir, I want to spend the day with Karen. I really appreciate the time you and have spent together this morning, as it has been both provocative and informative. However, I want to spend the rest of the day with Karen, as she and I have a number of things to talk about."

They stood up, shook hands, and expressed niceties. Mr. McIntosh surprised JW saying, "You're the best thing to happen to this family in a long time."

JW then looked around the yard. There were stacks of folding chairs and tables. As long as JW has known Mr. McIntosh, which was a long time, JW knew he never put anything on the grass without a good reason. JW was thinking to himself, "Why all the chairs and tables? Are they having a party of some kind?" JW didn't remember any mention of a party when he had talked with Karen the day before and wondered if maybe he wasn't invited to whatever it was. The two men started walking into the house without discussing the chairs and tables. Mr. McIntosh mentioned that Karen should be good for about six or seven kids and not to let Karen tell him any different. JW had to shake his head at how the conversation had changed from when Mr. McIntosh has greeted him at the front door just a short time ago.

As the two men entered the house, JW saw Karen. She was dressed with her bathing suit under her clothes and was kind of bobbing her head as if to say, "Let's go!" JW was more than ready to leave the strange conversation behind and nodded his agreement.

As the two started for the front door, Mr. McIntosh picked up the basket from the table. He pointed to the basket with his right forefinger and in a low voice to his wife, asked, "Is the special package in there?" JW saw her nod her head, "Yes." Mr. McIntosh then tapped JW on the shoulder and said, "Here, you need to carry this. Nothing in there I need."

JW took the basket in hand and continued with Karen out the front door. He placed the basket in the back of his truck beside the one his mother made for them. JW smiled at the two baskets and knew they would have plenty to eat for the day ahead of them.

JW moved around to the front of the truck and opened the door for Karen. The doors on his truck opened and closed just fine so Karen could have opened her own door. JW just liked opening and closing the door for the one he loved. He decided it was just one of the many things he liked to do for Karen.

As the two of them drove off, JW could see in the mirror of his truck that Mr. and Mrs. McIntosh were talking on the porch. Later he would learn what they said to each other and would think back to the picture they made standing together.

What he learned was this. Mr. McIntosh said, "That boy is damn lucky I didn't kick his ass."

Mrs. McIntosh turned to enter the house as she told him, "I don't think that would have happened."

"What the hell are you talking there, Woman? Bring me a damn beer and shut the f--- up."

His wife responded with, "Sure now you're going to start drinking out front?"

"Drinking in the f------ front my ass, I want to watch the worms eat your G… dam flowers! Now get me my beer!" Mr. McIntosh then laughed his booming Irish laugh and put his arms around his wife.

Mrs. McIntosh smiled up at her husband's red face and walked into the house with his laughter ringing in her ears. She couldn't help but think about the day ahead for her daughter. If things worked out the way they all hoped, and with their diligently engineered scheme, her daughter would be smiling into the face of her own husband someday soon.

CHAPTER TWO
JAMES WEST

James was awoken by the voice of his mother calling up to him with a sense of urgency in her tone. He stretched and yawned while rubbing the sleep from his eyes. He could feel the presence of the gentle early summer morning in spite of the no-nonsense tone his mother was projecting his direction.

He could smell breakfast cooking, and with that he knew he had work needing to be done before he could eat. So out of his bed he jumped and donned his work clothes. While getting dressed, he could hear his mother talking, not so much to him but what she was saying was intended for him, "Sure would be nice to have fresh eggs and milk to go with breakfast!"

James ran down the stairs, a six foot, two hundred pound nineteen year old running at full speed down a narrow stair case with a small landing and a ninety degree turn at the bottom, then through a doorway measuring only five foot eleven inches. Yes, a few times it had been ugly.

This was one more time he arrived safely in the living room after negotiating the narrow stairway with the ninety-degree turn and the doorway designed for a Munchkin. As James hit the bottom step, his dad said, "One of these days, Boy, you're going right through that damn wall!"

James replied with a laugh, "Well, I could use a short cut to the back door anyway, Dad!"

Looking over the top of his newspaper, his dad replied back with, "Where you're going, Son, they won't tolerate any smart mouth, and I don't want to hear any more of it my damn self!

Without breaking stride, James rounded the corner and entered the kitchen. His oldest sister was just coming out of the bathroom. When she saw James, she got a big smile on her face and reached out with her left hand to touch her brother on the shoulder.

She spoke with a quiver in her voice, "You're so lucky."

James gave her a puzzled look as he hurried on by. He bent down to give his mother a kiss on her forehead and a quick hug. His little sister, Judy, started giggling and wrapped her arms around his waist as best she could while she looked up at him and said, "When I grow up, I want to be just like you."

James reached down and picked up the scrawny little brown haired girl. He knew it would make her giggle even more and told her, "You don't want to be like me. You want to be better than me." He gave her a quick little kiss on the lips, set her back down on the floor, and then walked to the back door. He grabbed the milk bucket and the egg basket as he ran out the back door to complete his morning chores.

His first stop was the chicken house where he gathered up all the eggs and then gave the chickens fresh water and feed. After setting the egg basket down in a safe place, James headed for the barn. With the milk bucket in hand, he could hear the cow mooing quite loudly, a reminder that he was running way behind schedule.

The shortest path to the barn was through the pigpen. Upon arriving at the pigpen, James heard the young pigs grunting loudly. As a rule, the pigs would rub up against his legs. They seemed to enjoy being scratched behind their ears and generally liked some attention. Today James was running late and ran through their pen without petting any of them. They showed their disappointment as they gave chase all the way to the barn.

Once in the barn, James set the milk bucket down and hurried up the ladder to the loft. He grabbed a bail of hay and broke it open. Dropping down two cakes of hay for the cow, he returned to the ladder and scurried down. He put two scoops of ground corn in the feeder box for the cow to eat while he milked her. Then he grabbed the milking stool and the bucket, sat down on the right side of the cow, placed the top of his head in her flanks just in front of her right rear leg, and began to milk her.

As he was milking, he started thinking about what was said to him by his dad and sisters, "Dad always tells me to watch my mouth, but he also said 'where you are going'. I wonder what he meant? And the oldest of my sisters telling me 'You're so lucky' with a voice almost crying like. And Judy, wanting to be just like me! What could this all mean?" James pondered this for the next few minutes while he had a moment to slow down.

After making sure he had gotten all the milk, James patted the cow on her rump. He placed the one legged stool back on the wall (not knowing the future, a stool later he would come to hate) and turned to feed and water the pigs. They still weren't very happy with James but were content to be fed.

Grabbing up the bucket of warm milk, James started for the house. He still needed to take a shower before breakfast. As late as he was, his sisters would have the shower tied up and would leave no hot water for their brother.

With that thought in mind, James remembered the eggs and hustled back to the hen house for the egg basket. One of the eggs fell out and broke. James smiled to himself and thought, "That one must belong to one of my sisters, Ha, Ha." He entered the house through the back door, set the eggs and milk on the counter, and dashed off to get what would probably be a cold shower.

James was in luck and managed to sneak into the bathroom before any one of his sisters could tie it up for a long time. It only took him about five minutes, which meant there would be hot water for the girls. He was drying off when the thought occurred to him that the women in his life said they didn't take a long time in the bathroom. James knew from experience that men both young and old learned the hard way that the women were wrong. He shivered at the thought of all the cold showers he'd taken over the years while learning that lesson.

By the time James had completed his shower, his mom was starting the gravy and potatoes. The West family was a big family, ten of them altogether when James's big brother, Jerry, was home. Jerry had joined the army and had gone missing in Vietnam, but that was three years ago.

The family didn't talk much about Jerry after the parents had received the letter from Uncle Sam. If anyone talked about Jerry, his mother would get so damned depressed that she would start using President Johnson's name in vain. Dad would get so angry, he would start using God's name in vain with statements like, "Send that G - - D- - - F- - - ing General Douglas Mac Arthur in there, or old blood and guts Patton and this damn Vietnam thing would be over!" or, "I did my part in WW II and Korea. Why in the hell does one of my sons have to pay?" So they didn't talk about Jerry at the table.

Now James's mother could make a breakfast that would put a king's cook to shame. Maybe that had something to do with why he was six feet tall and weighed two hundred pounds. James was one inch shorter than his dad, who was seven inches taller than James's mother. James sat down at the table, and his mom reminded him to wait for the rest of the family as she finished the final touches on the breakfast.

James went in the living room to help his dear old dad read the newspaper, knowing his father greatly disliked anyone trying to read his paper at the same time as he. James thought, "What the heck, I'm nineteen and he's forty nine, and I'm sure I can outrun him. And to a nineteen year old, forty-niners are like, way over the hill."

James's dad looked over the top of his paper as his son entered the room. With his head tilted forward, eyebrows raised and his eyes on James, he rolled his eyes to the left, let out a long breath, and went back to reading his paper. James nearly laughed as he imagined his father thinking, "Oh shit, here he comes again!"

James placed one hand on the arm of his dad's chair and his other hand on his own leg as he began reading. You see, James might be young but he was not stupid. He thought of his dad as old but knew he was not slow. James wanted to be ready to jump if his father made any sudden moves.

James was shocked when all his father did was drop one side of his paper, look James in the eye and calmly said, "If you think I'm going to chase you down before breakfast, you have another think coming. However, you might want to keep an eye out for me later!"

James was not too worried, as he knew old men took naps after eating. Besides the work he did was for other farmers. It wasn't too likely that James's father would chase him down at one of those places just to get even with James for reading the newspaper over his dad's shoulder.

If James could have seen the future, he would have known this would be a day and a breakfast he would remember for the rest of his life. For now, everything seemed just like a normal morning in the West home as James's mother called her family to eat. After all nine of the Wests gathered at the table, it was little sister Judy saying grace. The family sat down and began passing the food around. They had sausage and eggs with hash browns, biscuits and gravy, fried eggplant and sliced tomatoes. Last but not least, was the fresh milk and butter. Most of this breakfast came from their own garden and small farm.

Sitting at this table was a time to talk. It seemed that this was the most important time for the family, as it was one of the few times they were all together and could talk about anything. This included sex, even though in the 60's sex was considered a taboo. They could talk about almost anything with the only exception of talking about their oldest brother, Jerry.

The rotation of the table was counterclockwise starting with Dad, then the oldest child to the youngest, and ending with Mother. A space was always left for Jerry, and at no time did family or friend ever fill Jerry's space. Dad made sure of this.

Dad always said, "As long as a space is left open, there's a chance he may come home."

With breakfast started came some of the best conversation that anyone could want. However, this morning it seemed that Dad and Judy had worked something out. Judy was talking to James just to sidetrack him so his dear old dad could slap James on the backside of his head. James looked at his dad, who had a shit-eating grin on his face as he told James, "Well, you weren't talking with your mouth full." With his lips half closed and to one side, he said, "Hum, must have been something to do with the newspaper. What do you think, James?"

James had a big smile on his face, and kind of hung his head. What happened at the breakfast table was a once in a lifetime thing. It was a very good thing as they all had a part to play. The family must have all needed a good laugh, because never before had such a thing taken place at Mother's table, and it all started with a slap on the back of James' head.

James could hear his little sister's snicker change to a giggle. He turned his head to face her with his left eyebrow raised, which caused her to giggle all the more. Laughter is very contagious and can spread like wildfire. Well it did that morning! Even James's mom gave in with a laugh, along with his other five sisters and younger brother.

James's little sister had a giggle that would provoke laughter from a troll with a bad toothache! Before long they were all laughing harder and harder, with Judy giggling, Barbara laughing and milk jetting out her nose, and Jo coughing and spraying food all over their little brother. Little John laughed so hard he started farting. Mom was laughing so hard, she farted and made a wet spot that ran all the way to the floor. Dad laughed so hard his upper plate landed in the gravy bowl.

All of the West kids had laughed from time to time, and so had their mom and dad, but never this full, never this hard, especially at the table with all of them together. The last time they all laughed together was just before Jerry left for Vietnam. That was three years ago with no word from him in all this time. They all needed a good laugh, and God knows they had one. As all good things do, a good laugh and a good breakfast came to an end.

Knowing he needed to get going, James asked his mom if she needed him to help with the dishes. Just as he thought, she said, "No, Son, your sisters and I can do them. Thanks for asking. Do you need me to pack you a lunch?"

James replied, "No, I will be at Mr. and Mrs. Loveless's place by noon, and you know how she likes to cook for the people who work for her."

Then his mother asked, "Do you like her cooking more than mine?"

James replied, "Mom, you know I don't like cold food. Besides, I'm six feet tall and weigh 200 pounds. Now who wants to pack a lunch for someone like that?"

"Well, try not to be late, Son. Disney is on tonight at 7:30, and it's about that 'Morgan Horse' you said you wanted to see."

While his dad was still coughing from the laughter, James said, "I know, Mother, I should be home in time to help John with milking."

Still coughing, Dad said, "Son, your mother and I have something to tell you when you get home. And, Son, it's important."

James replied, "I will try, Dad, but I have a lot to do today."

James reached out with his big arms, picked up this wonderful woman he called mother, and gave her a big kiss on her cheek along with a big hug. Letting her gently back to the floor, he placed one hand on each side of her face and gave her a kiss on the forehead.

James's dad was still coughing from breakfast and looked a bit red in the face as he covered his mouth. James asked, "Are you okay?"

Still coughing, Dad nodded his head "yes" and waved for James to go on. So again, James hugged his mom. The hug he got in return felt so good. It was the kind of hug you can only get from your mother. One can get a hug from a dad, a sister, or even a brother. One can get a hug from a wife, but none will ever even come close to the hug a young man will receive from his mother. A mother can reach deep, deep inside and hug your very soul. That's the kind of hug James received from his mother. It was a hug that made him tremble to the bone.

As James looked her in the eyes, the thought crossed his mind to stay home. The thought was short and fleeting so he said, "See you later." He turned away and blew a kiss to his sisters and brother, and out the door he went. Could he have known then what was to happen later, he would have stayed home.

Closing the screen door behind him, James could hear his mother's voice rise in surprise. His legs were in gear and at full throttle so he didn't even slow down as he remembered all the times his dad was always grabbing and hugging and kissing on James's mom. From time to time she cried out, playing along. Maybe that was why there were eight West kids.

James ran down and through the garden and on through the pasture into the woods. He crossed over a water pipe that ran across the family property feeding the oil wells of their neighbor's property.

Just as James jumped over this water pipe, he was surprised when something hit the back of his head and then hit the ground behind him. It felt like his dear old dad's hand had felt earlier that morning at the breakfast table but somehow different. It gave James a chill like the hand of death. The feeling of death was a sensation James would become far too familiar with and know far too well later in his life. For now, it was strange and a little frightening as he looked around. When James heard a small sound that seemed to come from above him, he looked up at the lower branches of the large oak tree he was standing beneath. He saw a gray squirrel sitting on a branch with his front paws clasped together. He thought the little squirrel looked as though it was praying.

It had been years since James had a nightmare and his mom or dad had to come and save him. It had been years since he had even been afraid of the dark. Now he was a big man and told so by many he worked with. He had no reason to fear the dark or much else, but this "praying" squirrel scared the poop out of him in broad daylight. From the corner of his eye, he saw his dad and all his fears vanished as quickly as they had arose.

His dad said, "I thought you might want some company so I'm here to tag along."

James replied, "Are you sure you want to tag along with me with all I have to do and the places I have to go? Dad, I'm walking or running to all these places. Are you sure you want to tag along?"

"Yes, Son, I'm sure. You see, Son, there are things in your head you're not yet sure of, and we must try and cover them. And I need you to help your brother Jerry. And just so you know, Son, there will only be two more time that you and I will have a chance to speak before your death. Now, Son, let's get underway."

James was surprised to hear his dad speak Jerry's name without cussing. When his dad said, "Son, let's get underway" that was a term used by the Navy and his dad was in the army during WWII and then Korea. James knew the whole conversation was strange but thought, "Well, I'm just a young man, what do I know?" He and his father started off towards his first stop.

The first stop was Mr. and Mrs. Loveless's farm and ranch where James helped take care of stock cattle. His jobs included dehorning, inoculating, and castrating. James told his dad, "This will take up most of my day. And the chances of me getting hurt is better than not."

While walking, his dad said, "Son, you're a lot like me when I was your age. Now I need you to help Jerry."

James thought to himself, "Here's another strange statement about my brother Jerry." Down the dusty trail they walked, bumping shoulders every other step or so, and James was in the height of his glory. He was a young man walking and talking with his dad. In spite of the odd comments his father was making, James enjoyed the rare chance to be with his father without all the other West children around.

When they arrived at the Loveless farm, James found he was so late that he was relegated to cleaning stalls and feeding the stock. This might bother some people but James knew he was late and it was no one's fault but his own. He got the jobs that were left and was proud to work no matter what the job. His father had other ideas, "Son, go and talk to Mr. Loveless, you're better than this."

James turned to his dad and asked, "Would you not do the same for someone who showed up late for work?"

His dad shrugged his shoulders and replied, "I guess you're right, but Son, anything's better than doing this shit."

After about three hours James was finished. He approached Mr. Loveless and expressed the job was completed and he needed to leave if there was no other work to be done. Mr. Loveless reached out and shook James's hand, "I was just told late yesterday afternoon, and I wish you all the luck in the world." He went on to say, "I didn't have time to go to the bank, so please accept my apology for not having all your money. I've only $28.00 on me. I'll bring the rest to your house on Monday if that's cool? That's the new term you young kids use, isn't it?"

James chuckled a bit and said, "Yes, the new term is cool for OK and it's Ok with me." Then Mr. Loveless handed James the $28.00 dollars. Someone called Mr. Loveless to the phone and he walked away before James could say anything else. James was really wishing he had been able to ask Mr. Loveless what he had been told yesterday but guessed he'd find out eventually.

James started walking toward the next farm where he worked. With his father beside him, he brought up the conversation with Mr. Loveless, "Well that was strange what Mr. Loveless just said. Why would he be bringing the rest of my pay to the house? Like I'm going some place." He shook his head and told his dad, "I know I told Mom I would be eating at Mr. Loveless's place but I'm running late. By eating at Mrs. Johns's place, I will be back on schedule. And don't tell Mom about the food we will get at Mrs. Johns's!"

His dad agreed, "I can never tell her, Son."

On they walked for about forty-five minutes and talked the whole trip. They talked about Sara Beth and James getting married, and what James wanted for his life with Sara Beth, his place in the family and that he hoped to bring six kids into his mother and father's life, and that he wanted them to help Sara Beth and him to raise the kids just as his grandmother and grandfather had helped his parents.

Suddenly his father grabbed him by his forearms, looked in his eyes and said, "Son, don't wait, start your family now! Time is shorter than you think. You have a task ahead of you that will require much of your time! Go, take Sara Beth and get married today and start your family."

For the first time in his life, James pushed his dad away, "Dad, that wouldn't be right, as I don't have a full time job or a solid source of income and besides I want to go to college before I get married!"

His dad continued, "Marry her now! You have a task ahead of you that will require much of your time. Start your family now!"

Never before in James's life had his father been this imposing and for the second time in his life, he pushed his father aside and walked on. As they arrived at Mrs. Johns's, James could see the pigs were running all over, and Mrs. Johns was standing on the porch calling for the animals to get back in their pens. James broke into a run and chased the pigs back towards their pens. These darn pigs can run in more directions than any two men. James watched them run right past his dad with total disregard to him.

After all the pigs were in their pen, James looked around and saw his dad by the gate. He yelled for his dad to close the gate, but the gate remained opened. So James ran across the pen, closing the gate his damn self. James felt the frustration grow as he wondered about his father's strange behavior during the last few hours. First it was the intensity of ordering James to begin a family and now this.

James could see his dad at the far end of the pen. He looked at James like he had done just fine. At that point, James knew his dad just didn't hear him. That was something that happened when working with animals, given the noise they make and everyone calling out all the time.

After about two hours, all the animals had been corralled and fed. Mrs. Johns seemed very happy, as she announced it was time for the workers to eat. God knows James was hungry and by now sure his dad was as well, so they stopped to eat.

They sat at the picnic table about fifty feet from the back porch of the house. James's dad sat facing him, and James faced the porch. Mrs. Johns was sitting on the porch. As James sat talking to his dad, he noticed Mrs. Johns looking at him as though he was doing something wrong. James checked the end of his nose and then his chin. He was thinking he had something on one of them but found nothing and still she kept looking at him.

James mentioned this to his dad, who just chuckled, "Son, you're young, and she's lonely."

James responded with, "Bullshit, Dad, she's a survivor like you and Mom have always told us kids. She's the soul survivor of her immediate family, surviving the sinking of the Titanic in 1914."

His dad corrected James on the year, "Son, it was 1912."

James said, "Ok, whatever the year. Dad, I'm young enough to be her great-grandson!"

Mrs. Johns disappeared into the house. When she reappeared moments later, she called James to the edge of the porch. She handed him $8 dollars and said, "James, this is all I have at this time. I didn't know until late yesterday afternoon. I will bring the rest of it to your house on Monday or Tuesday, will that be ok?"

James stared at Mrs. Johns for a moment and not knowing how to answer her, just said, "Ok!" As he accepted the money from her hand, he asked, "Would you like me to wash the dishes we've used?"

The answer was, "No, but please set them on the porch." James walked back to the picnic table. As he picked up the plates, he noticed his father's plate was still full. Nothing had been eaten. James shook his head in confusion, as he was sure he had seen his dad eat all that was on his plate. He returned the plates to the porch and set them down.

Mrs. Johns said, "One more thing, James."

James asked, "What might that be, Ma'am?"

"James, will you grant this old woman a small kiss?"

Of course being a young man and thinking about what his dad had just told him, James was flattered and a little embarrassed as he replied, "Yes."

Mrs. Johns placed both of her hands, one on each side of his face, placed her thumb and fore finger on his earlobes, and pulled outward ever so gently. She placed a kiss on his lips that was more like a peck as apposed to a kiss. Now this only lasted about ten seconds, but in this ten-second kiss, James lived a lifetime.

He could hear a young girl screaming, and realized she was screaming for her mother and father as well as calling for her brothers and sisters. It was all to no avail as she was being held by someone she didn't even know. James could feel the biting cold on her feet from the bottom of the little boat she was in, and still the screams for her family went unanswered. He could hear the prayers of other people along with her prayers that were never answered. He saw a huge ship sinking, breaking in half, and the back half finally going under. Then all he saw was darkness. He felt the sense of loneliness on a sea of darkness, lit only by the stars. He could feel the tears running down the face of the young girl and then feel the tears frozen on her cheeks.

James saw the next few moments from the eyes of the young girl as she went to another large ship and on into a very large city. He saw time pass her life quickly as two people came to get her. He saw her find love and lose it, find another love and lose. At the very last particle of a second, in the briefest moment of this very short kiss, James realized this wonderful old woman not only loved him but loved life and all that it had to offer.

Mrs. Johns told James to be very careful when he went upon the seas. She stressed that not always are prayers answered. She then added another strange comment in a day that seemed too full of strange comments, "And, James, you really shouldn't talk to yourself."

James answered, "Yes, Ma'am." As he walked away, he was wondering what everyone seemed to be talking about. James thought, "This must be what's called a hangover." Behind him he could hear Mrs. Johns's phone ringing. In all the time he had known this old woman, this was the first time he had ever heard her phone ring. He wondered who might be calling this wonderful person who had just revealed so much of herself to him in that brief kiss.

James and his father went on to Mr. Gilmore's and then to Mr. and Mrs. Gamefish's farm. James talked with his father off and on as he worked but noticed that wherever they went, no one else even said hello to his father. These same people kept telling James that he shouldn't talk to himself. Each one of them explained to James they hadn't been told until late yesterday, and didn't have time to go to the bank. To James these statements made no sense but he was too confused to ask questions. Besides, he didn't want to be rude. James mentioned the strange comments to his father but his father just smiled and looked lovingly at his son's face.

As they arrived at Mr. Johnson's place, the day was starting to take its toll. James had fifty postholes to dig for a fence. He collected the tools from the tool shed and checked with Mr. Johnson to be sure where the fence was going. James got a drink of water and some to take with him. After placing the tools and extra water in the wheelbarrow, he took off to start digging. James was keeping an eye on the sun, as he knew if it got too low on the horizon, how he would possible be late getting home. He thought about being with his family and how he was looking forward to watching the Disney show.

His father talked as James worked, and he asked James to stop and take a break a few times. Each time James simply said, "If I stop, I might not get every thing done, so you talk and I will work." They talked till late in the afternoon. As James approached whole number fifty, he was just about done in and his dad convinced him to stop just one time. After sitting down for a while, James got back up and completed whole number fifty.

James put all the tools away while Mrs. Johnson made him a sandwich. Well actually, she made him several but nothing for his dad. James was paid $35 dollars and was told either Mr. Johnson or the misses would bring the rest of the pay to James' house. Mr. Johnson said they hadn't been told until late yesterday, and it would be hard to find someone to replace James.

James finally tried to ask, "What were you told late yesterday?" Just then the phone rang so James told Mr. Johnson, "Never mind. I'm sure I will find out when I get home."

As they left the doorstep, James looked up at a jet airliner going overhead. He asked his dad, "What is this thing everyone was told late yesterday and why does it sound like I just got fired?"

His dad replied, "That's something you will need to ask your mother when you get home."

As they continued on their way, James asked his dad if he would like to stop for some refreshment before getting home.

His dad said, "No, Son, I don't think I need that kind of refreshments. Besides, you need to get home, and I need to go this way." His father pointed in a different way then they had been walking. James had learned that questioning the directives given by his parents was not always an option, and he sensed that this time was not appropriate for any option. Besides, he was tired and really just wanted to get home. However, he did remind his dad that the way he intended to go would take him around the lake and through the cemetery.

Normally when his dad spoke, he would stand in front of James till he was finished talking and then walk away. This time his dad was speaking to him as he walked away, "I know, Son. You see I need to go this way as this is where I now belong." His dad added, "I love you, Son" as he disappeared into the tall and uncut growth of the woods.

James watched his dad disappear into the wild growth and the dusk of the day, then turned and started for home. After crawling over a three-strand barbed wire fence, James could hear a truck coming down the road. It seemed to be traveling rather fast for this old county road. When the pickup passed by James, he could tell it was Mr. Johnson, the man who owned the farm James had just come from. Mr. Johnson was looking straight ahead and never saw James standing off to the side of the road.

Now in all the time James had known Mr. Johnson, he had never seen Mr. Johnson drive like that. The old pickup might fall apart being driven like that over the old county roads. James could see the sun was getting low in the west, meaning the time must be after 6pm. If he kept up his present pace, he could be home in about twenty to thirty minutes.

As James topped the wooded hill overlooking their small family farm, he could see many vehicles around the house. One of them looked like his grandmother's car, and she lived way over in Carlinville. James had never known his grandmother to be at their house this late in the day because she didn't like driving after dark and was never out late the day before Sunday. It would take an act of congress for his grandmother to miss church. James also could see Mr. Johnson's old truck. As he stood there, he wondered what could be so important that would bring all these people to the house this late on a Saturday.

James entered the clearing just west of the barn and could see his little sister, Judy, on the back steps of the house. As soon as she saw James, she started running towards him in a dead run while calling out his name. She ran across the yard and through the garden, still calling out his name, "James! James! It's Dad, James. Dad----." When this little three and a half foot girl came to a five foot wooden gate, she cleared it in one smooth move, just like she'd seen James do so many times. She hit the ground running, while still calling out his name. There was still about one hundred fifty feet between the brother and sister when James could hear Judy saying something about Dad. Although he couldn't make out all the words, he knew something was definitely wrong and it had to do with their dad.

When this little sixty-pound girl was closer, James could see tears streaming down her pretty face. Her light brown hair waved in the breeze behind her while she cried out, "James! James! Dad died!"

James clearly heard what she said that time. He couldn't believe what she was saying, because he had just spent the day with their dad. James just knew there had to be some mistake and would straighten it all out when he got to the house. It was then that Judy reached her brother and leapt into his arms.

Although James was close to twice her height and outweighed her by one hundred and forty pounds, when she landed in his arms, this little girl forced him back two or three steps. Her long brown hair wrapped around his head and shoulders, and her tears splattered onto his face. His little sister's wet nose ran down his left cheek and neck.

With her face buried against James's neck and shoulder, she cried uncontrollably. Between sobs she told James how they were trying to get hold of him all day. She told her brother that their dad had died after James left the house that morning. Then she looked him in the eyes with one hand on each side of his face. Through her big brown tear filled eyes and a runny nose, she said, "James, why didn't you come home we needed you so bad?"

James had finally taken all he could of this strange day and angrily said, "Judy, why would you say something like that? I just spent all day with Dad!"

Judy replied, "No, you didn't! Someone came and took Dad's body away about nine o'clock. James, Mom was crying so hard and calling your name. Oh James! Why didn't you come home?"

James shook his head in disbelief and whispered, "I didn't know, Judy, I just didn't know."

James carried Judy all the way back to the house, only letting her down when they reached the back porch. James opened the door and Judy ran in. James entered right behind her and the first thing he saw was one of his cousins standing in the kitchen, smoking a damn cigarette.

James walked up to him and growled, "You know my mom and dad don't allow smoking in the house. So you need to take your ashtray smelling mouth and that damn cigarette outside. And don't smoke in this house ever again!"

James turned for the living room and could see the breakfast dishes and food were still on the table. Wall to wall aunts, uncles, and cousins from both sides of the family were standing around. As James passed by them, cousins and uncles patted him on the shoulders and arms, as did some of his aunts. Most of his aunts gave him a hug.

He found there were more relatives waiting further in the living room. Grandmother West was sitting in his dad's chair. She was the only one who could sit in that chair, as even James' dad would never say anything to her. Then his eyes fell upon his mother sitting on the couch, crying openly and uncontrollably. Judy had sat next to their mother trying to consol her with her statement of, "I found James!"

When his mother looked up and saw her son, she started crying even harder. She stretched out her arms and pleaded, "James, please come here!" James found himself on his knees before his mother and started crying with her. It flashed in his mind that the last time he saw his mother cry this hard was when they got the telegram from Uncle Sam stating Jerry was missing in action. James knew something terrible was wrong and maybe what Judy told him was true. James just didn't understand how that could be when he had just spent the day with his dad.

James explained the events of the day that he had just spent with his father. He told his family a short version of what they had talked about as they went from one job to another. When he had finished, a hush had fallen over the room. His grandmother came over to James and put her hand on his left shoulder. She knelt down beside him and said, "James, as long as you believe in God, all things are possible."

Several family members nodded in agreement. James looked into the face of his grandmother and saw his father's eyes for a fleeting moment. James looked to his mother and knew that both tales of the day were true. He had spent the day with his father and yet his father had died that morning.

After about an hour or so, two of the aunts came over and said, "Mary Ann, we'll clean the kitchen and make something to eat. Is there anything you had planned for dinner or something special you might want?"

James's mother looked at them and said, "I planned something really nice for dinner but it was never taken out of the freezer."

The cousin who had been smoking in the kitchen spoke up and said, "Aunt Mary, I have twenty dollars and can go to the store and get some hamburger meat. Would that be Ok?" While his mother nodded her agreement, James realized that his life had changed that day and would never again be what it once was.

CHAPTER THREE
THE ROPE

After completing the twenty-eight mile drive to the park, JW was surprised to find they were the only ones at the park. Given the time of day and the perfect weather, this was very unusual. JW looked at Karen in surprise, with his eyes open wide, and said, "I've only seen this happen once before."

Karen replied in a soft voice with a smile on her face, "When was that, John?"

"You remember when that guy from Gillespie asked Sharon Stone to marry him? I think it was maybe two years ago."

"Oh, yes! I remember," Karen replied, as JW helped her out of the truck.

Closing the truck door, JW grabbed the two baskets from the back of the truck and said, "Seems to me Sharon asked a lot of people not to show up till late that day."

As they walked down the path entering the park, JW said, "Karen, I tell you this is weird, nobody being here like this."

Karen kept walking and answered, "John, I swear the only difference between men and a box of rocks is the rocks are smart enough to get in the box."

"What do you mean by that, Karen?"

"Never mind, John, just never mind," replied Karen with a smile and a shake of her head.

Now the lake was just over three quarters of a mile across at its widest point. There was a well-worn path around the lake. It was a short walk, about two miles, when holding the hand of someone you loved. As JW and Karen walked down this path, they encountered many clearings. Young people and families used these clearings to have picnics. Branching off the main path were smaller paths leading to more secluded areas farther away from the lake.

Blackberries and wild gooseberry plants, as well as maple and oak trees, lined the path. There were a few willows also mixed in with some Black Walnut trees. The trees were full of twitters from birds and the furious activity of squirrels. On the ground, rabbits scurried to hide and a few brave squirrels looked for a free handout. The main attraction of the park was a very large, very old oak tree. The oak stood about 150 feet tall and was growing fifteen feet from the lake water's edge and twenty feet from a creek that flowed into the lake constantly feeding the lake with fresh water year round.

On the water side of the tree grew a large branch that jutted out over the lake. On this branch was tied a long rope that was used by swimmers to swing out over the water and drop down into the water. Swinging out as far as possible, the drop to the water was about twelve to thirteen feet into the deepest part of the lake, which was fifteen to sixteen feet deep.

This was farming country and the park was completely surrounded by fields of wheat, corn, soybean and hayfields. Two of these fields were in plain view of the big oak tree and belonged to a young black man, known quite well by all as Roscoe E. Benjamin and better known to his friends as "Reb". Reb was a good friend of both Karen and JW.

Karen and JW walked around the park together. Since no one else was there, they took what was known as the coveted spot under the big oak tree. After spreading the blanket on the grass-covered ground, JW started to arrange the food from the basket his mother had prepared. It contained two large thermoses of Kool-Aid, egg and potato salad, fried chicken, a big dish of coleslaw, grapes, sliced apple, and oranges. For dessert she had added cake that was left from his sister's birthday party.

As JW reached for Karen's basket, Karen placed her hand on top of it saying, "Let's not get everything out just yet. We do have all day." A mischievous smile appeared on JW's face, and he nodded his agreement.

JW was sitting close enough to Karen to smell her perfume and this excited him. Although JW had been excited by Karen's perfume before, this time JW was excited in a very different way. JW didn't fully understand this new feeling, but he knew something had been stirred within him. Rising up on all fours, he placed a kiss on the lips of the woman he loved.

Now this kiss only lasted about ten seconds. However, what JW felt in those ten seconds was astounding. Starting with the warmth of her lips, then the smell of her perfume and her hair touching his face, a tingling ran through every fiber of his body. This caused his soul to stir. JW felt his soul stir only one other time and that was when he had given himself to God. He had been awakened by the touch of God, but this time was different. JW was suddenly awakened in a totally new way.

Near the end of this kiss, JW had a vision of Karen walking slowly towards him. She was dressed in white and a soft, white veil covered her face. Music was a jumble of lyrics in his head. He heard pieces of songs running the gambit of *From a Jack to a King* to *I got a Brand New Pair of Roller Skates, You got a Brand New Key.* The moment the kiss ended, so did the vision.

Karen opened her eyes slowly to see the man she loved with his eyes still closed and seemingly ready to fall. Karen placed her right hand on the left side of JW's face and kissed him again. This time Karen knew without a doubt that the man she loved with all her heart, the one who fought for the chance to sit next to her in the school lunchroom, felt the same way about her and was hers until the end of time. While she kissed JW a second time, Karen said a silent prayer to thank God for bringing the two of them together.

Karen smiled at JW even though his eyes were still closed. They were both on their knees in front of each other, and Karen asked, "John, are you ok? Do you know where you're at?"

JW replied, "Karen, I've never been better in my life!" He put his arms around Karen's svelte, toned waist and said, "As far as where I am? I'm right here with my arms around the woman I love. I'm right where I've always wanted to be." JW pulled Karen closer and held her tighter in his arms as he gently and tenderly kissed her neck.

Karen felt a great weight lift from her slim shoulders and knew all her dreams would soon come true in the arms of this man. The surprise she and other family members had planned for this evening was worth all the hard work to bring everything together. For this special night, the secretiveness had been justified. It had been difficult keeping the surprise from JW but it would be worth it.

JW interrupted her private thoughts and said, "How about going swimming? I think I need to cool off a bit."

As he and Karen stood up, Karen replied, "I need to cool off, too. John, can I go first on the rope?"

"Only if I can help you swing out on it," JW laughed.

As JW helped Karen with the rope, he thought to himself what it would be like to spend the rest of his life with her. He could have given her an engagement ring had he not put new tires on his truck. The idea crossed his mind to ask his mom and dad for the money to pay off the rings and then ask Karen to marry him. Watching her now and thinking about how being with her made him feel, he wasn't sure he wanted to wait much longer to make her his wife.

After an hour or two of swimming, Karen became tired and hungry. Karen asked, "JW, do you want to stop and eat now?"

JW replied, "You betcha! I'll race you to the shore."

Karen arrived first as usual. However, she knew it was because JW always let her win. After drying off, JW hung the towels to dry on a branch of the large oak tree. Karen set out the food and prepared each of them a plate. After JW finished three helpings compared to Karen's one, they settled back on the blanket and started chatting about whatever came to their minds. Karen, just a bit cold from the water, snuggled close to JW.

JW stretched out on his back and placed his left arm around her shoulders. Continuing with small talk, both could hear a farm tractor laboring in the nearby field. After a short time, Karen rolled on her right side and placed her left leg over JW's legs. JW moved his right hand to her side and began kissing her. Karen moved JW's hand down to her left hip and kissed him more vigorously. JW responded as heat built inside him.

It was about three in the afternoon, and the sound of the tractor had ceased. It wasn't until JW could hear crunching of twigs and other vegetation that he became aware that the tractor had stopped. He listened as the crunching of twigs approached their secluded spot. Suddenly, a shadow came across his eyes, and JW knew for certain that someone was there.

Looking up at the sun through squinted eyes, JW tried to see who had joined them. Before he was able to make out the face, he heard a startled gasp from Karen. He knew immediately who the intruder was when he heard a big guffawing laugh that was like fireworks booming across the sky on the Fourth of July.

Karen blurted out, "Reb! You're not supposed to be… I mean what are doing here? Don't you have dirt to dig or something like that?"

JW reached up and shook hands with Reb, one of the best friends JW ever had.

Reb said, "Hey, JW, how yawl doing? I see the both of you have plenty to eat. That's a good thing, cause no one brought me anything out to eat. Do the two of you mind if I help myself?"

Karen spoke up before JW had a chance to answer, "Reb, don't you have some dirt to play with or a pig to milk or some kind of 'farmy' thing to do?"

Reb and JW looked at each other and started laughing. Reb bent over and slapped at his leg as he laughed.

Karen looked at Reb with a glare that could kill, then said, "And just what's so funny?"

JW asked through his own laughter, "Reb, just how do you milk a pig?"

Reb, still laughing as well said, "I don't hardly know, JW. I've never milked a pig in my life!"

Karen huffed and retorted, "I'm glad the two of you think that's so funny." However, Karen could no longer hide that by this time she was laughing along with the men. After a moment or two, the laughter started to die down and Reb again asked for a sandwich.

Karen apologized and said, "Here Reb, please take two-- they're small. And please, don't let John and I keep you from playing with your tractor over there in the dirt. Goodbye, Reb!" She then softened her dismissal with a smile. Reb took the dismissal in stride and returned to plowing. He didn't disturb either of them for the rest of the day.

Karen and JW settled back to small talk on the blanket, and then went swimming again for about an hour. After getting out of the water and returning to the blanket, JW dried off with one of the towels. Then reaching for the other towel, he dropped to his knees. He began to dry Karen's legs and feet. When he stopped to look up at Karen, all he saw was a smile on the face of this beautiful woman. Karen placed a hand on each side of JW's face, which started his heart pounding like a base drum. Karen leaned close to him and whispered, "John, I love you." She put her right hand on the back of JW's head and pulled him against her tummy. In a softer voice that JW could barely hear, she said, "John, I will always love you."

With all of his new found feelings, JW put his right hand and arm around Karen's legs just below her butt, with his left arm around her waist, he held her very close and tighter as he told her, "I've loved you since the fourth grade, and I will always love you with all my heart!"

JW and Karen looked into each other's eyes. She could see the tears forming in his eyes and felt answering tears well in her own eyes. Her knight-in-shining-armor was on his knees before her and made her feel like a queen.

JW said, "Karen I have something I want to ask you."

Karen heard a quiver in her voice from the lump in her throat as she asked, "Yes, John, and what might that be?" She could feel the strength of his arms as they circled her tightly. Slowly a tear trickled down her face as she looked down upon the man on bended knee before her. She knew in that moment that she would love this man for the rest of her life.

JW asked, "Karen, would you do me the honor of being my wife till the end of time?" He hesitated a little before adding, "Karen, will you marry me?"

Karen didn't notice the big tears running down the cheeks of her face. The tears could do nothing to dampen her ear-to-ear smile as she dropped to her knees and put her arms around JW. She held him as close and tight as she could while she answered, "Oh! John, I've waited so long for you to ask me that! I would consider it an honor to be your wife till death us do part. Yes, John, I will marry you! But only if you're willing to be my husband till the end of time."

JW replied, "Karen, I'm so sorry I don't have a ring to give you. I still owe $65.00 on the set I'm buying for us."

Karen then said, "That's ok, John, its time you take a look in the basket I brought."

With a puzzled look, JW reached to his left to grab the basket. As he opened the lid, he saw a small box sitting on top of the potato salad. His hands began shaking as he picked up the little box. JW knew what was in this small box because he had picked it out at the jewelry store and had it sized to fit Karen's left ring finger. At first he thought Karen might have paid the balance. He then remembered what Karen's mom and dad had said in the kitchen before they left on this picnic, "Did you put the special package in there?"

Karen could feel the trembling in JW's body and was quite surprised that a man his size would be afraid of such a small box. Of course, she realized it wasn't the size of the box but what the box meant that caused his trembling. JW held the box against his left hand and opened the box with his thumb, thus exposing the three rings contained inside.

JW removed the engagement ring with his right hand and placed the box on the blanket. He took Karen's left hand with his left, watched Karen extend her left ring finger, and gently placed the engagement ring on the finger of the woman he intended to marry. As he did this, JW again asked, "Karen, will you marry me?"

As she tearfully nodded and demurely whispered, "Yes," he slipped the ring on her finger.

Karen and JW shared a kiss that lasted only a minute, but its memory would last a lifetime. JW's first dream had come true. He was to marry the woman he not only loved but he adored.

A short time later, after eating a small meal, which was very unusual for JW, Karen asked, "What time is it?"

"Don't know; just a minute; let me check. Wow! It's 5:30, where did this day go?"

"John, we need to get things picked up so we can get going. It will be close to 6:30 before we get home, and we both need to shower."

A moment later Karen said, "John, you have that lost look on your face again. Hello, are you in there, does a squirrel have your tongue?"

"Ok, Karen, I will pick up this stuff and take it to the truck. Will you please pick up what I can't? Carry that basket and these two towels. And Karen, please don't you open the door. I will open it for you."

After placing both baskets in the truck, along with the wet towels and used paper items, JW opened the door for Karen. After Karen was seated, JW leaned over and lightly kissed Karen on the lips and gently closed the door of the truck.

JW got in on the driver's side and placed his right hand and arm on the back of the seat behind Karen. For a long moment, JW looked in the eyes of his woman, then without saying a word, pulled her to him and kissed her again.

A short time later while driving down the road, JW said, "I think I just figured it out."

"Oh, and what's that's, John?"

"There was no one at the rope, just like the time when that guy proposed to Sharon Stone. Now you and I are engaged!"

Karen laughed, "Very good, John, you get a cookie. Maybe there's hope for you yet."

JW said, "I don't get it, Karen. How did you know I would propose to you this day?"

"John, you're so sweet! How about you just be the husband, and I will be the wife?"

"Ok, Karen, but what kind of answer is that?" Karen just laughed and moved to sit next to her future husband.

After returning to Carlinville, Karen asked, "Where are you going, John?"

JW's reply was simple, "Your house, where else, Karen?"

"No, John, we need to go to your house first. I had my brother bring a change of clothes for me over to your house."

"Well, ok, Karen, but I think your dad will kill me!"

As JW turned the truck into the driveway, he said, "I don't think my mom and dad are home."

Karen said, "John, you're as sharp as Sherlock Holmes, describe your first clue. No wait. Don't tell me. The lights are out!" Karen was finding humor in JW's reaction to the events of the day while JW was just growing more confused.

JW opened the truck door for Karen, and they both walked to the house. Just inside the house, Karen saw the clothes her brother had dropped off for her. Turning to JW and giving him a kiss, Karen asked if he would like to shower first.

"Yes, I think I will, if you don't mind. It seems it takes women longer, leaving little or no hot water." Then he added, "You know, Karen, it's strange my little sister isn't here."

"Well, John, maybe they all went somewhere to eat."

"Yes, I guess that could be, I know I'm hungry again. Hey, Karen? While you take your shower, I will get the stuff out of the truck, and then we can go somewhere to eat."

"Don't worry, John, when we're done we'll be going somewhere," she said mysteriously. "I need to use the phone while you're in the shower, ok?" JW turned and headed for the bathroom to take his shower throwing an "ok" over his shoulder as he reached the door.

Karen walked over and picked up the phone as soon as she heard the bathroom door close. "Hello, Mom? Yes, we're at John's house and John is in the shower." With a bit of a quiver in her voice, Karen went on to say, "Mom, it went just the way you, Dad, Mr. and Mrs. Walker, and I planned it. I will soon be Mrs. John F. Walker. Oh Mom, I'm so happy! Please tell everyone and I will see you soon bye, bye."

JW came down the stairs a short time later and said, "Ok, Karen, your turn."

As Karen started up the stairs, she stopped and asked, "JW, did you pick up your towel from the bathroom floor? Never mind, John, I will pick it up for you."

"Thank you. How did you know about the towel? Oh by the way, Karen, there's a lock on the inside of the bathroom door that's only controlled from the inside."

"Why thank you, John. Do you think I will need to use it?"

JW thought for a moment, and then as a sheepish smile slid across his face, he said, "I'll clean out the truck."

Later as Karen came down the stairs, JW met her at the bottom. He put his arms around her and told her, "You look great, and you smell sooo good. I just want to hold you in my arms forever."

"Why thank you, John…John, I want to be held by you and be kissed by you until the end of time. And John? You're right, there is a lock on the bathroom door, but I didn't use it."

JW looked in Karen's eyes for a long, quiet moment. Then JW said, "Where would you like to eat?" Karen placed a kiss on the lips of the man she planned to marry and said, "Can we please go by my house first, and then we can decide?"

With a chuckle in his voice, JW said, "That's a good idea. We can show your father your ring and that you are ok!"

The drive to Karen's house took them down the street that passed in front of James West's grandmother's house. JW, noticing the dark house, said, "Now that's strange. Mrs. West is always home before dark."

"Well, maybe she's out to dinner some place. You never know, John, we just might run into her wherever we eat."

"Gee, Karen, seems like everyone might be eating somewhere right now except us." JW was always hungry and tonight was no exception.

After turning onto Fairmont Street, JW said, "I love you, Karen, and today you made me the happiest I've ever been in my life."

"John, I love you, and just like you, this is the happiest day of my life so far." With a devilish grin she added, "What could I tell you that would make this day even better?"

"Ask me that after we're married," JW replied with a laugh.

"Oh, I will, John, but what could I tell you that would make THIS a better day?" she insisted.

"I'm not sure. Hey! What the heck's going on at your house?" JW looked at all the cars parked out front and said, "There's the chief of police's car, the mayor's and the minister's car and isn't that the fire chief's new car? I'm thinking that's the governor's car next to my mom and dad's car. My mom and dad? What is going on here?"

"Karen, there's a large number of important people here. I sure hope your dad didn't kill someone!"

As JW parked next to his mom and dad's car, his little sister ran up to the truck, "Hi, John, Mom and Dad are waiting for you in the backyard."

"Well hi, Honey, what's going on?"

"Don't you know, John?"

"No, Honey, I don't."

"Oh, well I better get back. Jeremy and I are playing hide and seek. Bye, John."

"Well ok. Karen, what's going on that I don't seem to know about?"

"Gee John, how would I know? I've been with you all day. How about we go inside and find out?"

"Ok, I'll get your door."

As Karen and JW walked through the empty house, it became quite clear that whatever was going on was taking place in the backyard. JW remembered seeing the chairs and tables stacked out on the grass earlier that morning while he was talking with Karen's dad on the back porch. Although he still didn't know what was happening, he realized what ever it was had been planned before today and that something big was going to happen in the backyard.

Karen and JW finally reached the back of the house and looked out the window. They saw the people milling about the backyard while they were eating and drinking. Some of the folks were enjoying a cold beer, and some were holding mixed drinks. The people included the chief of police, the mayor, the minister from their church, the fire chief, the governor, and the senator of Illinois. There were a number of other people neither JW nor Karen recognized all mixed in with young men and women Karen and JW went to school with.

JW thought about the strange mixture of people. There were people he knew quite well, and some he only knew in passing. They all seemed to know what was going on, and yet he didn't know anything.

Karen started to open the door. However, JW put his hand on the door to prevent her from opening it. JW said, "Karen, maybe we shouldn't go outside. Those are some very important people out there, and I don't remember being invited."

"John! I'm sure those people won't mind if we join them. After all, over there is your mom, dad and your little sister. Over there is my brother drinking a beer. What? Drinking a beer? I'm kicking his butt!"

"Hold on, hold on, Karen! Now just what's going on? Except for my mom and dad, I can't think of any reason why any of these people would want me at their party.

Karen, I'm not anyone special. I've never met the governor, and that other fellow over there I think is the senator?"

Karen said, "John, open the door, Honey!"

"Ok, Karen. But I wish you would tell me what's going on."

JW opened the door, and he and Karen stepped out onto the porch. The talk among the crowd stopped as all eyes were suddenly on Karen and JW. Karen's dad was the first to approach JW with his arms and hands open wide. Mr. McIntosh gave JW a good bear hug, and then stepped back, patting JW on the sides of his shoulders with his big hands.

He then said, "Welcome to my family, Son. You no longer need to knock on the door any more. As part of the family, you may walk in anytime."

Then Karen's mom, brother, and the fire chief were all saying how proud they were of JW while the rest were talking over each other saying similar things. Next were JW's mom, dad, and sister. His sister put her arms around him as best she could while looking up into his eyes and said, "I'm so proud of you. I love you, John, you're the best brother anyone could ever have."

His mom and dad told him. "We knew you could do it, Son. We are so proud of you."

With Karen at his side, JW said, "I don't understand all this fuss. All I've done is ask Karen to marry me."

Karen and JW's dads both had big smiles on their faces, as JW's mother said, "You will understand soon, my son. First, I want you to meet the governor and the senator. Then as soon as your friend, James, shows up, we can get on with the rest."

Karen asked of the group in general, "James's grandmother isn't here yet?"

Mrs. McIntosh replied, "No dear, none of the West family have arrived yet. Is there a problem?"

Karen replied, with concern in her voice, "Perhaps not."

Now with JW's mom, dad, the governor and senator along with Karen's mom and dad standing on the porch, the phone rang. Karen was the closest to the door and said, "I'll get it!" A moment or two later Karen cried out, "O my God, John! John!"

JW turned and raced for the door. Karen's dad headed for the back door as well, answering the cry of his daughter.

JW placed his left hand on the shoulder of Karen's dad and pushed him to the side like a feather. JW grabbed the handle of the screen door and swung it wide open. The only reason it didn't hit the side of the house was because it hit Karen's dad square in the face.

As JW entered the house, he could see Karen holding the phone and crying. With the sight of those big tears running down her beautiful but contorted face, JW demanded, "What's wrong, are you okay, Karen?" While still crying, Karen simply handed the phone to JW. By this time, Karen and JW's parents, the fire chief, and the minister were coming into the kitchen area. JW took hold of the phone. Again in a very demanding voice, JW spoke into the phone, "This is John Walker. Whom am I speaking to?"

All who were in the kitchen as well as those looking through the windows could see the expression on JW's face change from a demanding look to a look of total shock and then sorrow. Then JW spoke in a voice almost crying, "Judy, would you like for me and Karen to come over? Are you sure? Judy, tell your mother and James, if you need anything, just call. Well, I love you, too. Good-bye, Judy."

JW held Karen in his arms while tears streamed down his face. His mother asked, "What's wrong, my son?"

JW looked around the room trying to regain his composure. When his eyes landed on Karen's father, he asked, "What happened to your nose?"

"I was attacked by that damn screen door, imagine that. Now what the hell's wrong with my daughter, John? Why is my daughter crying?"

"That was Judy West on the phone, my friend James West's little sister. James will not be attending these festivities tonight. James and Judy's father died this morning, but James didn't know until late this afternoon," as JW spoke these words, his tears fell into the bright red hair of Karen.

Nobody said much of anything for a while, including the governor and senator who loved to talk. A somber hush had fallen over the group. Finally, the fire chief spoke up saying, "Let's get this shindig going, because I'm hungry and I'm sure some of you are hungry as well. So let's get Mr. McIntosh to work on cooking our dinner. What say ye?"

Karen's dad was slow to start, but finally went about cooking. Like the rest of the group, he was just going through the motions after the shocking news. However, when Reb and his mother arrived later, Mr. McIntosh gave both of them a long hard look. Karen approached Reb and his mother with tears in her eyes, and her hands out. Reb took hold of Karen's left hand as his mother took hold of Karen's right while asking, "What's wrong my child, didn't JW propose like you planned?"

"Oh, yes Ma'am, men are just the way you explained it."

"So, you're crying because you're so happy?"

"No Ma'am, you know James West? Well his little sister Judy called about an hour ago. James and Judy's father died sometime early this morning, and James didn't know about it until late this afternoon. Because of this, John hasn't been told about the surprise yet, so please be careful when talking to him."

"Not a problem my child. Rosco, you mind your mouth as well."

"Ok, Mom."

Shortly thereafter, with the smell of food and flowing drinks, the crowd started livening up again. Soon it was practically like a real party. The food comprised of halves of chicken barbecued to perfection, egg and potato salad, fried eggplant, baked potatoes, black and green olives, sweet and dill pickles, homemade and store bought bread along with biscuits, butter, and cottage cheese. There were even mushrooms sliced and fried.

JW brought Reb and his mother each a plate. Karen carried two more plates for herself and JW. While most of the other guests drank beer or mixed drinks, JW, Karen, Reb and his mother each drank a Pepsi. The small group talked quietly about James and his family, and of course, the fact JW had proposed to Karen.

After eating, something JW was not shy about as he was exceptionally hungry, he was sitting with Karen by his side when the governor and senator jointly said, "Let's get to the point of this party."

The two men stepped up to the podium and began by praising Mr. and Mrs. McIntosh as good and very gracious hosts. They thanked them for the fine dinner and congratulated them on their daughter's betrothal to JW. Then they asked Mr. and Mrs. McIntosh to join them at the podium, as well Mr. and Mrs. Walker.

JW turned to Karen saying, "I hope they're getting some kind of an award. Cuz I can't see making such a big fuss over you and me getting married."

"John, it could be a kind of award for them. I guess it's how you look at it. And John, after all we are uniting our two families."

"Well, I guess so, Karen. But how does that call for the appearance of the governor, not to mention a senator," he then looked at Karen suspiciously. "Karen, I see that smile on your pretty face. Now just what's up?"

Then JW's dad spoke, "I would like to ask my soon to be daughter-in-law to join us at this time."

As Karen stood up, JW looked into her eyes with a bit of a surprised look on his face.

As Karen walked towards the podium, JW marveled at the way she held herself. Just looking at the shape of her body excited him. JW knew he had seen Karen walk before, but never had her shape and walk excited him as it did now, and the smell of her perfume...the smell of her perfume weakened his knees just to think of it let alone smell it.

Then the governor spoke, "We are gathered together for the purposes of commemorating the actions of two young men. Unfortunately, only one can be with us this night, although both will receive the same commendation for being a person of high standards, academics and all the other good shit we're looking for. The senator and I consider it an honor to have participated in acquiring this most prestigious appointment, giving respect and prestige to the recipients of this great honor." Then Karen spoke about how she and JW had grown up together, and now she would soon become Mrs. John Fredrick Walker. She would be proud to be the wife of the man she had loved since the sixth grade.

Karen then asked, "John, will you please join me up here?"

Now JW was thinking, "Did I save someone's life? Did I prolong someone's life? Did I do something special?" The answer to each question was 'no' so JW was totally dumfounded as to what this might all be about. All he knew for sure was that it had something to do with James and himself.

Reb and his mother, Ruth, were still sitting with JW and could clearly see the facial expressions change on his face as he listened to all that was being said. Reb's mother said, "Reb, now that's a man in love."

Reb replied, "Yes, Mother, I believe you're right about that."

When JW arrived at the podium, Karen gave him a hug and a kiss then said, "I know you've been real patient with all that's happening this night, John, so I want you to know I'm so, so proud of you. Now the governor and senator have something to say to you."

"Young Mr. Walker, I would like to congratulate you on your upcoming nuptials and your fine choice for a wife. However, that's only part of why we're all here. Do you have any idea what this might be about?"

JW's honest response was, "No, Sir, I don't"

"Well, Mr. Walker, it's taken a lot of work to get to this point, and you sure seem to be worth that great effort that someone took to make this happen. So without further ado, I'm going to turn this over to the senator. Senator, if you please."

"I would like to thank the governor for bring this to my attention. After looking into your qualifications, and all the diligent work that someone put into promoting you, I now believe we've made the right choice. For the most part, I usually get to say how someone is perfect for something when they're really not. However, this time I feel absolutely, positively correct."

"Now I do a great deal of talking on many subjects. And I know I could talk on this subject for a while, but I'm not going to. But I will say this."

"I've been watching a young lady tonight, and she seems to be very much in love with the young man who is the reason for all this hoopla. She's responsible for the governor and me being here. She got the ball rolling that has brought us all together. So I'm turning this over to her. I'm sure she will find the correct words. If I may be so bold and premature, I would like to honor the two of you by calling her Mrs. Walker. So, the future Mrs. John Fredrick Walker, it's all yours."

Before Karen could speak, JW looked around and saw the faces of the governor, senator, and Karen's dad (whose nose looked like it had lost a fight with a meat grinder), Karen's mom, and JW's father and mother as well.

JW could see tears of joy welling in Karen's eyes as she met his gaze. Even knowing they were tears of joy, he felt a sharp pain deep inside his heart to see tears of any kind in her eyes. He loved her so much; he never wanted to ever see her cry, whether it was because she was happy or sad.

As Karen looked at JW, she began to speak. Her lower lip quivered a bit as she held John's right hand with both of hers. She then said, "John, I love you with all my heart and I always will. You told me one time there was a very special and particular college you wanted to attend. However, you felt it was too far out of your reach; it would only be a dream, never a reality."

Now in the trembling voice of joyous crying Karen added, "John, I've loved you since the sixth grade. So I decided to try to see if I could make your dream come true."

"With the help of our minister, school officials, the police and fire chiefs, I started the tedious task of getting things moving. Of course, I had help from your mom and dad, as there was quite a bit of paper work to do. Even my parents helped because they believed in me, and I believed in you."

"You see, John, my dad knows the mayor, and the mayor knows the governor. Now it took some time to convince the governor, but he finally came around. Then the governor contacted the senator who was a bit easier to convince, I think because the governor was a true believer in you. However, John, we found we needed a congressman. By that time, we discovered we were running out of time for all the paper work to be completed and submitted for this fall semester."

"Then disasters struck. The congressman was a bit different after we submitted all the paper work to his office. The statement from the fire chief was lost, along with your school records. Recovering your school records was easy; but the fire chief was on vacation in that big sandbox called Arizona. Finally, Congressman Menstop completed his paper work, and even had the papers signed by the president in time to file for this upcoming semester."

"So my love, you will be starting classes this fall at a college on the east coast. John, I love you so much. I want all your dreams to come true. Come this fall you will be attending Annapolis."

JW closed his eyes, leaned back slightly, and let out a long breath. With a lump in his throat and tears running down his face, JW bent down, put his right arm around and under Karen's butt, and picked her off the ground. He put his left arm around Karen and pulled her close and tight. Then in front of everyone, he planted a kiss on the most wonderful woman in the world: the one he adored, the one he loved, and the one he would marry. JW was astonished to think she was the one who made two of his most important dreams come true all in one day.

JW turned to his parents. While still holding Karen and with a bit of a cry in his voice, he said, "Mom, Dad, please welcome your soon-to-be daughter-in-law into our family. I proposed to her today and she said yes. All this while she had planned this big surprise for me. She's the most wonderful woman in the world, and I have to be the happiest man in the world!"

JW's parents put their arms around the two of them. Shortly thereafter, Karen's parents joined in on the group hug. While this group hugging was going on, JW continued holding Karen in his arms as they both cried tears of joy. Their tears mixed together to form a single stream, as Karen whispered in his ear, "Honey, your friend and mine, James West will be attending

Annapolis with you!" JW drew back a few inches and looked lovingly into Karen's teary eyes, and then hugged her even tighter.

After a while, JW let Karen down to the ground. Then the rest of the visitors came up to shake hands and give hugs and kisses along with congratulations for JW's dreams come true. When the minister came up, he told JW and Karen, "Let me know when, and I will do my best to make the church available."

JW and Karen told the minister, "Give us a couple of days, but it will be soon...very soon!" Everyone laughed as the newly engaged couple hugged each other. The guests formed a line to congratulate both of them on their news. It was a cheerful evening even though James West and his family stayed in everyone's thoughts. Tomorrow would be soon enough to deal with the sadness. Tonight was meant for celebration.

Chapter 4

The Wedding

Six weeks after the day JW had proposed, Karen, JW, and JW's parents were coming out of the Farmer's First National of Carlinville. Karen and JW were now the proud owners, with payments, of twelve acres of land located seven miles south of Carlinville, one mile southeast of an apple orchard and just under a mile east of the B&O Railroad tracks. JW's parents had cosigned for the house and property.

JW's dad said. "How about we all take a drive out there and take a good look at this new place you're going to be calling a home?"

JW's mother said, "I think I would like that. It will be my first chance to see where my grandkids will grow up."

All were talking during the drive, making the seven-mile trip seem very short. As they turned into the long driveway leading onto the property, they could all see the workers busily trying to get this old, somewhat dilapidated, farmhouse ready for the newlyweds to move into.

Karen and JW saw people from their church helping out as well as others they had helped in an earlier age. All were busy as bees hustling here and there to turn an old farmhouse into a palace, or what Karen thought was a palace. If it fell short of being a palace, then it would at least be habitable. A new roof, siding, and windows were well under construction. The trees were being trimmed and landscaping had even begun.

Boy and Girl scouts were helping as well as members of two or three different chapters of the FFA, who were mostly working on the barn and stock area.

Karen and JW walked into the house with Karen holding tightly onto JW's hand and arm while looking at all the work being done to the inside. The plaster walls were being torn out, as well as all the old wiring. A new staircase was being installed. The high ceilings were being replaced with lower ones with central heating and cooling.

Karen almost flipped out over the changes being made in the kitchen. The ceilings were lowered for recessed lighting, the walls were completed, new cabinets and counters had been installed. The cabinet under the window now had double sinks and a new thing called a garbage disposal and a new laundry room and bathroom had been added...not yet completed but added.

Karen approached the counter just in front of the window. JW sensed a strange feeling coming from Karen when she touched the counter top just in front of the kitchen window. JW could see her hand tremble, as she seemed to be looking for something. Then she quickly looked towards the living room area with a strange expression on her face as though she was very surprised and seemed perhaps ready to cry. JW asked, "Karen, is something wrong?"

Karen replied, "No, my dear, just something I thought I had seen before. Déjà-vu I guess. It's nothing."

Walking back into the living room, Karen again stopped while placing her hand on the doorframe for a moment, then proceeded into the living room where a man and his son were working. The man said, "Mr. and Mrs. Walker, the stairwell is good enough to use if you care to look upstairs. I'm sure you will be pleased with the changes."

Being called Mrs. Walker pleased Karen a great deal even though they were not yet married. Karen didn't correct the man. She smiled in reply as she and JW and walked up the stairs.

The second floor had been changed to the absolute delight of Karen and JW. It used to be three bedrooms and one bath. Now, it was still three bedrooms but had two full baths. The ceilings had been lowered for central heating and cooling. The master bedroom had a large window on the east and a large walk in closet on the west with a full private bath.

Karen looked JW in the eyes and with a big ear-to-ear smile said, "I think we're going to enjoy this room!"

JW responded with a smile, "I think you're right about that!"

JW gave Karen a hug and a kiss. Turning around, JW was surprised to see his mom and dad standing there with smiles on their faces.

As Karen and JW started to walk by them, JW's dad said, "Soon my son, not before but soon."

Karen and JW walked downstairs and out to the back to take a look at the barn and chicken coop and his parents followed. JW said. "Well, Dad, this all looks good, but I'm thinking this will cost Karen and me a great deal of money."

JW's dad responded with, "You're young my son, don't worry!"

JW looked at his watch and replied, "Well, Dad, Karen and I have an appointment with the minister. Would you and Mother care to join us?"

"No Son. I have some paper work to complete at the plant. Your mother can go if she wishes." During the drive back to town, JW's mother decided she had something else to do.

JW then asked, "Well, Mother, do you think Karen and I could use your car, if it's ok with Dad?"

JW's dad said, "That's fine with me."

JW's mother added, "In that case, yes, Son you and Karen may use my car."

Later that evening with the minister, Karen and JW worked out the order of events and the words of their vows and, of course, the date and time. When they were finished, Karen and JW stopped at a local restaurant and had something to eat. After eating, JW took Karen home where they sat talking with Karen's mom and dad till 8:00 pm. By this time, JW said he was a bit tired and needed to get his mother's car back and he would return the next day with some paper work from Annapolis, which needed information on Karen. He also mentioned going to visit James and his family.

Next day, Karen and JW took the completed paper work to the post office and then stopped to eat. After eating they gassed up his truck and drove to the home of their friend, James West. After visiting for about five hours, Karen called her mother to say she and John were on their way home. After completing the drive back to Carlinville, JW stopped to gas up his truck again, while Karen called her mom to let her know they were back in town and were going to stop and get something to eat.

Karen's mother said, "Oh please come on home. John's parents and the banker are here. We are getting ready to eat, too."

Karen and JW arrived, cleaned up and sat down to eat with Karen and JW's parents and the banker; just like one big family. After dinner the table was cleared and cleaned. The banker brought out the paper work he'd brought for Karen and JW. He explained to Karen that she would need to use her married name. He then went on to explain, although the forms were blank, he still needed the papers signed now because he had found a three thousand dollar savings at the close of business, so he grabbed the forms and came on over.

JW spoke, "Didn't you tell me never to sign any blank papers? And you're the banker; can't you keep the bank open if you need to?"

"Well yes, I did tell you that, and yes, I am the bank president, but these papers need to be filed with the county recorder's office, and they're closed. You and Karen have a number of things you're trying to complete; I'm just trying to save the two of you some time. As your banker, I would not mislead you. And after all, I do have a reputation to uphold."

Karen looked at JW waiting for direction on what she should do. JW looked at his dad and Karen's dad while thinking for a moment. His thoughts kept coming back to the banker always being very adamant about not ever signing blank papers, and yet, he had a reputation to uphold. JW's dad and Karen's dad were never very good friends, but here they were in the same house having dinner. Was this all because he and Karen were getting married? JW came to the conclusion that if both fathers and the banker thought this was the right thing to do, then it must be okay.

JW then said, "I guess you're right. Go ahead, Karen, let me have the pen when you're done."

Karen started smiling as she signed her name as "Karen Walker" and then said, "I will be so happy when it becomes official."

After the new property paper work was completed, the banker excused himself and left. Karen was always on the inside track of knowing what was going on, but this paper work was a surprise to her. Karen looked at her and JW's parents, as though asking, "What's up with this paper deal?"

The next day Karen came over to JW's house really early. As she opened the door and walked inside, she heard some sounds coming from the kitchen area. Entering the kitchen, Karen saw Mr. Walker sitting at the table reading the paper and drinking coffee. She walked quietly up behind him and before she said anything, without turning around, Mr. Walker said, "Good morning, Karen."

Karen was stunned, and surprised to say the least. So she said, "Good morning, Sir," and "How did you know it was me?"

Mr. Walker took a long deep breath and spoke while letting it out, "Your perfume Karen," and continued to read his paper.

Karen put her hands on Mr. Walker's shoulders and said, "Can I get you a cup of coffee? I'd like a cup myself."

Mr. Walker replied, "Yes, please." Karen returned with the coffee and she and Mr. Walker talked for a while. Then Karen put her empty cup in the sink and seemed to disappear.

A few minutes later, not hearing the front door open or close, Mr. Walker walked from the kitchen to the living room where he saw a beautiful young redhead, soon to be his daughter-in-law curled up on the couch fast asleep. He covered her up with a blanket that was kept in the living room for just this purpose. Mr. Walker went and gave his wife a kiss, then left for work.

About an hour later JW woke up and sauntered into the kitchen. Looking in the sink and seeing two coffee cups, he thought his mother must be up but then he smelled something familiar and began sniffing the air with a big smile on his face.

JW returned to the living room, where the scent was stronger. When his eyes fell on a redhead curled up on the couch under a blanket, his heart rate and pulse charged rapidly.

JW walked to the couch and knelt down, staring at the most beautiful face in the world, the woman he planned to marry. JW returned to his room to get a blanket and pillow from his bed and placed the pillow on the carpeted floor in front of couch. Lying down and covering up with his blanket, JW was now lying next to the woman he wanted to spend the rest of his life with-- apart, but almost together.

About forty-five minutes later, JW's mother walked in the living room heading for the kitchen. Just after entering the kitchen she stopped, turned and looked back into the living room. What she saw was Karen lying stretched out on the couch with her right arm hanging down and her hand on John's chest. Her son was lying on the floor, his left arm leaned against the couch, and his left hand held Karen's arm.

Mrs. Walker had seen her son sleeping many times in his life, but she couldn't remember seeing him look so peaceful. About ten to twenty minutes later, JW came into the kitchen and sat down across from his mom and asked if he could talk to her. "Mom, I didn't have time to talk to you and Dad, and it seems a lot of things are happening real fast for me here lately."

His mom said, "Let me see, you're not sure of what to do on a special night coming up?"

JW looked down at the table and then said, "Yes Mom, that's one of the things. But it's not the only thing."

"Well Son, your father needs to talk to you about that special night; but perhaps we can talk about the other things."

"Thanks, Mom. I feel better already."

Karen walked in, put her arms around JW's neck, kissed him on the cheek, and then said, "You feel better already about what?"

"Oh, nothing. Just something I need to talk to my dad about."

"Oh, I see. Would it be anything like 'the father and son talk' would it?"

Karen and JW's mother both had a good laugh at JW's expense.

"Yes, it would be, now can we change the subject?"

"Ok, how about we talk about our wedding day?"

"Sounds good to me," responded JW. "I will get the paper from the meeting with the minister."

"John, would you and Karen like some breakfast?"

"Yes, Mom, that sounds good to me. I'll be right back with the paper."

After eating, talking and checking dates, talking to Mr. Walker on the phone and Karen's parents as well, the wedding date was set. The wedding would take place on May 10, 1967.

JW made one more phone call. That was to the *Mariner Inn* in St. Louis, located six blocks from *Bush Memorial Stadium* and four blocks from the mighty Mississippi River.

Then JW announced, "We've got the bridal suite for two nights, at $85.00 per night."

JW's mother spoke up in a much higher voice, "**John, you got what? For how much?**"

"We got the bridal suite for two nights for $85.00 per night. What's wrong with that?"

Still in a higher voice his mother shouted, **"You're paying $85.00 a night! What are you getting for this $85.00 per night? John, that's a week's pay per night!"**

"But Mom, we get 'free TV'."

"Oh John! You need to talk to your dad NOW! I thought we taught you better than that. I think that's a waste of good money, John!"

JW looked around the room, only to see Karen kind of laughing, as he said "free TV".

That night during dinner Karen and her little brother were at JW's house. Karen's brother sat next to JW and JW's little sister. JW's little brother was away attending a Boy Scout camp. The topics discussed during dinner revolved around the wedding and included flowers, tuxes and, of course, the two-night stay at eighty-five dollars per night at the *Mariner Inn*.

To drive home the frugality point, JW's mother reminded everyone, "Don't forget he gets 'free TV'." JW's dad was looking down while making notes. He looked up with his eyes only while shaking his head.

JW said, "But, Dad, it's free TV and I think it might be color."

Mr. Walker put his elbows on the table and covered his face with his hands while shaking his head in disbelief. He then looked up with his left hand across his mouth, sliding his fingers below his mouth, and then running his fingers back and forth across his chin all the while looking at his wife, then to JW, then back to his wife.

Then he said, **"John, my son, we've have got to talk!"**

Karen poked JW in the ribs with her left elbow and whispered, "Free color TV no less. Hum."

Karen's brother asked, "John, are they going to show cartoons? I've been told they're in color by the way."

JW's dad said, "Now tomorrow John, I want you to go to Martin's Market and get two bags of ice, one six-pack of Pepsi and two six-packs of Pabst Blue Ribbon. Put the Pepsi and beer in the ice chest and cover them with the ice. I should be home just after five."

The next day, JW had followed his father's instructions to the letter. His dad arrived just after five. After showering and changing clothes he said, "Let's go, John." JW and his dad returned home at 8:40pm and after getting out of the car, JW fell in the front yard. Karen had witnessed this and ran over to JW.

"John, are you OK? What's wrong my love?" then looking up she said, "Mr. Walker, what did you do to him? How many beers has he had?"

Mr. Walker stood over Karen and JW and said, "Counting the one he spilled, three." Then he went on to say with a laugh, "Karen, you might have woke him up inside, but little honey, I just turned the light on for you."

JW had trouble talking, but managed to say, "The couch in the house is wrong, and Karen? I don't think we're going to need the free TV, color or not."

Karen looked up to Mr. Walker again and asked, "The couch? What the…? Is he going to live?"

Mr. Walker responded, "Karen, as long as you keep him away from beer and on Pepsi, I think there's a chance."

After an hour or so, Karen was able to get JW up and into the house with a little help from JW's mother. They were able to get JW into his bed and his mother left while Karen sat for a long time on the edge of the bed, watching him sleep. She never felt so much love for him as she did at that moment.

The next week, one week before the wedding, Karen, her mother, and her maid of honor went to be fitted for their gowns, while JW and James were being fitted for their tuxes. James' fiancée, Mary Beth, tagged along with Karen's entourage.

Family members from both sides were starting to arrive, and the little motel on the southeast side of town was filling fast. Karen and JW's house were being used for immediate and closely related relatives, with the exception of the master bedroom.

Time was starting to run short and they were starting to run short of bed space, therefore, some relatives were relegated to sleeping on the floor. There were so many things to do each day, and with all the extra mouths at breakfast the kitchen looked as if a naval unit had been invited.

JW's dad asked if he and Karen were driving his truck on their honeymoon. JW responded, "No Dad. Mr. McIntosh is lending us his Mercedes-Benz."

It was finally May 7, only three days before the wedding. JW borrowed one of his dad's company trucks and went to Karen's house to pick up her personal things. Then with Karen joining him, they went to JW's house to pick up his personal things. As JW carried the last of his things, which he would not need the next three days, out the door JW's mother started crying, just like Karen's mother did earlier in the day.

JW put his arms around his mother, just as he did with Karen's mother, and asked her to calm down and not to worry as she wasn't losing a son, but was gaining a daughter. This calmed her down some and so he also added what he thought was an extra bonus by mentioning that with his leaving she would have less work to do like laundry and cooking. Unfortunately, this backfired as his mother began to cry even harder.

Through her tears she said, "But John, that's my job to take care of you and your wife, and some day my grandkids. John I've taken care of you all your life. I've changed your diapers and given you baths when you were younger. I helped you with your homework from school. I've sat up all night with you when you were sick."

"And you did a fine job, Mom, but there comes a time when all fledglings must spread their wings and leave the nest."

JW wiped the tears from his mother's eyes, then giving his mother a kiss and a hug, he said, "I'll still be here until the morning of the tenth; besides, I'm sure Karen and I will be stopping by often."

"When you and Mrs. McIntosh finish setting up the house, while Karen and I are on our honeymoon, would you please bring the last of my clothes and things out to the house?"

"I guess you're right, Son. When Karen's mom and I finish setting up your new house, I will bring the last of your things." She then turned to Karen and asked, "Does your mother have a good idea as to how you want your kitchen set up?"

"Yes, well she should anyway."

"I love you, Son. And Karen, I love you; you take good care of him."

Karen said, "Oh, I will Mrs. Walker. I promise he will be well taken care of."

Karen and JW turned and walked to the truck. After Karen climbed in, JW closed the door for her and he looked back as his mother stood on the steps of the porch, with big tears running down her face. They waved at her and she waved back as they drove away.

As JW drove, Karen talked of how nice it was to see all the aunts and uncles arriving for the wedding. JW agreed about seeing the relatives and how happy he was at finally meeting some of her relatives.

After arriving at their new home, two of Karen's cousins helped to move all the things into the house, and

Karen went about checking out her new home. Then Karen went upstairs with JW. While making sure things were put away where she wanted them, her two cousins went downstairs to help with furniture arrangement.

Karen shut the bedroom door while looking at JW. Karen quietly said, "John, do you realize this is the first time we've been alone in three weeks and we still have three days to go?"

JW took Karen in his arms and held her close as he gently kissed her lips. JW said, "Karen, I don't ever want to be without you. I want to hold and kiss you forever. Karen, I ask God every night to let me have you for the rest of my life, to love and hold forever."

"John, I ask God for the same thing; I don't ever want to be without you. I want you to love and hold me forever too."

"John, tell me you will always be mine forever. Because John, I want to be yours till the end of time!"

JW drew Karen even closer and tighter than he had ever done in his life and kissed like he never kissed her before. When the kiss ended, Karen could tell certain changes were taking place within the man she loved so she quietly asked, "John, would you like to stay here for a while?"

For a long moment JW looked into the eyes of Karen, the woman he held in his arms, the same woman he wanted to marry, then in a soft voice said, "I believe I understand what you just offered me, and I'm so very temped to partake of the pleasures of the flesh, but I feel the fruits of that pleasure would be better as man and wife. Besides, I'm afraid by the time we stop, everyone would know."

"Karen, I know it will be our first time, and I don't want anything to go wrong. I want us to take our time and have it last forever. When we make love, I don't want there to be any reason for us to be disturbed or worry about time."

"Oh, I love you, John!"

"I love you too, Karen."

Driving back to town and when he was not shifting the truck, JW placed his right hand on Karen's left leg, which pleased Karen greatly.

Then Karen said, "You know what, John? We have our rehearsal tonight."

"Oh, gosh Karen, I'm so sorry, honey. I guess I forgot."

Karen and JW returned his dad's truck to the company yard, jumped into JW's pick-up and dashed off to the church. After rehearsal practice, JW and Karen returned to Karen's house and had dinner with both sets of parents. After dinner both fathers and JW sat outside on the back porch. Unknown to JW they both had a question to ask him.

"Seems like it took a long time, moving your and Karen's things into your new house. Is there anything you want to talk to us about?"

"Well Dad, seems Karen is particular where things go; some things had to be moved more than once."

"We thought that might be the problem...and that is all it was, wasn't it Son?"

"Yes, that's all there was to it."

Then JW's mom walked up, "John, can you drive to Springfield tomorrow and pick up your little brother? It seems the bus won't get in until late, about 8:30 tomorrow night."

"Well Mom, I had planned on visiting with relatives, but I guess I can. May I use your car? The water pump is going bad in my truck."

"Son, I've got a number of things to do tomorrow, and shopping is one of them."

Okay Mom, I will ask Mr. McIntosh if I can borrow his car."

On May 8, 1967, only two days before the wedding. JW was awakened by his dad at five a.m. JW jumped in the shower, dressed and shaved; he then went downstairs only to see wall-to-wall people sleeping on the floor. Entering the kitchen, JW saw his mom making breakfast while his dad was reading the paper.

JW's mom set his plate in front of him on the table; breakfast consisted of pancakes, eggs, and bacon with a tall glass of milk to wash it all down.

JW asked his dad, "Do you have twenty dollars; I've only five on me, and I am not sure how much gas Mr. McIntosh's Mercedes-Benz might burn. I am sure that in the four or five hour drive I'm bound to get hungry and want something to eat."

Mr. Walker replied, "So will your brother, so here is forty and be sure and bring me the receipts."

Mr. Walker dropped JW off at Karen's house. JW went inside to get the keys for the Mercedes and there was Karen holding the keys in her hand. JW got a kiss and a hug from her (something he wanted anyway), the keys for the Mercedes, and then went out the door heading for Springfield, Illinois.

JW arrived in Springfield at nine a.m. Due to some construction, he had a bit of a problem getting to the Scout camp. By eleven a.m., he was on his way back to

Carlinville with his little brother. They stopped at Stucky's where the two of them each had a cheeseburger, fries, and a large chocolate shake. After gassing the car, they were on the way again.

His brother asked, "Why did you come and get me? I could've returned on the bus?"

"Well, you need to be fitted for your tux and you need to be at the rehearsal."

"Ok, but I've already been fitted for my tux. But I guess I do need to rehearse my part of the wedding. John, why are you looking at me like that? Oh shit, I'm sorry you didn't know I had already been fitted."

"What else is there I don't know about?"

"Uh, huh. Nothing, John, nothing at all!"

After returning, JW picked up Karen and together they checked on the flowers, then the final fitting for Karen's dress and JW and his little brother's tuxes.

After all this JW said, "I don't mind saying, I'm a bit tired."

"Well John, we still have one more rehearsal tonight. Then you can sleep in tomorrow. This is nothing compared to what's happing on the tenth. You do remember the 'Free TV' don't you?"

JW chuckled and said, "It might be in color." Then all three left for the church.

As JW turned left off the road into the driveway of the church, Karen screamed, "John! Stop! Stop! My God, John! Stop!" JW stopped the car as quickly as possible, while asking, "What? What's wrong Karen?"

JW's brother ran into the church, as Karen bounded from the car. She ran some two hundred feet into a newly planted wheat field. With her hands out from her sides, palms turned up, turning slowly around in one spot, Karen started crying.

Leaving the car door open and engine running, JW ran to Karen, putting his arms around her and asking, "What's wrong, Karen? What's wrong my love?"

As Karen looked at JW, she could see other family members coming from the church, Karen said, "Something very important will happen here; and it involves you."

"Ok, what is it?"

"Oh John, I don't know."

"Are you sure you're okay, Karen? Do you want to go on with the rehearsal?"

"Yes, yes I do, John. I don't want anything to go wrong with our wedding day."

"Are you sure you're okay, Karen?"

As the crowd gathered around someone murmured, "I think she has the new bride jitters. I'm sure all-new brides experience the jitters to some extent."

The rest of the rehearsal went well without a hitch, and everyone went to Mr. and Mrs. McIntosh's home for a big barbecue. On the way to her mom and dad's house, Karen told JW, "I was asked to go with some air force officer. The helicopter I saw in my vision was unlike any I have ever seen in my life. It had something to do with you, John. I have no idea what it was about." Karen then curled up next to JW in a loving fashion as he drove.

May 9-1967. One day to the wedding and JW had been up about 20 minutes when Karen came in and said, "Well I hope you slept well last night, because I tossed and turned most of the night."

"So did I, my love. I feel like if I were to lay down, I could go right to sleep and I just got up some 20 or so minutes ago."

By now, everyone was starting to awake from sleeping on the floor and in corners of the house. After folding the blankets, a large number of relatives descended upon the kitchen. Even with three coffee pots going at one time, it was still hard to keep up with the empty cups looking to be filled and breakfast. Breakfast at best, was a nightmare.

JW asked Karen, "Did you ride your bike over here?"

Karen responded, "Yes, dear I did."

"Would you like to ride to my dad's shop with me, so I can get my truck?"

"Okay, let's go! John, are you going to peddle or am I?"

"I'll peddle first, when I get tired then you can. Ok with you?"

Karen and JW stopped back by his house after getting his truck. JW's mom fixed them a plate of eggs and potatoes with bacon. JW also had a large glass of milk. The two sat around talking with relatives till 11:30 a.m. when JW's mother asked, "What time are we supposed to migrate towards your house, Karen?"

"My mother said any time after 10:00. That will give her time to complete breakfast."

"Okay, I will start getting everyone headed that way. Karen, can you and John stop at Martin's Market? Your mother and I have an order to be picked up."

"Sure, John has his truck anyway."

After picking up the supplies from Martin's Market, Karen and JW returned to Karen's house, which by now looked like the makings of a revival with all the cars and people that had gathered there the day before the wedding.

A number of relatives helped carry the food in from JW's truck. The supplies consisted of hamburger meat, steaks, hotdogs and potatoes, as well as bread, milk, sodas, pickles and olives; and last but not least, watermelons, cantaloupes, and apples.

As the women started cooking and preparing a variety of foods, JW and some of the others started playing football, while the younger kids were playing hide and seek and board games.

By mid-afternoon the steaks, hamburgers and hotdogs started hitting the grill with Karen's father wearing the BBQ chef hat. This type of cooking he was very good at.

About four in the afternoon, when everyone had eaten, it started looking more like a large slumber party was taking place in the yard. Karen and JW went to sleep on a blanket near the back porch, while both parents sat in some yard chairs talking. Mr. McIntosh asked, "What do you think that deal was yesterday with Karen running into that field? I've never known Karen to do anything like that before."

Mrs. Walker said, "She saw something. And I think it has something to do with the future and John. I heard her say something to John about a helicopter landing there. But it wasn't like any helicopter she has ever seen. That she and John's youngest son, I think she called him Patty Boy? Well, it seems that Patty Boy evidently ran into the church yelling they found him."

Mrs. McIntosh asked, "What do you make of that? What could it mean? The youngest son's name is 'Patty

Boy'? Who in God's name would name a son 'Patty Boy'?"

"I just don't know."

The conversation changed from that to other things such as how Karen and John would be gone for three days on their honeymoon and how all of them would finish cleaning and setting up the house for the newlyweds.

Now just a little after 6:00 pm, everyone started waking up from drowsy naps. Some were hungry while others wanted beer.

As the evening moved along, Karen and JW were being asked, "How many kids do the two of you want? Will the two of you always live here in Carlinville? How long do you expect to be in the Navy?"

Soon the evening came to an end. Karen and JW anxiously waited the coming day and the start of the next step in their lives; a life filled with hopes, dreams and uncertainties.

May 10, 1967. The Wedding Day. Karen and JW didn't sleep that entire well but were up early getting ready because this was finally their wedding day.

After one last massive breakfast, all the relatives started heading for the church dressed in their Sunday best. JW was all thumbs; his mom had to tie his tie; his younger brother told him he had his shoes on the wrong feet; his sister told him twice to close the barn door before his little horse got out.

Soon the Walker family arrived at the church with JW in tow. JW could see the Mercedes-Benz sitting under the driveway cover with cans tied to it. The windows were marked with white shoe polish 'Just Married' and balloons on strings were taped all over the car. Inside there were many envelopes taped to the windows with family names on them.

After entering the church, JW was met by his best friend and best man, James West. James asked if JW is ready for all this. He added a teaser by telling JW that he had seen Karen in her wedding dress, and how beautiful she looked. Reb, who was also present, expressed that he had never seen Karen so beautiful, radiant and happy before.

"James, I'm about as ready for this as I can get. Did Karen really look good in her dress? James, you know I've been waiting for this day for a very long time; I hope it all goes well. James, did Karen really look good in her dress?"

"JW, that's the second time you've asked me that question, and yes, she looks beautiful! Now you're not nervous are you?"

JW replied, "Maybe just a bit, James, maybe just a bit."

The minister was getting everyone in place and ready for the ceremony to start just as JW looked out over the pews filled with friends and relatives. He recalled all the years leading up to this moment as the organist began to play *Mendelssohn's Wedding March*."

As "Here Comes the Bride" began, Karen started her walk down the aisle on the arm of her father. When JW saw Karen in her wedding dress for the first time, tears came to his eyes as he looked upon the most beautiful woman in the entire world, and she was walking towards him, taking his hand, giving hers to him in marriage.

With each step she took, JW recalled all the things he and Karen had done together; going to the movies, picnics, swimming, going to church and of course, fighting for the right to sit next to her in the lunch room at school. JW thought how small she looked next to her dad and how proud he seemed to look, as he was about to give his beautiful daughter away to the young man who used to mow his grass. JW could see tears in this big man's eyes, as the minister asked, "Who gives this woman in marriage?"

Mr. McIntosh stood proudly while saying, "Her mother and I," as he placed Karen's hand in JW's. Then taking hold of JW's arm he whispered in a low voice and a tear in his eye, "John, you take good care of her, or I will rip your F---ing lungs out."

JW and Karen now faced the minister; a man who had baptized the two of them and helped them to read and understand the Bible and the teachings of God and who was now going to join the two of them in holy matrimony. This was the moment in history the two of them had waited for so long in their lives. It was a time when the two of them would become as one in the eyes of God and to raise their children with the teachings of God: all from the training they had received from their parents on how to face the perils and uncertainty of life together; forever in each other's arms.

The ceremony was beautiful and everything JW and Karen had prayed for. The minister began with, "We have gathered together here this day to join these two in Holy Matrimony. Should any one for any reason, having just cause that this union should not take place, let them speak now, or forever hold their peace."

"John Fredrick Walker, do you take Karen McIntosh, to be your wife, to love and hold in sickness and in health, for richer or poorer to be forever together in each other's arms until death you do part?

"I do."

"Karen McIntosh, do you take John Fredrick Walker to be your husband, to love and hold in sickness and in health, for richer or poorer, to be together for ever in each other's arms until death you do part?"

"I do."

"Then by the power vested in me by the great state of Illinois, and in the eyes of God, I now pronounce you man and wife. You may now kiss the bride." JW and Karen began to kiss as the minister added, "What God has placed together, let no man put asunder."

The kiss was unlike any kiss that Karen and John had ever experienced. This kiss came from deep, deep inside. It was as if their souls had embraced, kissed and become one. After turning to face the audience of relatives and friends, the minister said. "At this time, I take great pride in introducing to all of you Mr. and Mrs. John Fredrick Walker."

As Karen and JW walked out of the church, the waiting relatives and friends tossed rice on them and congratulations were bestowed on them in the receiving line. Karen told everyone that they were going to drive around the town of Carlinville for a few minutes giving the town a chance to see them as newlyweds and then return to her mom and dad's for the wedding reception. This tactic allowed everyone a chance to get from the church to the reception before their arrival.

After arriving at the reception, Karen and JW had trouble being together, as everyone was congratulating them, giving them advice, and pulling them this way and that and apart from each other. The women were giving Karen advice about her 'first time' and the men were doing the same to JW.

Then it came time for the first dance as man and wife. Karen had always been good at dancing. JW always seemed to have three left feet. This night, however, he danced more like Fred Astaire as he and Karen danced their first dance as man and wife. When it was time to dance with anyone else, JW's three left feet returned.

After eating, it was time to cut the cake and all the men were telling JW how to feed Karen her cake. Even Karen's dad was telling him how to feed Karen her share of the cake by mashing it into her face. He warned him, "You won't get a second chance." JW decided not to do what was suggested as he had something else in mind. He gave Karen her cake very carefully and then took a napkin and wiped the specks of frosting off the corners of her mouth very gently.

Karen took the advice of the women, and JW had cake all over his face. After giving everyone a chance to take pictures with cake on his face, JW bent down and gave Karen a big kiss, making sure the cake on his face transferred to Karen's, much to the delight of the wedding guests. Then JW picked up a piece of cake in his right hand, with his left hand he pulled out the top of Karen's dress and stuffed the cake inside. Then patted it shut and said, "That's for later."

As guests hooted and whistled Mr. Walker smugly spoke up and said, "That's my boy, taught him everything he knows."

JW and Karen had one more dance and then opened the wedding gifts and cards. The gifts were all the things newlyweds would need; many of the cards were not only congratulatory but came complete with money. Among it all was one plain white envelope with a single five-dollar bill in it. This came from JW's cousin who was in Chicago's Children's Hospital and was unable to attend. This was a brand new five-dollar bill, minted in 1967; on it were written these words, "I love you so much, John, and I'm so very proud of you. May God keep you safe for ever."

By now it was about 7:30 pm and just getting dark. Karen asked JW if he was ready to go. "You and I can just take off, I'm sure our moms and dads will pick up everything."

"Ok, Karen. I will let my mom and dad know we're taking off."

"John, we don't need to tell anyone, let's just go. You and I no longer need to ask if we can go anywhere together."

Karen's little brother soon reported that the Mercedes-Benz had left the driveway, and he didn't think Karen had asked permission to leave. Karen's dad patted her brother on the head while saying, "Son when you grow up, if you live that long, you won't have to ask permission either. Now get started cleaning the yard, it looks like hell."

Karen and JW had enough clothes in the car for the next three days. There was no need to make any stops till the two of them arrived at the hotel, called the *Mariner Inn* located in St. Louis, Missouri.

After arriving at the *Mariner Inn* and checking in with the front desk while still dressed in their wedding clothes, Karen asked John, "Would you mind if I sign us in? This would be my first chance to sign my new name." It took three cards before Karen wrote it right.

JW told her, "Walker is spelled 'W A L K E R', the name Walker starts with the letter 'W' not the letter 'M' and I love you Mrs. Walker."

The man behind the counter was very patient as he could see her embarrassment as well the pride she was taking in signing her new name. He smiled graciously as he handed her the third card, which was finally the one she managed to write Walker on.

JW told the man, "We wish to not be disturbed for any reason, unless of course the building is on fire." The manager smiled while JW continued, "However, we would like room service only when called for, and tomorrow we have tickets to the Cardinals game, and would like to have a two-hour reminder call."

The manager said, "Mr. Walker, the *Mariner Inn* wishes to assure you and your wife that you will not be disturbed for any reason, except per your instructions." He then instructed a bellhop to take the Walker's bags to the Honeymoon Suite.

Karen and JW followed the bellhop to the Honeymoon Suite and the bellhop placed their luggage just inside the room and disappeared without saying a word or even waiting for a tip.

JW picked Karen up in his arms, gave her a kiss and told her how much he loved her. JW then carried her through the door, using the back of his right foot to close the door.

Four days later JW and Karen arrived at their home, the newly remodeled farmhouse. As they walked up to the door, JW opened the door and again picked Karen up, carrying her across the threshold of their new home where their children would grow up, learn how to ride bicycles, mow grass, care for stock animals, and learn how to read and write, and go through all the bumps and bruises that come with all the trials of life. This would be their new home for a long time.

As JW held Karen in his arms, he again told her how much he loved her, and how proud he was that she chose him to be her husband and that all he is, and all that he might ever become, he would share with her without any reservations, "So help me God!"

Karen said, "John, I feel the same. You will never be alone, and I will help raise our children in the eyes of God."

After letting her down, the two of them started looking around. JW said, "Well they changed out the couch." The living room was arranged in a fashion that JW was used to as well as Karen. On a small table was a display of wedding cards and one large manila envelope. Karen picked it up and opened it while JW went to the restroom. When JW returned he could see Karen was crying and asked Karen, "Why are you crying?"

She handed JW the papers from the vanilla envelope. As JW read the papers, he too started to cry. It was the paper work from the bank, pertaining to Karen and JW's property. It had been stamped in bright red letters "Paid in full."

JW took his new wife in his arms and said, "It's all ours my love, it's all ours."

In another envelope from Karen's mom and dad contained the free and clear title for the Mercedes-Benz, with insurance papers covering JW's truck as well, paid for two years in advance and a check for a thousand dollars, and paid to Mr. and Mrs. John Walker.

From JW's mom and dad was the paper work showing ownership of JW's parent's company giving Karen and

JW forty-nine-percent of the family business and a letter from the Illinois power company stating the power had been paid, and would continue to be paid by Walker Construction and Truck Bed Manufacture Company. There were many other envelopes containing cash, and checks and yet still there were envelopes taped to the inside of the car and as yet unopened.

Other than to call their parents to let them know they were home, Karen and JW stayed home that night.

April 14, 1967. JW and Karen only had six weeks to settle into their home before JW had to report to Annapolis and this time would pass quickly, and a lot quicker than they could even imagine. One week before JW was to leave for the Academy he was told he would be a father in about seven and half months. JW was in the height of his glory, as well was both sets of parents. Everyone was suggesting his or her favorite names for what the child's name would be. Finally, Karen spoke up, "Our first son's name will be John Fredrick Walker III in honor of the best man I have ever known."

Karen and JW's mother both said when Karen got far enough along she would come and stay in town with them. JW told the two mothers he knew he could depend on them and when he was home, he would need them to show him how to properly care for a small child. The days passed so quickly and it was soon time for JW to leave.

Karen took JW to the bus stop, along with JW's and Karen's parents. JW gave them all a kiss and a hug good-bye. To Karen, he gave a special kiss and hug, telling her to be ever so careful and take good care of the very special gift she was carrying and he would return as soon as possible. After one last kiss and hug from Karen, JW stepped on to the bus and took a seat next to James.

CHAPTER FIVE
ANNAPOLIS

Annapolis Naval Academy is a four-year prestigious naval military college in what is now historic Annapolis, Maryland. George Bancroft, the Secretary of the Navy at that time, founded the college in 1845. Attending Annapolis was both a privilege and an honor. From plebe summer to graduation, Naval Academy Officers Development is a program based on a four year integrated continuum, focusing on the attributes of integrity, mutual respect and honor.

Although excited with his opportunity to attend the academy, JW was sorrowfully aware that he would be away from his family and friends, as well as his new wife. He also knew he would most likely be called John instead of JW. James would be there to call him JW, so his connection to home would still be somewhat intact. JW thought he would surely make some new friends as well.

JW knew that moral and ethical development would be a fundamental part of all aspects of his Academy experience. As a midshipman he would one day be responsible for priceless multimillion-dollar equipment and the lives of other young men and women. He was aware that as a midshipman, his academic program had a core curriculum that included courses in science, the humanities, social science, mathematics and engineering.

These courses were designed to provide a broad based education, qualifying him for just about any career field available in the Navy.

JW knew he would have to work very hard. Even though he had graduated first in his class, he would be competing with other young men and women from all over the country who were just as smart and determined as he.

The first eight weeks at the academy proved to be a true test of JW's strong will and determination. In the first two months he saw many other cadets fall to the wayside and drop out, while other cadets were being asked to seek different careers. However, the class commander and JW seemed to hit it off really well. After the second week it seemed they would most likely become good friends. This became a reality as the first year at the academy flew by in a blur.

When the first year was suddenly a part of their history, James and JW were informed the class had suffered the loss of only twenty-five percent of the cadets. This number was considered low, but then again this was only the first year. Both men were pleased they had survived this initial year of training.

Before JW and James left for their first three-month cruise, one of the professors sat the two of them down and gave them some pointers on what to study. This information would help the two of them over the next three years. As important as the information was to them, they were excited to be on their way to their families and friends. James and JW left for home during the customary leave with plenty of books to study, but the journey seemed to last far too long. Finally pulling into town, the two could see JW and Karen's fathers standing on the sidewalk. The two men seemed quite anxious about something. JW and James felt their own anxiety grow as they wondered what had happened in their absence.

James asked, "You think something's wrong with Karen?"

JW replied, "I hope not, besides she's not due for two weeks!"

When JW stepped from the bus, his dad and Karen's dad met him. The two men hardly gave JW a chance to wish James good luck on his studies and to have a good time while they were home when the two fathers started going on and on about how Karen was in the hospital. As the two men whisked JW away in route to the hospital, JW learned Karen was in delivery and he was about to become a father. JW reminded his dad and father in-law that Karen wasn't due until next month.

Then his father in-law asked, "John, you and my daughter did wait until your wedding night didn't you?"

JW in a bit higher nervous voice responded, "Yes, we did!"

After arriving at the hospital, all three men rushed towards the delivery room where a nurse who was holding a gown met them. The nurse asked, "Karen's husband, John Walker?" She then placed the gown on JW and attempted to tie the gown while they ran into the delivery room.

The second Karen saw JW she said, "I love you, John, thank God you're here." A minute and thirty seconds later John Fredrick Walker, III arrived. He was nine pounds, seven ounces and fully equipped with all

God had intended. Karen and JW looked over their new son with awe while they counted ten tiny toes and ten tiny fingers. Karen looked up at JW and saw big tears running down his face. John was biting his upper lip, as he lovingly gazed at the wonderful child God had just given them.

JW then looked at Karen. He bent down and placed a soft, tender kiss upon her lips. While his tears fell on her face and on his new son, JW said, "Thank you from the bottom of my heart, honey, thank you."

A few minutes later, the baby was taken away and given his first bath, and Karen was taken to her room for some badly needed rest. JW went out to the waiting room and told everyone the baby was a boy and his name was John Fredric Walker, III.

The women went to Karen's room and left JW to be dragged off by his dad and father-in-law to celebrate the birth of their first grandson. They took along a box of "it's a boy" cigars to pass out to everyone they met. JW wasn't much of a drinker and often jokingly told people, "If I walk past a liquor store, I will have a hang over the next day." However, this was indeed a special time. James had decided to get off the bus with JW and had waited at the hospital. He joined them for the celebration as well. Unlike JW, James liked a drink now and again; so all four men took off for the local watering hole, the Carlinville Moose Lodge. After arriving at the Moose lodge, the proud grandfathers started handing out the cigars. In no time at all, free drinks of all kinds began to arrive at the table.

James, being a good friend as always, and JW's dad and father in-law tried to keep the table cleared of drinks as best they could. It was soon apparent they were greatly outnumbered and it became a losing battle. JW managed to down only two drinks. With everyone patting him on the back, it was much like shaking up a soda pop and then taking the lid off really fast. JW barely made it to the restroom before the big eruption. When JW returned from the restroom, he asked the bartender for a Pepsi or a root beer with no liquor. The bartender obliged JW and gave him a Seven-Up to help settle his stomach.

After about six hours, James and JW's dad and father in-law were all quite limber. With legs made of rubber, they were pouring more drinks on themselves than in. Their mannerisms of speech seemed quite impaired as JW announced, "I think this party is over, time to go home."

With the help of the bartender, who was the only other sober person within the confines of the lodge, JW managed to get the three of them into the car where they passed out. JW went back to the hospital to see his wife and baby. After visiting for about an hour, JW told Karen that he was going to his mom and dad's house. He also shared that his dad, her father and James were all passed out in the car.

JW returned to his mom and dad's house and went inside to call his mother-in-law to let her know where William was and that he was safe. After hanging up the phone, JW stretched out on the sofa and went to sleep.

When JW awoke the next morning, his mother was sitting at his feet watching the Price is Right on TV. She said, "When my show goes off, I will make some breakfast. Would that be okay? And maybe you can try and get the others out of the station wagon. John, when did William and Mary Beth get a station wagon?"

"Mother, it's not a station wagon. It's a Lincoln Continental!"

JW's mother put her hand on JW's leg and patted it while she said, "John, I may not know much about cars, but I think I can tell the difference between a Lincoln Continental and a rusted station wagon.

JW sat up and rubbed his face with his hands. Then he sat next to his mother until the Price is Right was over. The two then started talking about his new son, her new grandson, "Mom, I counted eight fingers, two thumbs and ten toes. I think Karen did a fine job. What do you think?"

"Yes, I think you and Karen did a fine job, Son. However, given Karen's height I don't think he will be as tall as you. He might, but I'm thinking he might be just a bit shorter. You both are real smart, so I think he will be at the very least a grandson to be proud of. And no matter how tall he might get, he will be a big man much like you. By the way, you're going to have him circumcised right?"

JW looked at his mother, squeezed his legs together and said in a bit higher voice, "Mother!"

She laughed at her son's reaction and said, "Well Son, I will start some breakfast. Will you please try and get the others out of the Lincoln Continental station wagon?"

JW's mother was in the kitchen when JW opened the front door. As he looked outside he said, "Oh shit, it is a station wagon. God, I hope the owner isn't pissed."

His mother called from the kitchen, "What'd you say, John?"

"Nothing Mom, I will try and get them out of the car."

JW had to hose James down to remove some of his stomach contents from the front of his clothes. William was a bit different; he was a furry Irishman, so some of the drinks he had the previous night were causing his shirt to stick to the hair on his chest; JW's dad was about the same.

James was the first to enter the house and take a shower; William was next and then JW's dad. JW called Mrs. McIntosh and asked her to bring some clothes for Mr. McIntosh. JW picked up their clothes and put them in the washer after he had his shower. Mrs. McIntosh arrived and was surprised to see all the men sitting around the table eating and drinking coffee with only a towel around them. But the first thing she asked was, "Willy, where is your car? And whose station wagon is that out front?"

JW's father in-law spoke up and said, "How would we know? John drove last night. I think."

The next three months passed very quickly, as JW spent as much time as possible with Karen and their new son as well as with their two families. The rest of the time he spent studying all the books he had brought home with him.

Two years later.

After James and JW were informed they had moved into the top ten of their class, JW received a letter from home. The letter informed JW of all that was happening with the two families in Carlinville and announced another new Walker was on the way. It didn't take JW long to figure out that he may not be there in time for the birth of his second child.

JW fired off a letter to Karen letting her know he would do the best he could to be with her during the birth. Given the approximate time of the birth and all the tests he must complete, he might be a day or two late.

JW and James determined the trip could be made quickest in a car, taking some twenty two to twenty six hours. A bus was totally out of the question since it would take something like three days. Unfortunately, there were no airlines that can do much better given such short notice and the closest airport was in St Louis. However, James and JW had a classmate who lived in Cape Girardeau, Missouri. The three of them would make the drive as quickly as possible. JW could only hope that Karen would hold on as best she could till his arrival.

After the completions of the ceremonies, the three men jumped into the car and hauled ass. They stopped only to water the flowers along the way and get gas and oil with a quick bite to eat. The drive was made in just over twenty and a half hours. The car arrived in front of the hospital where JW's dad could be seen waiting out front. Mr. Walker helped rush his son inside to a birth that had happened just five minutes earlier.

The first thing JW asked Karen, "Honey, are you okay?"

Karen responded, "Yes, I am fine. John, will you check on our new son?"

John had a surprised, proud new father look on his face as he tried to speak.

Karen asked, "What's the matter, John. Squirrel got your tongue?"

"We have a new son? Aw, aw, aw, sure I will check on my new son," JW turned to view a new baby boy who was being check out by the doctor and nurses. JW counted all the fingers and toes and sure enough there was a stem on the apple.

JW turned back to Karen and put his arms under and around her. As he gently drew her close to him, he placed a kiss on her lips. With tears in his eyes, JW said, "Thank you, thank you Karen for our second son. Honey, you're the best!"

Karen said, "Honey, you were late. My dad was here, and he wants to name him Paddy boy. Is that okay with you?"

"Sounds like a good Irish name to me."

Karen and John spent the rest of his summer break with their two boys while visiting with relatives. JW had some work to do around the little family farm and what seemed like endless studying.

Three days before John left, returning to Maryland for his last year of the Naval Academy, he sat down with Karen and expressed that he wasn't sure where in his class he might graduate. He felt he would be lucky just to graduate considering the educational level of the other cadets. They had come from all over the country and were all well educated.

Karen replied, "John, how can you say something like that? Going to the Naval Academy has always been your dream. All I have done is try to help make it come true. What you learn there may determine your survival in adverse conditions and ultimately our future!"

JW looked lovingly into Karen's face and said, "Karen, you and our boys are the most important things in my life. You're more important than this little farm. Karen, you and my boys are more important to me than my mom and dad and the three of you always will be. Except for Jesus and God almighty, I hold no one higher than you and my boys." John then placed a tender kiss on Karen's lips while putting his arms around her and caressing her tightly.

Karen lay back on the couch. The shirt she was wearing gently pulled up as she raised her arms above her head and exposed her bellybutton as she wiggled softly into the couch. As JW gazed upon her the thought occurred to him that this was something like his mom and dad used to do when he was a small boy and later would come a little sister or brother.

John moved his body to accommodate the position of Karen's on the couch. As John started kissing her neck and upper chest, John found she was more than willing to accommodate his ideas and intentions. As the passion of love they shared rose and they started removing each other's cloths, a little voice came softly, "Momma, can I have a glass of waa-ter?"

Karen and JW looked into each other's eyes as a smile came over their faces. JW said. "I'll get him a glass of water. Don't you go anywhere."

As JW got up, Karen said, "It's about two hours till his bed time. Do you think we can wait?"

With a big smile, JW said, "I've waited all my life for you. I'm sure I can wait two more hours," JW left to get the water for his son.

The next three days passed so quickly, it was almost unbelievable that it was time for JW to leave. JW's two boys (especially the oldest one, John) and Karen cried when he gave them all a kiss and then boarded the bus.

Seven months later.

After JW graduated thirty-seventh of two hundred and sixteen from Annapolis, Karen, and JW took their two sons to the wedding of Sara Beth and James. Then three months later along came James West Jr.

With almost no time to spare, JW was transferred to the Mediterranean going to Rome, Greece and Egypt. By late 1972, JW made full Lieutenant. He was doing really well and was respected by his superiors as well as the men under his command.

In August of 1973, JW was told he was transferred to a different carrier, which patrolled the Gulf of Tonkin and the South China Sea, an area located off the coast of Vietnam. He was given some leave time before reporting for duty because it would be a long wait before his next leave. JW rushed home to Karen and his boys.

When he arrived home, JW explained to Karen that he had been transferred to another carrier stationed off the coast of Vietnam. He also explained that as a new officer on board this carrier, it would possibly be a long time before he would get any more leave time.

Tears welled up in Karen eyes as JW told her this, especially when JW spoke the name 'Vietnam'. All Karen could see in her heart and mind were all the horrible things shown on the news. She remembered all the stories told by the other families from around Carlinville. Karen knew the war in Vietnam was deescalating, winding down to its end but still it was Vietnam.

With JW's dreams of attending the Naval Academy and being in the Navy, how could she be so selfish by putting the boys and herself ahead of her husband's dreams? Just what kind of a wife and a mother was she?

Karen resolved to make the best of what time they had. "Well, John, I'm thinking that we need to make the best of the time we might have."

JW replied, "What? I don't understand?"

"Well John, we need to make the best use of the time we have before you leave…and, Honey, the boys are in bed asleep."

JW replied, "Oh! Honey, I think that's an excellent idea!" JW scooped Karen up into his arms and carried her upstairs.

The next day after breakfast Karen and JW took the boys to visit with their grandparents, first Karen's then JW's. They told their parents that John had been transferred to another carrier operating off the coast of Vietnam.

The response was about the same from both families, "Can't he change his duty station?" Even though Vietnam was winding down, they all feared the worst. JW did his best to assure them that he would be in no danger. His duties as a Lieutenant would be confined to the carrier; that the Navy tends not to send Lieutenants into the jaws of death. His duties wouldn't have anything to do with shore duty. Should he go ashore, it would be most likely in Japan, not Vietnam.

JW went on to tell them that he had called Sara Beth, but there was no answer so he didn't know were James was located. In fact, it had been six or seven months since he had heard from James. He added that the last he had heard was that James was still floating around the Mediterranean.

Karen and JW later went to visit Reb's mother, Ruth Benjamin, and learned that Reb had joined the Marines.

He had become a helicopter pilot. Ironically and oddly enough, he was stationed on the same carrier to which JW was just transferred.

While talking to Mrs. Benjamin, something happened that would bond these two families together forever. Karen and JW's oldest son, John, placed his little hand on the arm of Ruth Benjamin and asked, "Aunt Ruth, can I have a glass of water?" The smile on her face was enough to show all of them her love for the family.

For the next three weeks JW spent all his time with his two boys and Karen playing games, working around the house and going to the rope. Oh yes, and making love to his wife. Two days before JW left, Karen wasn't feeling well, but she did her best not to show she was feeling down. The bathroom was so well built that no sounds could be heard outside the room when the door was closed. This insulation worked out well for Karen first thing in the morning and helped hide her secret.

JW was so filled with his boys and the good times with them and his wife that he never saw the signs of the beginnings of a new life within Karen. Karen knew it would be a long time before she would see her husband again. She didn't want to disrupt any of their very limited and precious time together.

Karen and the boys were so happy while JW was at home. They passed that time going to church, swimming, eating meals together, and playing games. The best part of all was just being together as a family.

Then came the day that John had to report for duty. Both sides of the family were present. All were crying and wishing John the best. Karen and the boys were crying the hardest while John Jr. and Paddy Boy were telling their dad. "Daddy please don't go, Daddy, Daddy, please stay here with us, Please Daddy, please don't go!"

As JW stepped onto the bus, John Jr. said in a very loud and clear voice, "Daddy, if you don't come home, I'm going to come looking for you."

JW looked at the driver. The bus driver gave JW a nod of his head. JW turned around, stepped off the bus, and picked up John Jr. He looked his little man in the eye and said, "Son, I'm going to hold you to that. And I'm going to depend on it. I love you, Son!"

JW again gave his wife and two boys a kiss and a hug before he turned and stepped onto the bus. As JW sat in his seat, a strange feeling came over him. It was a feeling of great hunger and thirst. He felt very dirty, like he hadn't bathed in a very long time. This feeling soon subsided, and the rest of the bus trip to Maryland went without any further thoughts of hunger or thirst. JW's call to duty was strong and loud.

At the exact moment JW was sensing the strange feelings, Karen was also feeling loneliness, hurt and pain, as well as great hunger and thirst. She felt a terrible sense of a great loss very much like death, as the bus roared down the street. She watched until it disappeared out of sight when it rounded the corner by what uses to be the old Chinese laundry but was now the insurance office of Moyer and Moyer.

Karen turned to both sets of parents and said, "I fear we have seen the last of John for a very long time. There will be two letters from him followed by nothing." Both sets of parents were stunned and could say nothing in response. As Karen took her boys to go home for the night, the two sets of parents were left standing on the sidewalk watching after them and wondering why she had made such strange statements.

JW arrived at his duty station on the aircraft carrier Kitty Hawk. The Kitty Hawk's duty station was called Yankee Station. Yankee Station engulfed the whole of the Gulf of Tonkin, which was located just off the coast of Vietnam and the South China Sea.

After settling in, JW began looking for Reb. This was a task that didn't take JW very long as the two men shared a quick handshake and smile. JW and Reb suddenly began dancing around doing something like an Irish Jig with a bit of the jitterbug. As other officers and enlisted men watched, these two men continued to dance around patting each other on the back and shoulders and hugging each other. When Reb and JW finally settled down a bit, the two men had made it very clear to all who were watching that they were the best of best, the greatest of great friends that God had ever put on this fine green earth. The song playing in the background was *The Ballad of the Green Beret* by Sgt. Barry Saddler.

When the two friends had calmed down enough to speak in normal voices, JW said, "Your mother told me to tell you that when you get that cast off your arm, you are to please write home."

Reb, with his big booming voice, just laughed as he said. "Hell, JW, I send a letter home per week and I'm in line for some leave time soon I hope. I am praying my turn for leave comes up soon as I want to see my mother…and I have someone special in Texas."

"Reb, you've got someone special in Texas?"

"Yes, I do and I'm told there's a new little Miss Benjamin. But, I've never seen her, except for a small picture. I haven't told my mother yet. I want to surprise my mom by taking her to Texas to see my baby in person."

"Reb, I didn't know you were married!"

Reb hung his head as he said, "We're not."

JW patted his friend on the shoulder and said, "Not to worry my friend, just make sure I get to see the picture." JW then went on to say, "Reb, I've been told it's hard to get away from here,"

"That's no bull, JW! I've been on this mobile island for eighteen or nineteen months."

"Well, maybe that will change soon. Reb, I understand the military will start evacuation procedures real soon. Yes, that means this Vietnam thing is pretty much over."

"JW, now that you're a Lieutenant Commander, you would be privy to that kind of information. Are you sure you want to share that kind of information with a lower ranking noncom like myself?"

"Reb, let's just say I was thinking aloud."

"I understand, JW, I do understand. It's nice to have someone thinking out loud from time to time. It helps the rest of us to keep our eyes open and out of the dark!"

The next three weeks passed quickly with Reb and JW spending as much time together as their duties would allow. With each meeting, it was very clear to all that Reb and JW were constantly reaffirming their very strong and deep friendship. The two could always be seen playing pool, watching TV, or writing letters.

At the end of those first three weeks, JW was requested to attend a high priority meeting.

Upon arriving at the meeting, JW was asked to show his ID and was then directed into a darker room where he was requested to be seated and remain quiet. After a few minutes, Admiral Glean entered and all eight officers stood at attention until told to be seated and reminded to remain quiet. The Admiral asked the Marine guards to repost outside and to maintain tight security in the hallway. No one was allowed to walk past this area until the meeting was completed.

The first thing the Admiral told the officers was, "You've been picked due to your rank, but this is totally a volunteer mission. After I describe this mission, should you feel you cannot participate, you will be excused and required to remain silent in the strictest sense of the word. This includes not telling your wives, girlfriends, etc. This mission will require each of you, to command an extraction team. You would be extracting personnel from areas the government has denied being in. You will be flying into northern Laos. Are there any questions?"

JW spoke up, "Sir, can we possibly choose our own pilots?"

The Admiral responded, "I'm going to say yes, if you think the pilot can be trusted. Any pilot you request will have to be cleared by N.C.I.C."

"Sir, I would like to request pilot Roscoe E. Benjamin, Sergeant U.S.M.C."

"Mr. Walker, I will have Sergeant Benjamin checked out and cleared for you."

"Thank you, Sir."

After the meeting was over, JW returned to his quarters and checked his mail but found nothing. He knew it might take a while for the mail to catch up to him. He seated himself at his small table and began penning a letter to his wife and boys.

In the letter, JW told about life on board the Kitty Hawk and about the great times Reb and he spent together. He also mentioned that he still hadn't heard anything from James, but was in hopes to run into him soon. JW went on telling Karen how much he loved and missed her and the boys. He asked that she give the boys a kiss and a hug from him; that he was depending on her to take good care of everything while he was away. He ended with, "I hope to see you all soon." Naturally, following his orders, JW never said anything about the mission he was preparing for.

The next day JW attended a preflight briefing. Each officer was given a specific coordinate and the approximate number of personnel at their location. The length of JW's flight would take six and a half hours total round trip.

JW returned to his quarters to change out of his uniform and into a flight suit. When he got to his quarters, he saw that his mail had arrived and there was a letter from Karen and the boys. However, as he started to open the letter, a lieutenant came by and informed JW that due to weather conditions, take off time for his flight has been moved up. It had moved up to immediately.

JW placed the letter back on his small desk and finished dressing into his flight suit, thinking he could read his mail when he returned. After all, his flight would only be about seven hours roundtrip anyway.

After boarding the helicopter, JW told Reb, who had been approved as his pilot, "Once were off the flight deck, head for these coordinates and advise."

About twenty minutes later, Reb called to JW, "JW, we're at the coordinates you requested."

"Very good, continue north to eighteen minutes fifty-three seconds, then west to one hundred five minutes forty-one seconds. Advise when arriving."

A longer moment later, Reb called to JW, "JW, are you sure about the coordinates you gave me?"

"Yes, Reb, I'm sure. Is there a problem?"

"JW, as a pilot, I've been given strict orders to never enter that area. So, I can't fly into the coordinates you've given me."

JW looked at Reb, thought for a long moment, then said, "Sergeant Benjamin, do you understand the coordinates I've given you?"

"Yes, of course I do, JW!"

"Sergeant, is this aircraft able to fly to the coordinates I've given you?"

Reb noticed a difference in the tone and the way JW was speaking to him so he decided to speak in a more military fashion, "Yes, Sir. But…"

"Then follow the coordinates I have given you, Sergeant. That's an order!"

"Yes, Sir, Lieutenant!"

Twenty minutes later, Reb called out, "Lieutenant Walker?"

"What's up, Reb?"

"We're coming up on land and the coordinates you gave me. Sir, can you see that small boat?"

"Yes, I do. Why?"

"Well, Sir, he's not fishing to feed his family. He's a lookout for anything approaching land. Let me assure you, Sir, they know we're coming. Besides that, we are being tracked on active radar. What would you like for me to do now, Sir?"

"Drop to the top of the water, head for the mouth of that river. Follow the river in for about one hundred and sixty miles. Advise me at that time."

"Copy that, Sir."

After running up river for about sixty miles, JW came up next to Reb and was amazed at how easy Reb made flying helicopters seem while following the curves of the river. Reb advised JW that they were about twenty miles from the second coordinates, when suddenly warning bells and buzzers started going off. Reb told JW, "Strap yourself in! It's going to get rough."

JW asked Reb, "What the hell is that? What's wrong?"

Reb shouted back, "We've got a S.A.M. trying to run up our six!" Reb started putting the helicopter through its paces, making hard left and right turns until coming to a fork in the river. He suddenly yelled, "Hold on to your nuts! This is going to be unbelievably close!" Reb waited till the last possible second before putting the helicopter into an all, but impossible ninety-degree right turn. Reb was strapped into the pilot's seat, but JW was hanging on to a safety strap and had a rough time trying to hold on.

Once the helicopter successfully completed the ninety-degree turn and evaded the S.A.M., they now faced something just as devastating and deadly. Before any sound could be heard, a large number of golf ball size holes started appearing in the helicopter. Instantly, the windshield on the left side disintegrated. The one on the right side became so damaged it was almost impossible to see through it.

Reb pulled back hard and to the left as he tried to get the helicopter up and over the tops of the trees and to some kind of safety. The bottom of the helicopter became filled with golf ball sized holes, all courtesy of a .50 caliber mounted on a riverboat below.

The interior of the helicopter became filled with thick black smoke. The two of them commenced coughing and gagging. It was unlike anything they had ever experienced. This thick black smoke was worse than being in a room filled with cigarette smoke. It was like a thousand little hands digging and clawing at their lungs and eyes. Then the interior of the helicopter cleared, leaving Reb and JW still coughing and gasping for air.

Reb called out to JW, "Are you hit? JW, are you hit?"

JW replied, "No, but I could use a clean pair of underwear!"

Then Reb was on the radio talking to the carrier. It was not good news he was relaying, "We just evaded a S.A.M., took extensive damage from anti-aircraft fire, losing oil pressure! Controls very sluggish!"

"JW, what do you want to do? We might be able return to the carrier! But we've got to haul ass right now!"

"Reb, is there a chance we might be able to make repairs if you had help and time?"

"JW, there's no way to know just what's wrong or if I can make any kind of repairs. The way this bitch is running, she may or may not restart. JW, I just can't be sure!"

"Reb, I understand. Now, can you see the left side of that small mountain? Well, just around the edge of it is where we're supposed to make the pickup. Reb, these men are depending on us."

"JW, I'm sure we can make the pickup point. If the men aren't shot up too badly, maybe they can keep these assholes off of us long enough to affect some kind of repairs. With a little luck, maybe one of them can help with repairs. But keep in mind, we will be trailing smoke all the way to the pickup point. That will most likely lead them right to us!"

The helicopter shook and vibrated badly as they approached a wide stream. JW was about to change his mind about the pickup point when all hell broke loose. The tail of the helicopter erupted in flames then disappeared, leaving a large gaping hole where the tail used to be. The helicopter was thrown into a spiraling descent and landed in the stream that was only six feet deep.

The main rotor blade chopped into the water, turning it into a frothy boil with the blade still turning at a very high rate of speed. The helicopter rolled on to its left side. This caused the blade to start digging into the bottom of the stream. What was left of the helicopter began to shake even more violently, similar to a paint can on a paint mixer.

As the last blade broke-off, it dug into the bottom of the stream and forced what was left of the helicopter to roll back over onto its right side. This caused Reb, who was still strapped in his seat, to be plunged under the water that was rushing into the helicopter.

A moment or two later, JW realized his friend was in trouble. Not being familiar with the straps and restraints, JW frantically tried to free his friend, who was unconscious. After what seemed like forever, JW was able to free Reb. As Reb's head came above the water, he gasped for air and started breathing. When Reb opened his eyes, the first thing he saw was his best friend. Reb placed his arms around JW, held on tightly and said, "Thank God for you, JW. I don't think I would have made it without you!"

Karen's dream

As Karen was sleeping, all warm and safe in her own bed some six or seven thousand miles away from the problem, she had a dream so realistic it was just like being there.

At first, she saw the holes appearing in the front and bottom of a helicopter. The windshield on the left side seemed to disintegrate. She could only see the back of the pilot as he pulled back and to the left on a stick shift of some kind. She could feel the emotions were running high with fear running the highest. Although Karen was conscious of all the feelings, she was also very aware of the smells. Karen knew she was seeing this through the eyes of someone else, but she wasn't sure how or why.

As the dream progressed, Karen could tell the helicopter was flying just over the treetops. Then as the helicopter came to a large stream or a small river of some kind, the back of the helicopter disappeared and left a large gaping hole. Karen suddenly realized that what she was seeing was happening to her husband John. She was seeing this all through his eyes.

Karen sat up screaming and calling for John. Karen's two young boys rushed into the bedroom. Trying desperately to calm their mother down, Karen's oldest son John said, "Mommy, please calm down, you're scaring us!"

Karen woke when she heard the cries of her two sons pleading for her to calm down. After taking a moment to collect her emotions, Karen put her arms around her boys and told them everything was fine. She assured them she had just had a bad dream and hoped she was telling them the truth. The two boys climbed under the covers next to their mother. As her sons fell asleep near her, Karen finally relaxed enough to sleep through the rest of the night.

Back in Laos

After making their way to shore, JW asked Reb, "Just what the hell happened?"

"I have no idea, JW! However, I don't think it was a S.A.M.!"

"Why is that, Reb?"

"Because we're still alive!"

"Reb, I'm thinking we should get the hell away from here!"

"And go where? In what direction? JW, we've got nothing but jungle in any direction we look."

"Reb, we'll head for the pickup point. That should be our best chance for rescue. When the carrier determines we're down, they will most likely send another helicopter to complete the rescue. So our original coordinates should be where the next rescue will head. Besides that, there's safety in numbers."

"Sounds good to me, JW. I'm thinking the distance to the extraction point is something like fifteen to twenty-five miles. This jungle terrain won't make our endeavors to reach the extraction point any easier. This terrain isn't anything like Illinois, and the locals don't much care for us at all."

After moving very carefully the rest of that day and on through the night, JW and Reb were about a mile from the extraction point shortly after sunrise. They looked up when a rescue helicopter flew over their heads in route to the extraction point.

"JW, that's our ride out of here. We've got to pick up the pace unless we want to walk home."

About thirty minutes later, the two of them saw the helicopter going the other way with the side door open. This allowed them to see the men inside the helicopter with what seemed like blank expressions on their faces.

JW and Reb tried waving and yelling at the helicopter, but this was all to no avail. When the helicopter was about a quarter mile away, the two men saw something streak up from the ground and strike the helicopter. They watched in total horror as the helicopter disintegrated before their eyes. Body parts of the men mixed with parts of the helicopter dispersed out in all directions and then fell to the ground.

Reb looked at JW and asked, "What do you think God has in mind for us?"

"I don't know my friend. But again, I'm thinking, we need to get out of this area."

They moved on until they reached the extraction area. They looked around and found some chicken eggs and a pan. For the first time in twenty-four hours, they ate. When they were done, they moved along the mountain ridge, which gave them a good view of the entire area below. Off in the distances, they could see smoke that was most likely from the rescue helicopter that had been shot down. The rest of the terrain consisted of trees, rivers and rice paddies.

Reb asked JW, "What the hell are we going to do now? We're in a foreign land where, per the government, no Americans are supposed to be and we don't even know the God d--- language!"

"Yaw, Yaw seems we have everything working in our favor, kind of scary, hum. And one more thing, Reb, I don't wish to hear you use God's name in vain ever again!" JW went on, "I need some time to think about what to do."

The two men sat still and quiet for about two hours while JW looked around. Then he said,   "Reb, do you think you can go two days without eating?"

"Yes, I think so. Why?"

"Well, I'm thinking. We can stay here for two days or so, letting things calm down and then try making our way back to the river, then out to the coast. Then maybe we could acquire a boat of some kind and maybe make our way out to sea and the carrier."

"Well, JW, that sounds good to me. Do you mind if I get some sleep?"

"Go ahead, I think we both could use some sleep. Besides, it's getting dark anyway."

JW woke up when Reb urgently said, "JW, JW wake up. JW, wake up, we've got company."

When he opened his eyes, the first thing JW saw was twelve to fourteen men standing around with their weapons pointed at him and Reb. Reb stood up and spoke softly to JW, "In case you don't know, those weapons they've got are not American made. They are AK-47's, Russian assault rifles," Then Reb whispered, "JW, I think I can take them."

"You're probably right, Reb, but wait till I get on my feet."   JW stood quickly and grabbed the one closest to him.   He used the man like a club against the others.

Reb was doing the same. "These Laotian soldiers went down without much trouble," he proclaimed, as he tossed the last one over the side of the mountain.

JW said, "That was just too easy, Reb. I know they are smaller than us, but that was just too easy." After he thought about it for a moment or two, JW said, "Let's pick up a weapon and whatever ammo is available. I'm also thinking we should get the hell out of here before someone comes up for a look-see when these people don't report in."

"What do you want to do then?"

"Reb, I guess we'll have to take our chances. Let's start towards the river."

After picking up as much weapons and ammo as they could carry, JW and Reb made a two-and-half day track back to the river. There they found a small boat and began their journey down the river to the coast. It took three more days to reach the coast. When JW and Reb were about two hundred feet or so from the open ocean, powerful searchlights came on from both sides of the river. With machineguns blazing away, a very fast patrol boat approached the two men. JW and Reb had no choice. It was surrender or die.

CHAPTER SIX

THE BEGINNING OF THE END

Reb and JW, after being removed from the small boat, received the first of many beatings. They held their own for thirty or so minutes, but the little bastards kept coming out of the woodwork as they swarmed over them like ants on a bug. This encounter with the Vietnamese soldiers was much different than their encounter with the Laotian soldiers some five or so days before on the mountain.

After being subdued, they were placed in a pit that was used as a holding cell, as well as their bathroom. The human excrement in this pit was knee deep. After being in this pit the rest of the night, just like clockwork the sun came up the next morning. The flies became unbearable.

Then two different soldiers came over and asked if they wanted anything to drink. The soldiers then pissed in the pit and asked if they wanted anymore. One of the soldiers made the mistake of sitting down to take a shit. After he was well seated and seemingly comfortable with all his family jewels exposed, Reb moved very quickly. He jumped up as the first turd started to come out, grabbed the soldier's family jewels and squeezed tightly to all three items, which are required for sex, producing children and taking a piss.

Now this person must've thought these items were important as well, because he sure screamed. He screamed like a girl and squealed like a pig. As this soldier shit all over Reb, he managed to get loose, but he was missing three very important parts. Neither Reb nor JW could see anything from the pit and waited for what would happen next. After a minute or two, they could hear some of the other soldiers laughing.

They remained in this pit for the next two days, but no one used it as a bathroom as long as they were in it. The morning of the third day, the wooden frame was removed. A ladder was placed in the pit, and they were instructed to climb out. When they got to the top, they stood and looked around at the soldiers who were keeping their distance. Some of these soldiers were the ones who captured them, and they looked like they had been in one hell of a fight.

One of these soldiers motioned for the two of them to move towards the river. As they moved forward, some of the other soldiers started looking in the pit. Reb said, "JW, you know what they're looking for don't you?"

With a bit of a chuckle JW said, "I think I have a pretty good idea."

Reb and JW sat on a large rock about ten feet out in the river and took off their shoes to clean them. Even though the river water was dirty, it was better than what they had in their shoes. When they came out of the river, they were directed to a truck where there were nine other men.

After about four or five hours in the truck, they came to a stop. The soldiers got some food to eat. When they were done, one of the soldiers put the leftovers with a bucket of water in the back of the truck for the prisoners to share. The truck kept moving north until sundown when they arrived at a compound in northern Vietnam.

The men were taken out of the truck and placed in a cell where they were told to be quiet, no talking. Someone said they were in Vinh and this was only a layover in route to Hanoi. A day and a half later, Reb and JW checked into the "Hanoi Hilton", which was located in beautiful down town Hanoi.

Up until now, they had been treated rather well, but that was all about to change; the good graces of the Vietnamese would never be seen again. They had started off from the river with eleven men, and along the way they had picked up six more. Two of these men needed intensive medical attention. One was shot up really bad and the other had a head wound and was blind because of his wounds.

When they arrived at the Hilton, they had asked for medical attention for the two wounded men. They were told not to worry about those men, as they would receive the attention they deserved. The rest of the group was ordered to move inside. As the gate closed, JW heard two short blasts from an AK-47 and none of them ever saw those two wounded men again. This gave them the first real understanding of what was to come.

They were pushed into a crowded cell with no idea how many men already huddled inside. At first Reb and JW were separated due to the sheer number of men in this cell. However, as there was no way out of the cell, Reb and JW found each other and were back together again soon after.

Reb asked, "How many of these men do you think you might know?"

"No idea, why?"

"Well, JW, I'm sure I heard someone call you by your nickname."

Then the guards came and removed some of the other men from the cell. After the sun went down, one of the new POWs started asking for food. Other POWs who had been there for a time told the man to be quiet before the guards came and took him away.

This new POW didn't listen and continued asking for food. The guards soon came and dragged him out of the cell. They could hear him screaming and then his screams were silenced with a short blast from an AK-47. The camp became quiet again, as quiet as a mummy's tomb. They never saw that POW again.

Two days later, four guards arrived with two big pots. One pot had what looked like table scraps with something moving in it. A closer look revealed that the moving parts were maggots. The other pot was water of some kind and smelled more like a urinal from some backstreet bar after a long Saturday night.

Some of the POWs who had been there for a long time began picking through the food. Reb said, "I think I will wait and see what dessert looks like."

About an hour later, more men were removed from the cell and again Reb and JW were not among the men removed. About an hour or two later, six F4 Tomcats and four A10's flew overhead but not a shot was fired. However, the guards of the camp went into a tizzy, as they began running around like chickens with their heads cut off. For the rest of the day they saw almost no guards at all, and it was very quiet the rest of the night. No guards harassed any of the POWs no matter how loud they became.

The next day four guards arrived very early. They took the two pots away and returned soon with two more pots. One pot contained fresh food, and the other pot was filled with fresh clean water. While the men were busy eating, several more Tomcats and A10's flew over the Hilton three times but still no shots were fired.

JW said, "Reb, that's the second time that's happened. What you make of it?"

"Don't know, JW, but take a look at what's happening out there!"

JW and Reb could see men getting a bath and clean cloths. The guards were not beating the men and were actually helping them. They were so engrossed in this new event that they almost missed a really low voice, almost inaudible, ask, "Reb? JW? Are you two deaf or just being unsociable?"

JW looked at Reb and said, "Even I heard it that time." As JW turned and looked towards the dark cell, he said. "I'm John Fredrick Walker, now who's calling for Reb and me?"

One of the other POWs was pointing towards the back of the cell, as he whispered, "It came from back in there somewhere."

As JW and Reb headed for the back of the cell, JW patted the POW on the shoulder and said, "Thanks, Buddy."

It was fairly dark in the back of this large cell, and JW stumbled over some men lying on the floor. JW said, "Excuse me I didn't mean to step on you, my friend."

Then they heard the voice again, only now it was a bit louder and clearer, "Don't worry about stepping on those guys. They've been dead for the last three days."

JW replied, "That voice, Reb. I do believe it sounds like... James, is that you?"

"You damn well bet it's me. Now would the two of you please give me a hand? I need some of that food and water out there."

After patting each other on the back and a couple of hugs, the three men started for the front of the cell. As James emerged from the darkness of the cell with the assistance of his two friends, JW and Reb were totally shocked to see his physical condition. JW was the first to speak up asking, "What the hell happened to you?"

"James, I know you're a pretty good scrapper, but what happened to you?" Reb questioned.

As James was stuffing food into his mouth, he told them what happened and how many it took to get the job done. Reb began checking James over while listening to James's explanation for his condition. Reb then asked, "Does this hurt?"

James almost passed out and said, "Hell yes!"

Reb then said, "JW, take a look at this."

As JW looked where Reb was pointing he said, "Holy shit, James!"

Reb quietly spoke, "JW, it's still in there and needs to come out."

James stopped eating long enough to say, "Hey look guys, I'm having trouble breathing. I can't get any sleep and something hurts like hell when I move. Now I don't know what you are looking at that needs removal, but if the two of you kill me, I'm sure I will feel much better!"

JW made a motion with his hands behind James and Reb shook his head in agreement. JW said, "James, you're one of the best friends I have in the world, so I wouldn't normally do something like this to you."

Before James could say anything, JW delivered a sharp blow to the base of the skull, and James went out like a cheap light bulb.

Reb asked JW, "How long will he be out?"

"I don't know, Reb!"

Reb replied, "You didn't kill him did you?"

"Well, I sure hope not! Now let's get that thing out of him."

Reb reached in with his fingers and fished around. After getting a good hold of the object, he removed a four and a half inch long piece of steel that was wedged between a rib and lung on the upper right side of James.

Then JW asked, "Do you think it punctured his lung?"

Reb's reply was. "I don't see any bubbles, and I know he's still breathing, so I'm going to say no. JW, all I have to work with is my standard field training. I may have given him some kind of an infection because my fingers are not all that clean.

Reb and JW continued to look over James's body while James was out cold. Other than bruises and abrasions, no other serious wounds were found. Reb asked JW, "Who do you think could've done this to James?"

"I don't know, Reb, but if I had to guess, I would guess the Vietnamese. So I'm thinking they wouldn't give this guy a fair shake. I'm sure they intended harm."

About three hours later, James woke up rubbing the back of his head. Reb asked James, "Well how you feel now that you've had a nap? Can you breathe better?"

"That's the first good sleep I've had since I got the shit kicked out of me a week ago. Yes, I can breathe better. What the hell did the two of you do to me?"

"Well first off, JW is the one that knocked you the hell out and I pulled a piece of steel out of your back. Now would you mind telling us how you acquired a piece of steel that size and why you seemed to be trying to conceal in your back?"

"Well, I can't pronounce his name, so I just call him Ping-Ding. His name is something like that anyway. It seems he and six or so of his friends decided to give me a welcome to Vietnam party. He and his friends don't seem to care much for Americans and Ping-Ding's idea of a good American is a dead American.

James went on, "I was told by one of the other POWs it took me a day and a half before I came too. That's why I was staying in the back of this cell. The other men kept me out of sight and, therefore, hopefully out of mind."

JW spoke up, "Guys, I really don't want to kill anyone, so if it wasn't for all this Vietnam shit coming to an end this Ping-Ding guy, as you call him, sounds like someone I might want to make an exception for and in the end appreciate killing. So I thank God it's all over."

As the three of them sat looking out from their cell, they could see what was happening out in the courtyard. They continued watching as other POWs were cleaned up and given clean clothes.

James finally answered JW's statement, "JW, Reb. Please don't try to take these Vietnam bastards on." As James struggled to his feet, he went on, "They won't fight with you one on one." He walked to the back of the cell and settled against the wall. It was starting to get dark, so

JW and Reb followed James to the back of the cell where all three went to sleep.

After the next week and a half, James, JW, Reb, and all the other men in the cell were being fed and cared for in a fairly decent manner. Some of the men were changed out for new men but generally the number of men in the cell was steadily rising.

The number of men in the cell had been approximately one hundred and fifty when Reb and JW had first arrived. Then the number of men dropped to about twenty when you counted those who were alive. At this time when they were being given better treatment, the cell was cleaned of the dead bodies and human excrement. Vietnamese peasants were hired to do this. However, JW later found out that although they were indeed Vietnamese, they were American collaborators and sympathizers. Therefore, they were thought less of than the Americans.

From their cell they could see the courtyard and other seemingly large cells filled with other American military men. These men seemed to be like the group JW was with as none of them were getting baths or clean clothes, either. JW was still grateful for the cleaner cell and the better food.

After about four days of receiving new arrivals, the population of the cell swelled to close to two hundred men. With this many men in the cell, they were constantly in contact with someone. In order to use the can, the only thing that could be done was the other men would turn their backs to allow at least some privacy.

JW guessed you could say the three of them were lucky, as they were in the back of the cell out of the weather and away from the can. Being in the back of the cell had its downside as well, as the food and water was delivered to the front of the cell. In order to get to the food or the can, they had to work through all the men and that took some time. Then they had to work their way back or lose the spot. It became of game of moving quickly to take care of basic needs and then back just as quickly to the spot they had claimed as their own.

Ten Days Later.

James was getting better and was able to get around quite well with only a little help from JW or Reb. However, with the larger number of men in the cell and lack of any personal space, some small arguments and fights broke out. JW and Reb kept James out of the way while other men quickly quelled the fights. They all knew it would be a bad idea to draw attention of the guards to their cell.

Then came the morning the trucks started arriving. One truck would pull up at a time to the front of the cell. The guards would load about thirty of the men from the cell into the truck. The three long time friends were in the last truck and began to think they were on their way home.

Oh yes, they were on their way home for sure. What they didn't know was that they would first make a twenty plus year layover in a POW camp.

After traveling two days in the back of the truck, Reb, JW and James knew they weren't heading south. None of them had been given food or water or a chance to relieve themselves during the trip. One of the men in the truck tried to piss out the back and was shot. The others watched as his body fell out the back of the truck. The man's body hit the ground with a thud, and they heard the sound of bones breaking and being crushed as the truck behind them loaded with guards ran over him.

Another man tried to hang his butt out the back of the truck. Without any warning, his lower belly and crotch area exploded, spraying chunks of flesh, intestinal fluid and blood all over the other men. He made no verbal sounds as he too fell out the back of the truck. Not unlike like the man before him, they heard the sound of his body hitting the ground with a "thud" and the truck following behind them hitting him and causing this man's bones to break and be crushed.

A man sitting just to the left of Reb suddenly slumped forward, as did the man seated just behind him. The man to his left was hit directly in the mouth and died without making a sound. Four men died within thirty seconds because one of them wanted to perform a body function that was as natural and necessary as breathing—a function even these Vietnamese bastards must perform from time to time.

Later on that same day, just before sundown, the trucks came to a stop. The men thought it might be another fuel stop, but to their surprise they were ordered out of the trucks and into a small field. They were told they could relieve themselves and drink from a small stream running through the field. A bucket of rice was delivered to each truck. The people delivering the food, although Asian, were not Vietnamese. Given the direction and distance of travel, they concluded these people must be Chinese.

After the guards were fed, they ordered everyone back into the trucks. Anyone who refused was shot and killed on the spot. Others were beaten with a rifle butt and then shot. After getting into the truck, James said "I don't think trying to fight these bastards right now is the thing to do."

Reb replied, "Well, when do you think the right time might be?"

"I don't know, Reb." JW answered. "I'm thinking as long as we are breathing we have a chance. If we were lying on the ground dead, we would have exhausted any chances of survival and retribution. Time for the most part is on our side and that one Vietnamese bastard, the one James calls Ping Ding? I hope to kill him one day."

After another two days, they were again allowed out of the trucks to relieve themselves and eat. This time the cussing at them was relentless, and the one with the biggest mouth was the one James called Ping Ding. Ping Ding told them he was going to teach them a lesson for touching a guard.

James asked, "Who touched one of the guards?"

JW spoke up. "I don't know, James, but there's two trucks missing. It might have something to do with the shit pit. What you think, Reb?"

The young man chosen for this demonstration was about five-foot-eleven with blue eyes and sandy blond hair. After two guards twisted the man's arms behind him, Ping Ding started pelting him in the chest and stomach with the butt of a rifle till the young man started puking blood. Then Ping Ding took the rifle butt to his ribs. With each strike, they could hear bones break.

As James and JW started to assist the young man Reb stopped them by yelling, "No, no not yet!"

Twenty or so armed guards came around the side of the truck and ordered them to back away, which they did. When the young blonde man was finally released, he fell to the ground with a thud and never moved again.

The prisoners were then allowed to eat a small amount of rice and a small drink of water before they were ordered back into the truck. They never knew why some of the trucks went missing, but the next time they were allowed out of the trucks four more trucks were gone.

This time Ping Ding's anger was aimed at a different truck. After being ordered out of the trucks and into a field covered in knee high grass, the man Ping Ding picked was a man Reb said had been in the truck with him and JW when they left the river. The thought again crossed JW's mind that Ping Ding really might be looking for Reb and himself.

They noticed a new and different vehicle had joined the convoy, but their attention was drawn back to what the wonderful and loving Ping Ding was doing or was about to do. After cussing at this young man and accusing him of something they knew and were sure even Ping Ding must have known he didn't do, Ping Ding seemed to take great pride in the butchering of this young man in front of them. The first thing he did was cut off the man's thumbs, then the big toe from each of his feet. The tool Ping Ding used looked like a pair of end cutters or the tool used for trimming horses hooves. As this Vietnamese bastard continued his butcheries, JW didn't think he'd ever heard such blood curdling screams in all of his life.

At this point the young man was glaring at Ping Ding, and Ping Ding didn't like that at all. Ping Ding started telling him that he was the son of a Goddamn American cur dog. He yelled that since the prisoner liked looking at him so much, he was going to fix it so he could look at him all the time. From a small sheaf strapped to his side, Ping Ding pulled a small knife and cut off the man's eyelids.

The young man must have figured he was about to die, because he retorted to Ping Ding, "Why are you doing this to your brother? I know you must be my brother, because my dad told me he was over here some years ago and had sex with a Vietnamese slut. He said she looked a lot like a pig and to me you look like a pig. Was your mother that bitch pig my father spoke of? Is that why you become angered with all you come in contact with?"

Ping Ding tilted his head slightly forward like someone looking over the top of his glasses. He turned slowly around and looked at all the POWs laughing out loud at him.

Still holding the small knife in his right hand, Ping Ding ordered a third guard to remove the man's clothes. Once this was done, Ping Ding started laughing as he pointed at the man's genital area. He then asked, "Do you got all da cur kids you want?" Then he took hold of the man's penis with his left hand.

The young man, now unable to blink or close his eyes, asked, "What are you going to do now? Do you want to suck my dick or beat me off?"

They were forced to watch this horrible act of human desecration as this Vietnamese bastard butchered this young man's manhood. There was nothing they could do, unless they wanted to die as well. Still holding the young man's penis in his hand, Ping Ding pulled out real hard. With the knife in his right hand, he sliced off the young man's penis.

Blood started running down the man's legs and squirted out onto the ground. As this young man again cried out in pain and agony, Ping Ding held the man's penis out like a trophy and turned around to show all that were present what he had done. While the young man was still screaming, Ping Ding turned back to grab the man's bag and cut it off, leaving the young man's nuts hanging in open air.

Suddenly, someone dressed in a semi dark gray uniform with the sleeves rolled up to mid way of his upper arms rushed past them. This person started yelling at Ping Ding to stop what he was doing. They could tell by his accent that he was Russian and by the tone in his voice, he was definitely in charge.

The two men exchanged words in a mix of Russian and Vietnamese. Ping Ding talked in a loud voice as he waved and flayed his hands and arms about while still holding the young man's bag in his left hand.

The Russian, on the other hand, was quite different. Except for the initial yelling to get Ping Ding's attention, the Russian spoke in a calm voice, which indicated a higher level of intelligence than that being expressed by Ping Ding. The stance of the Russian was similar to that of a gunfighter ready to draw in a shootout. JW, for one, hoped the loser would be Ping Ding.

By this time, the young man had all but stopped bleeding. When the two guards released his arms, he collapsed to the ground and didn't move or make any sound ever again.

Ping Ding was still talking in a high voice when the Russian unsnapped the cover of his holster and placed his hand on his weapon. Ping Ding then became very quiet, walked quickly to the last truck, got in and sat there without saying another word.

The Russian's stance was firm and commanding, as he never took his eyes off of Ping Ding until Ping Ding was settled in the truck with the door closed. Then and only then did the Russian pull his pistol and fire one round into the head of the young man on the ground. He then turned and talked to the remaining prisoners.

The Russian asked for all of them to gather so he could address all of them at one time. The Russian stood on the bumper of the middle truck, as some two hundred and fifty plus men gathered to hear what he had to say. To the best JW could later remember this was what the Russian had to say to all of them.

"You are all prisoners of war. There is no chance of escape and if you try, you will be shot. Your families and government have been told you're dead. Your dog tags have been turned into the American embassy at Da Nang."

"In a couple of days you will arrive at the farm camp. There you will have work to do. If you want to eat, you will work. If you don't work, you will not eat. If you don't eat, you will die, or I will kill you myself. If you touch or cause harm to any of the guards, you will be killed."

"I promise you as long as I'm in charge, there will be no more treatment like what happened to that young man over there. I believe that kind of treatment is wrong and I will not tolerate it."

Six Days Later

After the tiring travel of the last few weeks, JW hoped this ride would soon come to an end. Suddenly, the truck did come to a stop. Just like all the other stops, JW wondered if this stop would be any different. Hell, when you're a POW, no one asks you if you're tired or if you want something to eat or sleep, God forbid take a bath.

However, somehow this stop was different. From early in the morning, JW could smell something in the air that was quite unlike the bad breath of the men around him or the stench of all of them. No, stench was like someone talking about a bad smelling flower. The way we were smelling, would've caused a maggot to gage.

In the last few weeks, they had to put up with bad smelling gas and poorly tuned engines with black smoke rolling up around the back of the truck, as if the guards wanted to gas the men to death. JW thought to himself that if he was going down, he was going to take one of them with him. He hoped that one would be Ping Ding.

As the chain hooks were undone and the tailgate dropped, the words of encouragement came as always, "Out of the truck you pieces of shit, get the fuck out of my truck." As you might assume, they were assisted out of the truck with the butt of a rifle and a club. This place was different from the other places they had stopped. The air smelled fresh like the sea. This told them they were close to the ocean, and JW was thinking it was probably the Pacific Ocean.

JW's mind was trying to drift to a better place and better time. JW tried to clear his head because he didn't know where they were, and he needed to know what was happening around them. When he cleared his head, he knew he wasn't in Illinois and he was damn sure he wasn't in Vietnam any longer.

JW knew with all the easterly bound travel and all the towns they had come through, that they had to be on or near the coast of China. It wasn't until much later when they were rescued that they all learned their real general location. The POWs were being placed in various huts, which were more like lean-tos. JW thought a strong wind could have knocked them down. These were their new homes nevertheless and better than the back of a truck.

James, Reb and JW tried to stay together in one of the huts, but this was not to be. James and JW stayed together in one hut with about thirty other men who were all white. Reb was placed in a hut with some thirty or forty men who were all Negro.

———————————

As all this was happening to Reb, James and JW, one of Karen's visions was about to come frighteningly true. Considering all the time that had passed with absolutely no word from her husband, Karen was starting to resolve herself to accept the seemingly overwhelming possibility that she might never see her beloved husband ever again. Time was ever so slowly ebbing away at her beliefs. Time and what others were saying was taking its toll on Karen and her resolve that John would come home again some day.

It was a sunny and very peaceful Saturday afternoon. Karen was washing the lunch dishes when suddenly a vision she'd had some nine years before came rushing into her ears and flooding her memory. Karen was standing at the counter just in front of the kitchen window. The first time she had seen the vision had happened the first time she had stood at this same counter long before she had children to care for. She was again lost in that moment.

Suddenly, she could hear her two boys, John and Paddy-boy, who were just outside the window. The two boys were working on something when Paddy-boy spoke up, "If our dad was here, he could fix it!" At almost the exact same time, Kathryn, the daughter John has never seen or even knew existed, started crying in the living room. Karen went to the living room, picked up her daughter from the floor, and sat down on the couch while holding her daughter.

Karen said a prayer out loud as she cuddled her daughter next to her:

"Dearest almighty God, forgive me for I am weak and you are strong. I shall endeavor to never allow anyone to influence my belief in your love and compassion. God, you have given me a mountain to climb, I now ask you to help me to find the strength within myself to climb that mountain. Give me the wisdom to overcome those who would be a doubting Thomas. Dearest God, I hungrily await the time you allow my husband, children and I to be together again"

Karen had no idea what her husband was going through while life went on with their children. She only knew that someday, God would bring them together again. She had to put her trust the visions she had seen and believed the visions must be God's promise to her.

Meanwhile, life continued for JW and the other prisoners much as it had before Karen's renewed belief that her husband would return. The guards' shacks, as they came to call them, were quite different than the POW huts. They had glass windows and doors. JW didn't think their roofs leaked unlike the roofs of the POW huts. The guards also had running water, showers, and clean clothes. The POWs were made to wash the guards' clothes, and they pissed in the laundry water every chance they got.

Over the next two years, they lost over one hundred fifty men. The only time James and JW were able to see Reb was in passing while in route to their work duties. Their original numbers had declined to about one hundred men. However, from time to time fifteen to sixty POWs would arrive. With each new arrival or group of arrivals, there seemed to be less and less information arriving with them. The ones who would talk had information that was at least ten years old. As time went by, the POWs arriving seemed less interested in conversing in English. It seemed to them these POWs had been so mistreated that they not only did not speak English but also shied away from anyone who did speak English to them. Putting all these things together, James and JW had come to the conclusion that these men who were arriving were from other POW camps that had closed down for whatever reason.

Ten More Years Later

The last few years had been almost unbelievable. There were far less new people coming in than the number who were dying. When the Russian went on vacation or took some kind leave, Ping Ding would go on a killing spree. It was hard to believe, but they had come to rejoice in the return of the Russian. One time while the Russian was away, Ping Ding unmercifully killed four men just after sunrise. To them it seemed that he did this horrible act just for the fun of it.

JW came to firmly believe that Ping Ding was one sick bastard! Even though God said, "Vengeance is mine," JW felt God might not mind if someone stopped this worthless person from wasting any additional oxygen. JW, John Fredric Walker, planned on doing just that. Maybe not today and maybe not tomorrow, but one day JW knew that he would kill this godless person.

Given the poor food they had been forced to eat, JW could see the changes that had taken place in their bodies. They had all lost weight and more than just a little. They had all lost a lot of weight. JW could clearly see his ribs and the ribs of James. When they saw Reb, he looked like a walking skeleton.

From time to time, James and JW found some food down by the guard shack. They were not allowed to be out of the hut after lights out nor were they allowed to be down by the guard shack unless they were escorted by one of the guards. However, the need for food could drive any man to extraordinary acts of desperation when they knew that a box of food was there two to three times a week. This box of food was always in the same places by the guard shack and by a leaky old gas truck. The reason for the food and the gas truck was unknown to them. All they worried about was getting the food and getting away without anyone being the wiser.

Several More Years Later

After years of picking turnips, potatoes, and various other vegetables, the number of POWs had dwindled to a final count of ten. They were all placed in the same hut so JW, James, and Reb were together again. Unfortunately, the outlook for survival diminished with each passing day. Only three day earlier, the POW count had been eleven until some of Ping Ding's henchmen decided someone needed to die.

The last man killed was a man they had all come to know quite well over these last few years. He was a man who had been teaching them how to speak Spanish, Jose Hernandez. Jose told them he was born and raised in a small town located west of Phoenix, Arizona. It was called Buckeye and the best they could determine, Buckeye was a lot like Carlinville, Illinois.

Jose had been passing blood from his bowels for the last four days. They had all seen men doing this in the past. It would seem these men never lasted more than about eight or so days after starting to pass blood. On one day Ping Ding's henchmen wanted them to return to work. They all refused, stating they were too tired. The henchmen said, "No problem. Now someone must die. Which one of you American piece of shit want die?"

JW strongly believed Jose knew the inevitable outcome of his condition. So Jose stood up and placed his left hand behind him. He rolled his right hand in front of him while bowing from the waist. Jose told them in Spanish that he would be watching from the gates of heaven, as they entered the gates of hell. Two henchmen opened up with their AK-47's and Jose Hernandez passed into history, becoming one of the lucky ones.

Three Months Later

For the first time in what had been a very long time, a truck arrived. Now trucks actually arrived pretty much all the time, but what was different about this truck was that it carried two POWs. At first the two men were kept separated from the rest of them. However, eventually they were placed in the last remaining POW hut. In the beginning, they learned almost nothing about these two men except one of the two didn't speak hardly at all. Then something strange happened with one of these two men.

One man, the one who didn't speak, started doing something strange. He began to look at James for a very long time. He never spoke. He just stared at James. When James would walk or move around, this strange man followed James' every movement by the turn of his head. When he didn't turn his head, he followed James with his eyes.

When James called out JW, a change came over this strange man. A change of his facial expressions became quite clear. The next thing this strange man did surprised them all, even surprising the other POW he had arrived with. This man crawled quickly from the far side of the hut to James' feet and placed his arms around James' ankles and lower legs. He babbled in some kind of language they didn't understand. However, the man clearly said, "James".

James was very surprised by the actions of this strange man who was now at his feet. James spoke angrily, "What the hell?"

Reb asked James, "Do you know this man?"

James replied, "I don't think so," and then asked the man at his feet, "What's your name? How do you know me?"

JW asked James, "Could he be someone from your command or someone you've had a drink with?"

James replied, "That's possible, I've been on several different ships, and been in many ports of call. It could be he knows me from something like that."

Paul, the POW he arrived with, spoke up, "In all the time I've known him, you're the first person he's had anything to do with."

JW asked Paul, "What's the man's name?"

Paul replied, "I don't know. I don't think I've ever heard him utter a word!"

From that point on, this strange man held onto James unless they were working in the fields. Even though James tried talking to this man from time to time, he could never get anything out of him.

Many More Days Later

Over the last few years, James and JW had been slipping out of their hut every other night. They had discovered the box of food that was always located by the guard shack, but they had no idea why it was there. In the last few weeks, there had been more food in this box. They could only think it was because they were taking some of the food, but they had no way of being sure.

Then there was the old gas truck, as well. They had no idea why there was a gas truck in the compound. Most all of the trucks and equipment there seldom needed gas. This was due to the fact that they were just not used that much. There was a fuel tank, and it held about one hundred and fifty gallons of gasoline and stands above ground. They thought this old gas truck carried approximately two thousand gallons. They wondered what was the need for this gas truck other than to refill this above ground fuel tank.

They know this truck came from the west, but where it came from beyond that they don't know. When it arrived on the compound, it rumbled up to the guard shack and shut down for a while. After that, it rumbled across the compound to the east side where the sound of the truck became muffled. After about an hour or so, they would hear the truck leave the compound. When it left, it sounded different. It sounded less labored. They didn't know why, but they believed the guards were storing gas.

CHAPTER SEVEN
THE TRUCK AND THE BOAT

The POWs had grown used to hearing the old truck rumble around the compound. This was an activity that always took place after dark. The truck could be heard starting up and then rumbling off in to the distance. The sound became muffled after a time but could still always be heard. After about an hour or so the truck would return, but the sound the truck made while returning was different than when it left. It sounded like the truck was less labored. The POWs knew the sound of the truck and knew the routine night after night, but the POWs never knew until this night what the story was about the truck.

JW and James continued to sneak out of the hut at night to look for food. A small amount of food left in a box could be found near the guard shack. While they did not understand the reason the food was left night after night, JW and James were grateful. They took a small amount from the box each night and took it back to the hut to share with the other men. This small amount of food went a little farther than it used to, as over the years the number of men has dwindled to twelve. The last two POWs to arrive did not say much. What they did say was already old news. One of the two men seemed to hang on James for some reason.

James was on his usual run for food. As he approached the guard shack, he could hear the men inside as they talked. He realized that it was more of the Russian talking while the others listened. What James heard sent a cold chill down his spine, as he listened to the Russian lay out what was to happen in this next two to three weeks.

The Russian told the Vietnamese soldiers that this would be the last harvest of crops from this camp. The soldiers could return home and were not to come back. The camp was to be torn down, as the Chinese would no longer allow such an atrocity to continue in their country. One of the Vietnamese soldiers asked, "What's to be done about the last of the American pigs?"

The Russian's answer was short and to the point, "Bury them with the camp."

James heard someone coming and dove under the old truck parked there. Someone came up and put the box of food in the front seat of the old gas truck and closed the door. James could smell the gas that was leaking from the truck. He could also smell someone smoking a damn cigarette, which was not the wisest thing to do around a gas leak. As he waited, more guards came near the truck to stand around talking. After years with these guards, James had learned the language but there was nothing of any importance in their conversations. Some talked about going home while others talked about how gutless the Chinese were. For the most part, all were simply closing up the day and going to bed.

Not wanting to be caught, James hung on to the bottom of the truck. While he was hoping to be able to get back to his hut without further complications, he realized this was not going to happen soon as someone climbed into the truck and started the engine. He knew from the sound alone that this was the truck he had heard rumbling around the compound for so long. As the truck drove off, James hung on with all his strength. With potholes shaking the truck and gas leaking all over him, it was all he could do to hold on.

From what James could see from under the truck, it looked as though the truck passed through a gate and then started down a steep hill. James could see the truck was headed for the far side of the camp, which was an area where the POWs were never allowed. He thought this might explain the muffled sound of the truck he and JW had wondered about all these years.

James realized his strength was running out fast, as his arms and legs ached from holding on. The exhaust from the truck was all around him and made it hard to breath, but he knew he had to hang on if he was to survive this adventure. As the truck neared the bottom of the hill the tire ruts got worse, much worse.

The ruts became so bad it shook him loose from the truck, and he landed on the ground with a thud so hard it rattled his bones. His left leg landed in a rut in front of the rear truck tire. With the truck still moving forward, he knew his leg would be crushed from the weight of the truck. It was a certain fate then that the guards would find him and shoot him without any more feelings than someone would have from shooting a chicken-killing dog.

It seemed all was happening in slow motion. James watched the truck tire approach his leg. The only thing he could think of was all the good times he had spent with his wife, Sara Beth, his son, JW, Karen and their two boys. He was sad thinking about the fact that he would never see them again in this world. He worried what JW would do when James did not come back to the hut. As the tire was passing over his leg, he braced for the pain that would come as his leg was crushed by the tire.

To his surprise, the pain didn't come from his leg. Instead he felt intense pain from the right side of his head. The axle of the truck hit him in the head and turned him sideways. His leg was down in the old tire rut far enough that the tire passed over his leg without harm. The only thing that hurt was his butt from hitting the ground and the side of his head from being struck by the truck's rear axle.

As the truck moved away, James stayed where he was and looked up to heaven. He knew why he had been spared the serious injury and spoke quietly to God, "Thank you for keeping me safe. I don't know how but some day I will repay you."

Still lying on the ground, James looked at the truck that had stopped a short distance from him. He watched as the driver got out and walked around to the back. The driver picked up a flashlight from out of what must have been a toolbox and turned it on. James was sure the driver must have heard something and was going to come back for a look-see.

Instead the driver turned and walked the other way about fifteen or twenty feet. He then stopped and turned on a big light, which faced away from James.

When James' eyes adjusted to the light, he almost couldn't believe what he saw. A million ideas ran through his head, but the main idea was that he had found a way to escape. For the first time in his life, he used God's name in vain. In a breath of air no more than a whisper, he spoke these words, "It's a God damn power boat!"

As James looked at the boat, he was troubled with what kind it seemed to be. It appeared to be about seventy-five feet long and maybe fourteen to sixteen feet wide. Being a navy officer, this boat wasn't any kind he could seem to recognize that entirely well. He thought it might be from WW II and with that thought it came to him.

It was an old PT boat. James remembered seeing one in a movie he had seen in 1964 or 65. The movie was about President Kennedy and PT 109. He had thought that the PT boats had all been destroyed at the end of the war, but somehow this one made an escape of its own.

James watched the driver fuel the boat and place the box of food on board. Then he filled four other drums that were sitting on the dock. The driver retracted the fuelling hose, turned off the big light, and started back to the truck with the flashlight guiding his way.

James got up and moved towards the boat. He stumbled a time or two but reached the boat just as the driver was starting the truck. James grabbed some of the food from the box and ran for the truck. He knew he needed to return with the truck, as the gate would be closed and he would have no way back.

James ran as hard and fast as he could. He tripped and fell while his body throbbed in pain from the ride down and being hit in the head by the axle of the truck. Somehow he held on to the food he had grabbed from the boat, but he could not catch the truck.

As James stumbled up the hill where he was sure the guards would be waiting behind the closed gate, he thought about how he had spent his life trying to keep the commandments and lead people towards God. He believed that his current fate was God's punishment for his moment of weakness when he had used God's name in vain. James thought about how foolish he had been in his excitement in seeing the boat that he would do something he had known all his life to be unacceptable. He stopped walking long enough to say a prayer asking God to forgive him and asking God to save JW. If JW at least made it back home, then Sara Beth would at least know what had happened to her husband.

As Jams topped the hill, he stared in amazement that he could see the gate was still open and no guards seemed to be around. So he crouched down and took a long look around the area. There was no movement and no sense of there being any life. He slowly began to make his way forward and then through the open gate. Once safely through, he headed for the hut. He stopped to take a look several times, as the feeling of being watched crept over him. When he made it back to the hut, he wanted to tell JW what he had seen.

JW was the first one to greet him. With his hands trembling, James divided up the small amount of food. JW asked, "What took you so long? You've never taken that long before."

While James explained about the boat, the open gate, and no guards, he could see JW wasn't hearing much of what he was saying. James decided to wait and tell JW in the morning. Tonight he would get a good night's sleep.

It seemed like no time at all until they were being awakened in the usual manner. The usual manner was being screamed at while getting kicked and beat with a club. This was the normal wakeup call.

After the head count, and lets face it, it doesn't take long to count twelve people; they were given a small bowl of rice with some sort of meat. The men thought it was probably rat meat but no longer cared as long as they had something to eat. After this fine breakfast, they were then sent out to the fields to work all day. The guards' idea of getting the men motivated was to remind them they were dog mongrels and so on.

On this morning, Ping Ding had his mouth going non-stop. One might say he was trying to motivate the prisoners the best he could. Ping Ding was a short unintelligent piece of shit and weighed about one hundred pounds.

JW had a great dislike for Ping Ding. When Ping Ding started running his mouth about how the men would never see their homes or family again, all hell broke loose. James later thought that some of what he had told JW about the boat and gate might have gotten through, even though James had thought JW was asleep.

JW was about five feet from Ping Ding. JW rose to his full height, turned and took two steps. At the same time, JW drew back his right fist and let Ping Ding have all he had.

Ping Ding came about a foot off the ground and landed face down in the water. JW jumped on his back in less than a heart beat. He grabbed Ping Ding's arms and placed his hands together in the small of Ping Ding's back.

Ping Ding tried to raise his head up above the water. JW, still holding Ping Ding's hands, slid forward and placed his chest over Ping Ding's head. This forced Ping Ding's face back into the water and mud.

James was about twelve or fifteen feet away from JW, as he started moving towards him. James could see the Russian running towards JW. The Russian was pulling his pistol out, and the other guards running in towards JW pulled weapons as well.

James placed himself between JW and the Russian as best he could. He knew the worst was about to happen. He knew one of the best friends he had ever had was about to be killed right before his eyes and there was no way to stop what was going to happen.

By the time the Russian arrived, JW released Ping Ding and stood up. Ping Ding didn't move, as he was stuck in the mud.

The Russian spoke loudly and very clearly, "You know it is against the rules to touch a guard! As it looks to me he is dead, the punishment for you is death!"

The POW, who had been hugging James ankles to keep him from joining the battle, fell to the ground and curled up in a ball without making a sound.

The Russian jacked a round into the chamber and drew a bead on JW.

James did the only thing he could think to do. He spoke to the Russian, "If you kill him, you will have to kill us all and bring this crop in your damn self. And we're not half done yet."

The Russian's eyes narrowed as he looked at James. James felt his heart skip a beat or two. He wasn't sure if this was the end but almost welcomed it at last. This world of hell would soon be over and JW and he might soon become among the lucky ones who were free.

The Russian pulled the trigger. James could feel the bullet wiz past him. He heard JW call out in pain and knew when he turned around that his friend would be dead or dying. He knew there was nothing, not one damn thing he could do to save JW.

James stared at the big Russian for a moment before turning towards JW. All the things JW and James had done together as kids growing up ran through his mind. JW was on the ground as James expected but to his surprise and delight, JW was very much alive. It seemed the Russian just grazed JW's leg. The number of surviving me had almost become eleven, but JW would survive the gunshot to his leg. James was puzzled about the Russian, as in the past if the Russian pulled his gun, some one died.

The Russian said something to the other guards, and they backed away. The guards told us to get back to work and be quick about it. Only after the Russian holstered his pistol did JW return to work, and the guards took Ping Ding's body away.

"James, what do you think our chances are of us getting that PT boat?" JW asked quietly after the guard and the Russian were far enough away that they could whisper without being heard.

"I think they will be damn good. JW, let's talk about it tonight," James whispered back and then continued working. At least now he knew JW did hear at least part of what he had tried to tell him about the boat. The rest of the day went without any further problems as the men worked silently lost in their own thoughts.

At the end of the day, James told JW and the rest of the men what he had overheard at the guard shack. He then told them about his wild ride and what he thought was an old PT boat. He also told JW about the redhead who seemed to be around him during the night. This was the same man who had tried to hold Jw back when JW was fighting Ping Ding.

When it was daytime in the POW camp, it was night in the state of Illinois. At the same time JW was shot, Karen woke up screaming. She knew John had been hurt. She could see it as clear as day, but she had very few people to talk to about her visions. Some people were beginning to think she was loosing her mind from the stress of not knowing what had happened to her husband. Even the minister of the church was having doubts and wondering what he could do to help this poor woman and her children.

Karen had told her children, her mom and dad, and John's mom and dad when something would happen to John. She had explained that she could feel it and see it as though she was there with him. She believed he was still alive even after all these years of hearing nothing from John. She still believed even though the government assured her that all the POWs were supposed to have been released.

Fewer and fewer people believed in what Karen would tell them, but Karen never lost hope. She never lost sight of the vision she had so many years ago. She believed in her vision. More importantly, Karen believed in the strength of the love she had for her husband and for God.

As morning came, James and JW woke up without any help from the guards. That fact alone was as strange as a three-dollar bill.

As the other men woke, JW and James were already wondering what the hell was going on. The other men started asking as well, but there were yet no answers for them.

Soon two Chinese guards showed up with food and water. The two stood for a while and talked to each other while taking a long look at the twelve prisoners. JW could understand part of what the two guards were talking about, and James understood some of the conversation. Between the two, they were able to put most of it together. They moved to the back of the hut and whispered to each other what they had heard:

"Me no like what being done these mericans in my country. You know this not right. They maybe mad you me."

The other Chinese guard had then said. "You think they do us like yesterday man?"

The first guard answered, "You right, them no know us."

Then one of the guards asked for two of the prisoners to come out and get the food. Two men did so and then returned to the hut. After that, the two Chinese soldiers left. A short time later, the same two soldiers returned and ordered James out, "The one called James, you come out now. Russian sees you."

James started out, which meant he had to bend over to go out the door. It was made this way so that when any of the group was called to come out, the guards could start beating on him. That was the normal thing to happen whether they were called out to work or called out one at a time. The Chinese guards were not normally the ones who called or removed any of the men from the hut. They would seldom do any harm to any of the men. However, they did beat a man to death just outside the hut one time. It was something none of the men would ever forget, so none of the men would trust any of the guards at all.

As James went out the small door, he was not struck or assaulted in any way. When he could stand up straight, he asked, "Where you are taking me?"

"To the main guard shack. You see Russian. He wants talk you."

James turned and led the way to the guard shack with the two Chinese guards following close behind. Upon arriving at the shack, James was shoved through the door. He stumbled but was able to remain on his feet even though his legs were cramping.

James looked around the room and could see four or five guards. His eyes stopped on the Russian, who had his back to James. He seemed to be reading something, and then turned to look at James with a strange look on his face like he wasn't sure what to do or say. The first thought that came to James was that the Russian had somehow learned of the conversation between James and JW. It was right after JW had killed Ping Ding and then asked James about escaping in the PT boat. If this was the case and the Russian knew their plan was to use the boat, and the twelve men still alive would soon be going to heaven.

Always before the Russian had looked and spoke with absolute authority. James had personally noticed this when he first met this big Russian. Although James had lost track of how many years had passed since that first meeting, he knew the Russian had always been in control. He thought back to the first time he had seen him. Even then, the Russian had been in charge over Ping Ding and the other guards.

Over the years the Russian has come to the aid of the men a number of times, mostly in keeping the guards from beating someone to death. In all this time, James had never known the Russian not to complete anything he said he wanted done. He expected that everyone would carry out his orders to the letter.

James thought the Russian would use him as an example of what happens when someone touches a guard, not to mention kills one. James had stepped between JW and the Russian, and JW was still alive. This fact did not make sense with all James knew of the Russian. He was sure this would not be over until either he or JW were dead.

The Russian started talking about how things had changed in the world. James listened but it didn't really seem as though the Russian was talking to him. It was more the man was talking to himself. He said something about the Berlin wall coming down. He used a word James had never heard before that sounded like "perestroika" or something like that. Then the Russian stopped talking. As he looked around the room, his eyes narrowed and his face became trite as the Russian spoke these words, "You piece of shit, you are in my way and I'm tired of looking at you! Why don't you just die?"

In an instant, a Vietnamese guard put James on the floor so quick and hard it rattled his very frame. James wanted to rip the bastard's heart out and show it to him while it was still beating. He knew he had to remain in control of his emotions, but it wasn't easy. Since he had become a POW, he had seen men beaten, sometimes beaten to death. With the beatings he had received, he had learned to hate. This was a hate no man should ever have to know.

James sometimes wondered if this was the way the black man felt about the white man during the years of slavery. These men were separated from their families and beaten. Many times they were beaten unmercifully, even to death. They were forced to work hard, long hours, even when they didn't feel well. They had no choice where to live or sleep. Their food was often table scraps at best. All this ran through James' head as he thought that being a POW could not be much different than being a slave. He had learned not to make friends or try and find out very much about any POW, as they did not seem to last very long. Every now and then a new POW would arrive who had been a POW as long or even longer than James and JW. James thought about the two newest POWs who had arrived about two or three weeks ago with no new news from the outside world. One of the two had still not talked. It seemed all the man wanted to do was stay near James for some reason.

James snapped back to reality as the Russian yelled, "Turn him loose and get the hell out of my office!"

James was released and fell to the floor with a thud as the guards left the room. He was still on the floor when the Russian came around from behind his desk in a huff. James knew in just a moment that he would be feeling the Russian's boots in his ribs, back and legs. He was sure he was in for the beating that would be his last.

James watched as the Russian's left boot came at his hip. He tried to roll up on his right side as quick and best he could. He felt the boot just slip under his hip and buttocks. This rolled him on to his right side and exposed his back to the Russian. The Russian then pelted James' back with several kicks. Some of the kicks landed on James' legs and head. James wasn't sure if the Russian wasn't kicking hard or if his body had become so numb that he didn't feel the full impact of the boot. The thought crossed James' mind that being numb would be a good thing as he died from being beaten.

The Russian then forced James onto his back and put his right boot in the center of James' chest so damn hard that he thought his heart stopped. With his strength and his weight, the Russian rolled James back and forth like a rag doll. James lost track of just how long this lasted, but it seemed like eternity. He felt like he was dying and there was nothing he could do to stop his own death. He let his mind drift away from the torture and saw the face of his mother. He reached out and touched her face. He knew she must be able to see him, as she had tears running down her face just as he remembered she had the day his father had died.

James did not know if he was screaming out loud or maybe just inside his head as he called to her, "Mother, help me! I'm hurt and I can no longer help myself. Mother, please! Please Momma, help me!"

James heard his mother's voice comfort him through her tears, "I love you, Son, keep the faith and you will be okay! Remember what God said. He who believes in me shall not perish."

James was becoming desperate. He was struggling just to breath and was in tremendous pain. It was then that he saw his wife. As he reached for her, she started screaming, "I love you, James!"

At the same time, James told her, "I'm being killed! They are beating me to death. I no longer have the strength to fight back. Help me! Help me!"

"James, I'm trying, reach! Reach, James, I will help you, I will help you, James!" At that point, James saw the bedroom door burst open.   A young and powerful looking young man entered and said, "Mother, Mother calm down, calm down you'll be fine."

Suddenly, the young man looked up at James with a look of total surprise on his face. He turned to James and said, "Dad, is that you?"

James screamed again, "He's killing me!" The young man reached forward and had a good hold on James. He tore off a piece of the rag James had for a shirt and then James slipped away.

James saw all of this as he felt his life slipping away. He called for God to help him, and then all the pain disappeared. James felt so calm and peaceful. He experienced a peace like he had never known before in all his life. The terrible hunger and thirst of the years in the prison camp were gone. There was no pain, no hunger, and no thirst. Suddenly he saw the brightest light he had ever seen. It was a million times brighter than the sun, but it didn't hurt his eyes at all. He was at peace.

Within the light he could feel strength, power, and a love that was more intense than any he had known before. He could see a figure moving towards him. The closer it came, the more puzzled he became as who he saw was his dad.

James held his arms out so he could hug and hold his father. He knew his father had come to walk him the rest of the way to Heaven. James smiled, as his father looked exactly the way he remembered him the last day they had walked together.   James' smile began to fail when his father stopped just out of his reach. James said, "It's me Dad, your son, James. I've come to heaven. My captors have beaten me to death. Now we can be together forever. I know I'm dirty, but a good hot bath and I'll be just fine. I love you, Dad!

James' father then said, "I know you love me Son, and I love you, too. But it's not time for you to come to heaven. You still have much to do. You must return."

"Then why have I come so close only to be sent back?" James questioned.

"Son, God knows what you're going through, and He wanted you to know what's in store for you, as long as you keep the faith."

"Dad, they've beat me to death! I can no longer help myself!"

"Son, you will be okay, just follow your heart and keep the faith!"

James started to slip back away from his father. He reached both arms out as far as he could but he could not reach his dad. He pleaded with him, "Dad, please don't make me return. Please! God help me!"

It was then that James took the first breath since he had seen the vision of his mother, and all the pain came rushing back. He knew he had returned to hell. The next thing he knew was when a big s. o. b. grabbed him up from the floor. He held James in front of him and stared at James with a look of death in his eyes. James had just returned from the other side and no longer feared death. If this was his end, then he knew he could welcome it and be back in his father's arms.

The man holding James began yelling at him, while James was being violently shaken. James was sure his head or at least one of his arms would break off for sure. James realized it was the Russian still beating him. The Russian was screaming, "You American piece of shit, no guts dog American. I have beaten you and you know it! Don't you, don't you, don't you!"

When the Russian released James, he fell to the floor with a crash and a thud. James could only wonder what had provoked this big Russian into doing this. In the past he had been strong but always restrained. Now he stood over James and was taking a long, long look. The look on his face and in his eyes was different, and James was sure the man must have flipped out.

James had never before feared this big Russian the same way he had Ping Ding and the guards. It was more like a fearful respect for a man who could kill any of them but had some degree of humanity. Now what James was feeling was a real fear like he had never known. Years ago no man would have had a chance to kick and beat him like this big Russian has just done. James knew that the condition was in from being poorly fed, over-worked, and beaten that he was in no condition to take this Russian on without a weapon of some sort. His fear included his feelings of being totally helpless and at the mercy of a madman.

The Russian bent over and picked up a chair, setting it upright on all four legs. He then turned picked James up from the floor and sat him in the chair. James mind was locked on the chair with four legs instead of the type of chair they normally had a POW sit on. He was used to a chair with only one leg on it and so low it was hard to sit on. He knew any man sitting on such a chair would have trouble to keep from falling over because his knees were bent and keeping control of the chair was damn hard to do.

The Russian picked up a rag from his desk and turned back towards James with the rag in his hand. James was sure the Russian expected James to wipe the blood from his boots. To James' surprise, the Russian bent over and wiped off his own boots. He then tossed the rag to James and motioned towards the sink on the other side of the room. He said to James, "Would you like to clean up a bit?"

The Russian turned and stepped behind his desk. After the man sat down, James rose slowly from the chair using the arms of the chair to help him up. He found it hard to move because of the beating and then sitting for a short time had caused his legs, arms and back to freeze. Moving brought back all the pain.

As James sorely staggered across the room to the sink, he once again turned to the Russian. The Russian gave a slight nod with his head. James turned back to the sink and turned the water on. The water coming out was clean and clear. There was no scent of piss or shit. James saw and picked up a bar of soap. He washed his hands and face by cupping his hands to hold the water. He splashed the water again and again on his face. It was almost unbelievable how good the water felt on his face and how good it tasted as he rinsed his mouth out. This was good clean water and just to touch it was a pleasure!

As James stood there, he looked in the mirror. He could not remember the last time he had seen his own reflection and what he saw looking back at him was a dirty, beaten man. He knew this was not the man he remembered. In his own thoughts, the man he remembered was a young man, strong and well groomed. He was a young man who had shoved a man through a solid core door because that man had made a nasty remark to his wife and used God's name in vain all in the same breath. The longer James stared at the man in the mirror, the more he realized he was not sure who the man was looking back at him.

In the corner of the mirror, James could see the Russian still seated behind his desk and pouring a drink. James thought that it was probably Vodka. He stumbled back to the chair and sat down. He looked right at the Russian, as the man took down three more small glasses, one right after the other.

James knew the prisoners were not supposed to look at any of the guards or the Russian in the face, but he looked right in the face of this Russian and the Russian looked back at James. He looked at James as though they were friends who had been in a fight the night before and was not sure what to say the morning after.

The Russian turned and picked up another glass from the table from behind him. Holding the glass in his left hand, he tipped the top of the glass towards James. James returned his gesture with a yes nod. The Russian sat the glass on the side of the desk near James and poured the glass full. The Russian refilled his own glass and started to drink. He stopped drinking and motioned with his left hand for James to drink. James wondered silently, "This man just tried to kill me! Just what the hell could he be up to?"

James reached forward cautiously and picking up the glass, put it to his mouth. The Russian gave him a small salute with his glass. James returned the salute and then started to drink.

As the vodka poured into his mouth, it started to burn due to the open sours in his mouth from the beating he had just received. James also knew it was burning due to the fact that he had not had any alcohol in a very long time.

The Russian saw this and broke into a big smile as he started to laugh and ramble off in Russian. After having one or two more glasses of vodka, the Russian stood up and said, "You and me, we need to go for a walk."

This big Russian came around the desk and gave James a hand up that brought James about four inches off the floor. James was not sure if the Russian was that much bigger than he was, or if James just didn't straighten out but the Russian towered over him. The Russian helped James steady himself and out the door they went.

Once outside, the sun seemed really bright. James was sure part of the brightness was due to the alcohol he had just consumed for the first time in years. As they went down the steps, the guards started to follow. The guards had not taken more than three steps when the Russian stopped and turned. James, however, did not stop or turn and found he was face first into the Russian's chest.

The Russian steadied James, as he told the guards to stay on the porch. To James' he said, "Follow me. I'm sure you will see a day you have dreamed of." He took about three or four steps and stopped and turned. Again James ran into him. As he put his hands on James' upper arms, he said something to one of the guards. He then looked at James and said, "Easy Yank! You've still a full day ahead of you."

A bottle of vodka and two glasses were shoved into James' chest. The Russian asked, "Do you think you can carry them, Yank?"

The only thing James could think to say was, "I'll try" and so off they went. They walked to the far side of the compound where James had been just the other night. The Russian said, "Pour us a drink," and so James did.

As the two strange new companions stood near the edge of the cliffs, the Russian started telling James how the world has changed. He explained how the Berlin wall had come down. He talked about how he would be going home soon and most likely would never see another American again. He continued to talk on about all kinds of things.

The Russian walked James all over the far side of the compound. They them went up to the gate that was still opened and unmanned. They stepped outside the gate for a few steps, and the Russian pointed out towards the ocean.

James said, "Yes, the beautiful blue Pacific Ocean."

The Russian said, "You're right, it is beautiful," and went on to say, "When I was a boy . . ." The rest James could not understand as the Russian rambled on in his native language. From the gestures he was making with his hands, James knew it was something to do with fishing. The Russian must have caught a big one and needed help landing it. James had a feeling the Russian was talking about a time his dad had helped him catch a big fish.

Then the Russian quieted down, looked at the ground, and said, "Damn war." He then kicked some dirt and rocks into the air. Then in a louder voice and kicking more dirt and rocks he shouted, "Damn war, always damn war!" as he continued to kick more dirt and rocks.

The Russian stood with his feet apart, his hands shaking and clenched in fists over his head. In a very loud voice he said, "War, war always damn war! Why never peace?"

After a minute or so, he calmed down. James saw him wipe his eyes before he turned to James and said, "I must have got dirt in my eyes."

James said, "Well you sure put plenty in the air."

With a slight smile, the Russian said, "Yes I did, didn't I. Yank, I want to tell you one more thing about the pacific."

"What's that?"

"If I was going to Pearl Harbor this time of year, I would keep the moon just over my right shoulder. That is if I was going to Pearl Harbor."

From the gate they walked back the same route James had used the night he had returned from the P.T. boat. The Russian made a point of telling James that there was no need for guards on the gate. He looked James in the eyes as he said, "Cause you POWs don't seem to want to leave."

When they returned to the hut, the Russian said, "There will be no work today. I will have some real food and water delivered to your hut." He then turned and walked away leaving the hut unsecured.

JW and the other men could clearly see that James had received a relatively severe beating. They all wanted to know what it was about and why James smelled like alcohol. James regaled them with what had taken place in the guard shack, and that he had seen the faces of his wife, his mother, and his father. He explained about the brightest light he had ever seen and the love he felt within this light. He knew he had been with his father in Heaven but had been sent back. He went on to detail where the Russian and he had walked. He told the men that the Russian had told him to keep the moon over his right shoulder while in route to Pearl Harbor.

James explained that he felt he might have been being watched while on his way back from the gate the night he discovered the PT boat and that the Russian just walked him back on the same path he had used that night. The men spent the next few minutes trying to figure out what all this meant. They were wondering if it was another sick game their captors were playing or if they really might have some hope of escaping.

Soon the food and water arrived just as the Russian had promised. The men all sat together and enjoyed this food and water. After it was gone, most of the men slept through the rest of the day. Reb, JW, and James sat discussing the information and events. They came to the conclusion that the Russian had been trying to tell the something. They were afraid to trust the fact they were finally having a turn of good luck so they wondered what in God's name was this Russian trying to tell them?

A plan slowly started forming. After Reb went to sleep, JW and James came up with a basic plan for what might be a last ditch effort to escape. They knew the gas truck would be arriving that night as it did every night. When it went to fuel the boat, they could possibly over take the driver as long as there wasn't anyone else at the dock. They knew from the time James was there that there were other fuel drums on the dock. They could place some of the drums on the deck of the boat and then fill them as well. With the extra fuel drums, they could possibly extend the range of the boat by some two hundred miles or so.

The three biggest questions were: 1. Could they take the driver and what would they do if there were two drivers? 2. What if there were other people with the boat or even just on the dock? 3. The biggest question of all was could they move twelve people from the hut to the docks?

They came to the conclusion that the odds were indeed against them being able to take the driver. If there were other people on the boat or dock, the odds against them were astronomical. They knew the plans for their future at this camp and the chances of surviving if they stayed was even more astronomical than trying to steal the PT boat. JW and James felt they had thought this out the best they could and determined this meal the Russian had given them could be used as a farewell dinner.

JW and James finally went to sleep and were awakened by the sound of the gas truck rumbling into the compound. All the men who were still asleep were allowed to continue sleeping. JW, James, and some of the other men wondered what was taking so long for the gas truck to take off for the boat. James was sure it was like anything that seemed to take longer when you were watching or waiting for it to happen.

Soon all the men were awake and listened to the plans JW and James had developed. If everything went smoothly according to their plans, the whole group would be in the boat and headed out to sea in just a short time. They reminded the men of military protocol and explained that all their lives would depend on everyone giving one hundred percent of what ever they might have left. It was then decided Reb would bring up the flank, making sure all the men kept moving and didn't get lost.

Just before they started moving out, JW and James thought they heard what sounded like small arms fire. They thought they heard about six or seven shots, but the sound was so faint that they couldn't be sure. They decided to continue because the escape was tonight or possibly never.

As they moved out from the hut, their line became about fifty feet or so long, but they all kept moving. They only heard Reb telling one man to get up and keep moving while they were all in route to the boat. Although the moon was full and very bright, it was partially obscured by clouds, which made it dark and difficult to see anything.

When JW and James reached the open gate, they crouched down and waited for all the men to join them. They could see the path leading down the hill to the boat. They listened to ensure they had not been detected and no one seemed to be pursuing them. JW whispered, "James, I have this almost overwhelming feeling that we are being watched."

James replied, "I seem to feel the same. It's how I felt when I snuck back to the hut the other night when I had discovered the boat." They continued to listen and to watch the shadows but nothing moved. After about two or three minutes, they started moving through the open gate and down the hill.

About ten to fifteen feet past the gate, JW tripped over what turned out to be a dead body. Then two of the other men tripped over a dead body. When the clouds covering the moon cleared for a short time, they were able to determine the body count at six and all were shot through the head. They saw the face of one of the dead men and knew it was one of the guards. Continuing down the hill, they encountered no more bodies.

After arriving at the lower areas of this big hill, they could see the area was well lit with spotlights making it much harder to approach without being seen. They sat in the shadows of the gas truck, out of the intense lighting of the floodlights. Except for the driver of the gas truck, they couldn't see any other people around. They moved to the north end of the gas truck and awaited their chance to take the driver.

After waiting for what seemed like forever, the driver returned to the truck to light up and smoke a damn cigarette. James thought for the first time in his life how glad he was for someone who smoked. This cigarette would prove to be very hazardous to the driver's health. This placed the boat out of the driver's sight for a short time and it was at this point the twelve men took possession of the boat.

James decided it was time to visit the driver and possible shut down the truck. After a very short time of thinking, he realized the sound of the truck was important and this sound needed to be kept going.

JW was also moving towards the truck. He had seen on the dim lighted side of the truck that his best friend was moving forward in an attempt to destroy a human life. Although the driver of the gas truck was indeed a Vietnamese person, this person most likely had done no harm to any of them. He was not one of the guards who had beaten and killed prisoners over the years.

When JW got to the truck, he saw that James not only had this Vietnamese person on the ground, he had his foot positioned for breaking the man's neck. JW called out to James. As James turned to face his friend, JW thought he could hear a small snap. It was hard to say with the sound of the truck running, but the Vietnamese man no longer struggled. JW then said, "We need the truck running so anyone who is listening won't notice anything wrong. We also need the truck running to pump the gas into the drums we will be placing on the deck of the boat."

James walked over to JW and said, "You're right about the sound of the truck. We will leave it running."

The two men returned to the boat, climbed aboard, and started preparing to shove off as soon as the fuel and men were loaded. JW called down through a voice tube mounted at what appeared to be the control area and informed the men on the other end to start the engines.

James called to Reb, "Are all the drums on board and secured?"

Reb replied, "Yes, we have eight drums filled but the truck ran dry half way through the ninth one."

James and JW were very impressed that these men of various military and rank went to their stations of expertise without being ask. They found this to be so astounding. Hell, they even found they had two men who were very knowledgeable in marine engines.

With the engines running, they completed a head count. JW then asked for reverse of both engines. Slowly the old boat started moving backwards. They were all finally on their way home.

After clearing the dock, JW cranked the wheel hard to the right and asked for one third forward on the port engine.

Per JW's commands, the old girl moved slowly out towards the open sea and on into the vast expanse of the blue pacific.

After the glory of leaving their captors, most all of the twelve settled down and went to sleep, but only a select few remained awake. These were the ones required to operate the boat. This consisted of James West, John Walker, Reb, and two other men who had working knowledge of Naval mechanics had volunteered for and were placed in the engine room. The first few hours of the ride for the most part were smooth and uneventful. The dreams of returning home ran unchecked by anything they thought could happen.

The two men below in the engine room were cousins. One was from the great state of Tennessee, and the other was from the great state of Mississippi. Both states were of great beauty and were entrenched deeply in the rich history of the United States.

These two men acted more like young schoolboys at recess than two men who had been starved, beaten, and treated less human than a dog. For in their minds, they thought tomorrow they would walk up to one of their family reunions and be received with open arms. They dreamed they would be served food only fit for a king. They had visions of fried chicken, pork chops, mashed potatoes, corn on the cob with fresh cow butter, baked and fried potatoes with a salad of a head lettuce, turnip greens, and red onions and pies of all kinds: apple, peach, cherry, blackberry and blue berry. All the pies were topped with homemade, hand-cranked ice cream.

After about six or so hours, the rush of adrenalin had worn off. The thought of all the fine food made their stomachs growl. With urgings from JW and James, two men settled in to making adjustments to the very old and tired engines attempting to get maximum fuel range out of engines long, long overdue for a tune up. Reb assisted them as he shared his own mechanical knowledge he had gained from working his family's farm.

Reb reported to JW and James that all that could be done had been done given the tools that were available. However, one of the engines was running hot and leaking oil. Reb recommended that it be shut down.

James, with a surprised look on his face, asked in a commanding voice, "Reb, just how many engines are we running?"

Reb replied, "With three. All PT boats have three engines in them don't they?"

JW spoke up, "Yes, shut it down, and do it now! And Reb, lower the R.P.M's on the other two. My God, we've got to conserve all the fuel we possibly can!"

Reb disappeared back below deck. A minute or two later the sound of one engine shutting down could be heard reducing the vibrations throughout the boat. The groan of the other two engines was reduced to just above an idle.

Reb returned to the hatch and called for James and JW, "Are the current engine settings okay?"

JW replied, "Yes, we should be able to maintain heading and headway. The speed is approximately 25 miles per hour. As long as all is well, the men should try and get some rest." JW went on to say, "Reb, check one more time that things are okay and then please come topside."

After about ten minutes Reb came topside. He had grease and oil on his hands, arms, and face as he gave James and JW a report about the engines. Reb finished his report, walked away, found a place to lie down, and quickly went to sleep.

JW looked at James and said, "We may have traveled some one hundred to two hundred miles with three engines running but I'm not sure."

James replied, "I think you might be wrong about the distance. I'm thinking the distance might be closer to four hundred miles, as we've been traveling at approximately forty-five to fifty miles an hour for at least ten to twelve hours."

"Yes, James, and just what do you think that did with the fuel in the main tanks, with the engines running badly and over half throttle for the last ten to twelve hours?"

"JW, I don't think you or I ever thought we had the fuel to reach the Hawaiian Islands anyway."

"I know, James, but I thought we could make it out into the shipping lanes and hopefully be rescued before we ran out of fuel completely. I sure don't want to be drifting in these seas with no hope of someone finding us." JW was silent for a few minutes and then said, "I'm going to find a soft place on this deck and get myself some rest, if you don't mind. Wake me if you get too tired to stay awake or if President Nixon comes by for a visit."

"JW, how do you know if he's still president?" James asked.

"I don't, but he was president the last time I heard. I don't know anything differently so I may as well stick with him," JW and James shared a laugh as JW moved off to find a place to sleep.

Thinking about the condition of the men who had been beaten, starved, and were extremely tired, James knew he was no different. However, before sitting down on the deck and going to sleep, James tied off the steering controls. He was thinking that if he did go to sleep, the boat would at least keep going in the right direction. The right direction was out into the vastness of the beautiful blue Pacific and, hopefully, straight in the direction of the Hawaiian Islands.

James sat down on the deck next to the controls. He was feeling so damn tired from being up the last ten or so hours. Feeling weak from not eating and having little to drink combined with the rocking of the boat from the waves and the throbbing of the engines, James went to sleep.

James started dreaming of the last breakfast he had enjoyed with his family the morning his father died. As James dreamed, tears from his sunken eyes ran down his face. These were not tears of sorrow but tears of joy as once again James spent the day going from one farmer to another while working and talking to his dad. He could see himself and his dad, both in good health. He was not hungry, and he wasn't covered with sores, some of which were bleeding. His hair wasn't long and stringy nor was it dirty. He could feel that his hair was clean, cut short, and well groomed like he always kept his hair. He could see the rich medium brown color. In his dream he sat down, leaned against a shade tree to rest, and took a nap. Some time later, he could hear his name being called and felt a tap on the shoulder. He thought that when he opened his eyes that he would see the face of his father but this was not to be.

When James opened his eyes, he saw the face of a man he had known for years. This was the face he had spent the last 20 plus years with. He was looking into the face of a man with sunken eyes, his hair was long and stringy, his cloths were rags and dirty as well, his body was dirty. This man also had sores on his face, arms and hands. It was the face of a man whom had been his best friend since childhood. This was the face of John Frederick Walker, better known as JW.

JW spoke in a voice of urgency, "James, wake up, the damn boat ran out of fuel!"

James responded with, "Do what, Dad?"

"Wake up my friend, the damn boat has run out of fuel, and we are adrift. It's possible we could be in the shipping lanes with no way to move."

"But, JW, it's still dark!"

"No shit, James, and we could get run over by the very ship we want to be rescued by."

"JW, let's not wake up the other men just yet. Just let them sleep as long as possible cause I don't think there's much anyone can do in the dark," James stated as he looked around. Seeing one of the prisoners sleeping next to where James had been, James asked, "And why does this guy keep getting so damn close to me?"

"I don't know, James, but we need to keep a sharp eye out for any approaching ships."

After James stood up, rubbed his eyes and stretched his six feet, ninety-five pound body, his eyes fell on an object off in the distance. Again James tried to clear his eyes and focus on the object.

"JW, ten o'clock off the port beam. Is that a ship or not?"

"My God, yes! Quick, grab the flare gun, James!"

"I'm on it, JW, I'll jerk one out of my ass or maybe you can shit one?" James shouted back to his friend. They stared in horror as they realized there was no way they could contact the ship that was so close yet still too far away.

Within thirty or so minutes the ship off in the distance was out of site, disappearing over the horizon. JW had sat down on the fore deck on his butt, with his knees bent allowing his feet to be out to the sides, next to his butt. James tried to talk to him, but JW seemed to be lost in his own thoughts. He continued to sit there until after the sun came up and the other men were awake.

JW finally stood up from where he had sat the rest of the night hours. Even though other men were awake, no one approached him. This may have been due to the lack of energy. As he turned around, James and the other men could see vertical streaks running from his eyes down to the corners of JW's mouth and on down ending on his chin.

As JW walked from the fore deck, aft to just past mid ship where James was standing, JW's walk was more like that of a drunk. Part of his walk was due to his weakened condition and part was due to the rocking of the boat on the waves. The boat was at the mercy of the waves produced in the vastness of the beautiful blue Pacific Ocean because the engines were not running. Without the engines, there was no way to maintain any kind of headway. Without the ability to maintain headway, the boat would rock uncontrollably with whatever waves came their way.

As JW approached, James apologized for falling asleep while on watch. JW looked at James with a bit of a smile on his face and said, "Not to worry, James. We're all very tired and I don't think it would have made any difference had we all been awake. I'm thinking the boat would have run out of fuel anyway. What say we get after the task at hand and refuel this boat? Get some headway going and smooth out this ride?"

James, now with a sense of relief that his friend was not angry with him for falling asleep at the helm, simply said, "Let's get after it."

Reb, over-hearing the conversation, attempted to move one of the drums but failed with his first attempt. Reb, with a bit of a surprised look on his face, made a second attempt and again failed to move the drum.

James and JW saw their friend's failure to move the drum of fuel and quickly moved to assist Reb. One other man from nearby also assisted. The four men together moved the fuel drum into place.

James and JW both could see the bewildered look on the face of their friend, a friend they both had grown up with. Reb had once been a man who could have moved this drum without any help, but that was long ago before they all became POWs. It was before he had spent years being beaten, starved, and worked as hard as any slave of the early years of America.

CHAPTER NINE

THE LONG VOYAGE HOME

After the drum was in place for fueling the boat, the men then discovered they did not have a pump to transfer the fuel from the drum to the tanks of the boat. James looked at JW and said, "What the hell else could possibly go wrong?"

JW replied, "James, please don't talk like that. We will find another way."

Reb joined the conversation with another concern, "I've looked at the old radio on board, and I can't fix it. I'm think I can make a transmitter from the parts of it. It would only be able to transmit not receive. What would you two like for me to do?"

"Reb, you do whatever you can with the radio. James and I have something else to do if we can find a way to do it." JW turned to James and continued, "It seems to me, if I remember correctly, there should be a bilge pump stored forward in one of the lower compartments."

James cautioned, "Now JW, I remember reading about these old boats when we were in the Academy. Even then these boats were old and outdated. This boat is some fifty plus years old and has been used by the Chinese for forty years as some kind of patrol boat. So just what in God's name makes you think some old sump pump might still be on board, not to mention in some compartment in the lower deck?"

JW just looked at James. James opened his eyes wide, tilted his head from left to right, and then spoke, "Ok John, for Christ sake let's go and look for this damn pump."

JW and James walked forward towards the hatch. Their walk looked more like the stagger of two buddies coming home from the bar. This was caused partly by their weakened condition from being starved and partly from the boat being rocked from side to side by the two to three foot waves courtesy of the beautiful blue Pacific Ocean.

After making their way to the hatch and down to the lower deck, the two men found they needed to stop and rest. James said, "Damn JW, are we that old or just in that bad of shape?"

"Well James, I'm not sure. But I think it's the shape we're in, because I don't think I'm much over forty five or so."

After a few minutes, JW and James forced themselves to their feet and started forward. As James took his first step, the boat rocked. James tripped and hit his face into the bulkhead. As the boat rocked back the other way, James fell back against the other bulkhead.

JW couldn't hold back his laugh as he said, "Damn, bet that hurt huh!"

James, holding back a grimace, replied, "Let's get to looking for that pump."

As the two men started checking the compartments, JW said, "Hey James, seems most of these compartments haven't been opened in a long time."

"Yaw! And they have been painted over. JW, I still wouldn't hold my breath on finding some damn old pump."

After working through more of the compartment, JW and James again stopped to rest.

"CLUNK, CLUNK"

JW was talking about a PT boat he'd read about, "Kennedy's PT 109 didn't have much use for their sump pump."

"CLUNK"

James shook his head in surprise and said, "JW, where do you come up with this crap?"

"CLUNK-ting"

"All I said, James, was that I knew a PT boat that didn't need the pump."

"CLUNK"

"Hell no, they didn't need the pump, JW. The Japs cut the damn boat in two, now I'm thinking that might be a bit overwhelming for any pump."

"CLUNK"

"James, what is that noise?"

"CLUNK-ting"

"What noise?"

"CLUNK"

"That noise!"

"CLUNK-CLUNK-ting"

"Don't know JW, a loose screw maybe?"

"CLUNK"

"Keep in mind JW, this old boat's over 50 some years old and I'm sure it has a loose screw or two."

"CLUNK-CLUNK"

"CLUNK-ting-Clunk"

"James?"

"Yaw! JW I don't think I've ever heard a loose screw make a sound like that either."

"James, it sounds like it's coming from in there!"

James pulled on the door as hard as he could but still the door would not open. With a bewildered look of defeat on his face, he looked at JW and said, "JW, the door has been painted shut, and I can't get it open."

"CLUNK"

The two men stood silent, not saying a word. They listened to the sounds around them. They could hear the waves hitting against the sides of the hull, the creaking from the joints of the old boat, and the clunking behind a compartment door that would not open.

"James, if that's a pump in there, you know we need it to transfer the fuel from the drums into the fuel tanks. We've got to get underway in case we misunderstood the Russian's intentions or he changes his mind. I don't think we've traveled more that two hundred to three hundred miles in the last twelve to fourteen hours or so. That means we aren't out of trouble yet from being followed by that Russian. Of course, there's also the problem of floating adrift out in this ocean until we die of thirst or starvation. I don't think we survived that hell hole all these years to end up here listening to this clunking!"

"JW, what if it's just an old can of beans or spam in there? You know spam was real popular in the last big war."

"Well James, if a can of spam or beans is what's in there, then we will have something to eat, now won't we."

"Clunk clunk-ting, clunk"

"Now we've got to open that damn door!"

James' voice quivered as he replied, "I know, JW, I know but I'm so damn tired and hungry, I just don't have the strength I used to have. God help me, I just don't have the strength." At that point, a good-sized wave hit the boat and sent both men bouncing off the bulkheads.

After a minute or so, the two men once again stood before the compartment door that would not open and again came the sound from behind the door. "Clunk, Clunk-ting, Clunk"

James placed his face in his hands with his back towards the door. JW thought he heard James say, "Dear God, give me the strength to do what I must do."

A moment or two passed in silence. Then James clinched both fists. With all the strength he possessed and all he could muster, he drove his right elbow through the old wooden door. The door shattered from the blow and splinters fell in all direction, reminding JW of a time he had broke a glass windowpane.

James turned around and faced what was left of the compartment door. James reached in the compartment and felt around. His hand landed on something round and the "clunking" stopped. James turned to JW with a broad smile on his face.

JW was looking at James with his eyebrows raised. To JW, it seemed like an eternity before James spoke. JW thought James had a baffled look on his face, but it might also be a look of pain. JW could no longer stand the suspense and asked, "Well, what the hell you got?"

"JW, what I got is a right elbow that hurts like hell and is bleeding. Even my right hand is tingling a bit." Seeing the look on JW's face, James knew he wasn't asking about his tingling hand or his elbow. He realized that JW was also not in the mood for joking and quickly responded with, "Well, it feels like a rubber hose and something round with a handle on it."

"Damn it, James, does it feel like a pump of some kind?"

From the hole in the door of the compartment, James pulled out what at first looked like the green and dirty leg of a leprechaun. JW could see that it was a pump green with tarnish. The pump was at one time bright and shinny brass that was always well kept when the PT boat was new.

At first JW and James were so delighted, they grabbed each other in kind of a hug and managed to jump up and down a bit. They each gave the tarnished covered old pump a kiss. Then they looked at each other, pointed their fingers at one another, and started laughing out loud. Their lips and the tips of their noses had turned green where they had touched the tarnished pump.

After a time, the two men came back to their senses and started back to the upper deck. However, the boat started rocking even worse than before. Climbing back to the upper deck while carrying the pump took longer than they would have liked as they fought the rocking and their own fatigue. Shortly after they returned topside, the waves calmed down once again. The boat was still rocking slightly, similar to that of a rowboat crossing the wake of a powerboat.

When JW and James showed the rest of the men the pump that had been found, all the men started patting each other on the back and giving a cheer or three. Then the real job started. They had to get the pump to work. If they were lucky and could operate the pump, then they would begin pumping the fuel from the drums into the fuel tanks of the boat.

Reb had been working on the transmitter and had missed all the excitement. As he approached JW and James, he saw the green lips and noses of his friends. At first he stared in silence but then he could no longer contain his humor as he broke out in laughter. As he continued to laugh, Reb asked, "Did you two do something strange to a Leprechaun?" After a minute or two and still laughing a bit, Reb started explaining what would still be needed for the transmitter to work. His list included two pieces of fruit, a three-inch piece of zinc, and a piece of copper about the same length as the zinc. He explained that the two pieces of fruit would be used as a battery. Even then, he couldn't be sure if it would work or be on the right frequency to contact any of the ships they might pass.

James and JW both looked at Reb with blank looks of surprise. James' voice cracked with disbelief as he yelled, "What the hell are you saying? You know we need all the food and fruit we have just to feed all of us! Do you know what you're asking for?"

Reb replied, his own voice in a bit higher than normal, "Yes, I know what I'm asking for! But do you know what our chances of chasing down a rescue ship might be? Do you know what our chance might be without any form of communication?"

James blasted back, "You want to take food out of the mouth's of starving men for some damn radio that you said you are not sure will work. Then you said that it might not be on the right channel if it did work!"

Reb knew what he was asking. He also knew they had little chance to survive if he couldn't get the transmitter to work. He shook his head slowly as if to clear his thoughts and said in a much calmer voice, "I know what it sounds like, James. I know what it sounds like. And you're right. I can't be sure what channel it might be on or what channel we would need. I can't be sure it would even work at all. Truth is, I just don't know what else to do to try to get us out of this fix."

James and JW looked at each other, thought for a moment, and gave a short, quick nod to each other. James broke the silence, "Only take two pieces of fruit. Take the two biggest or the two smallest, whatever you need, but only two."

JW looked Reb in the eye for a moment and then solemnly said, "Reb, make damn sure it works."

Reb studied the faces of these men he had known all his life. He knew all their lives could depend on what he was able to do. He also knew they needed something to believe in just as much as he did. "You guys know I shined like a pewter dollar in a mud hole in Mrs. Boulware's science class. I might not remember everything. But by damn I did build a small transmitter from a kit and got an A+ for my project. I think I can build one from scratch. I just don't know if the damn thing will work or not, but you both know I will do my best! I don't plan on sitting out here on this old boat for the rest of my life."

Neither JW nor James answered right away. They thought back to those days from their childhood and both remembered how Reb had been able to fix all sorts of things that the rest of them just didn't understand. JW met James' eyes and then turned to Reb, "Reb, you work on the radio, and we will try and take care of the other things. Reb, I know you will do your best, and I think I saw something that looks like zinc in what's left of the galley in the lower deck. Take what you need. Reb, please, just do your best my friend."

Reb gave a reassuring look to both JW and James. He then turned and headed forward. James and JW turned and started helping with the refueling of the boat. After a few moments JW turned to James and asked, "Do you remember Morse code?"

"JW, I'm not sure how well I remember the code, but I'm sure I can tap something out. How about yourself?"

"Well, I'm thinking we can figure out something. But what do you think it should say?"

"I'm not sure. But I would think it should be short and to the point. Shouldn't it be something like 'small boat twelve men, no food or water west Pacific Ocean'?" James wrinkled his forehead as he tried to remember how to tap out even that small phrase in Morse code.

"Ok, James, I agree it should be short and to the point, but don't you think we should give some kind of location even if we don't know where we are exactly? I mean, do you think that 'west Pacific Ocean' is enough of a location?" JW asked.

"Not sure," James replied, "it might be better to let whoever might be listening do a triangulation on us. I guess if I knew exactly where we were, then I'd be more ready to try to tell someone our location. Since I don't think any of us really know, Pacific Ocean is about the closest I can guess."

"You're right, James. I sure can't give any better location. While the rest of the men take a turn at fueling the boat, let's talk about what we do know, and I know that's not much!"

"You're right, JW. So just what do we know? And let's not stop at that. We need to ask the rest of the men just to make sure we have all the facts to give our best position possible. And keep in mind, one degree could mean two hundred miles or more."

"I agree, James. But you and I should decide what info we need and what we don't need, as we are the ranking officers on this boat of POWs."

As JW and James started talking, the two cousins from the engine room were walking by to take their turn on the pump. James asked them, "What do you men know about where we are or where we came from?"

One of the cousins said, "Well I'm not sure but I did hear the Russian say one time he had a 600 mile drive to get home to see his mother."

The other cousin said, "I'm sure one of the Chinese guards said something like he had a drive of some three hours to get to his home town. Is that what you're asking?" James and JW both nodded their heads in a "yes" motion as they said, "Yes."

The next hour was spent with asking all but one man much the same questions. All the answers were similar. None of them really knew where they had been held captive and only had bits and pieces of overheard conversations to work with. James and JW were feeling a bit hopeless with getting any better information from the one man who was left, especially since this was the man who never spoke to any of them.

JW reasoned with James about talking to the strange POW, "Come on, James ask him. He seems to like you a lot." James looked back at JW with a strange look on his face. He considered what JW had just said.

When James finally spoke, he shared his doubts with his friend, "Ok, JW, but this man has been a POW for a very long time. I think he was held a lot longer than you and me. I don't think he's got all his marbles left."

When James moved closer to talk to him, the man put his hands up in a defensive posture, drawing his legs up as well. James tried to let him know he wasn't going to hurt him and only wanted to ask a question or two.

The man cried out in some mix of Vietnamese and Chinese and then clearly said, "James."

JW stopped James from going any further, "Let it go, James, I'm thinking he probably can't help us anyway. It isn't worth having him scared more than he already is, and I doubt he knows more than the rest do. Maybe it's better that we don't give our location just in case it's one of the enemies that hear the message. They would know for sure it's us."

James sat down on a wooden box without really listening to JW. A minute or so later the POW crawled over to James. The man put his arms around James' feet and started mumbling something in a mix of Vietnamese and Chinese. The only word this POW spoke in English was, "James". The looks on both James' and JW's faces was that of total and absolute surprise. James had thought the man had said his name before but now knew he had heard correctly.

"James, what's with you and this POW? He has been scarily attracted to you ever since he arrived a few weeks ago." As JW was speaking, the POW was still mumbling. JW thought the POW might have said, "Mom" or "Mother."

JW looked around and saw the other former POW who had arrived with the one at James's feet. JW asked the man to come over to them.

As JW watched the man coming towards him, he thought that it was likely this man was at one time a man of good size. Years spent as a POW had changed him but some trace of the man he once was still remained. His skin was darker than most of them except for Reb and JW thought the man might be Hispanic or American Indian descent. JW shook his head in dismay to realize that he had paid little attention to the newest members of their group. It had never been a healthy thing to get attached to any of the prisoners in the compound since none of them seemed to last very long. That was no longer the case as the twelve men were bond together in a new way. JW asked, "What's your name, my friend?"

The man tried to come to attention as best he could and then proudly stated, "I am Sergeant Paul A. Redbear, USMC."

James asked, "Just where are you from, Paul?"

"I'm from Eagle Butte, South Dakota."

James felt a spark of interest in this man he had practically ignored before, "I know almost nothing about the Dakotas. However, I know there are a number of reservations in that state. Do you mind if I ask the name of your tribe?"

"No, Sir, I don't mind. I am Cheyenne. Is that a problem?"

James answered, "No, that's not a problem at all." Then, with a bit of a chuckle, James said, "Even if I was related to General Custer, it would not be a problem."

Paul came back with a smile of his own and said, "I guess we did kind of fuck up Custer's day didn't we?"

Although JW had waited while the two men talked, he was more interested in where they were right now then where Paul came from. He interrupted the conversation and asked, "If you're all done with a trip down history lane, can you tell us anything about the man at James's feet?"

"Well, Sir, I'm not sure how much I can tell you. I don't know his name if that's what you're asking. He doesn't talk to anyone. In fact, you are the first person I've known him to have anything to do with in the last fifteen or eighteen years that I've known him."

JW asked, "You can hear him mumbling can't you?"

"Well yes, Sir, I can."

"Good. Do you understand anything he is saying?"

"Well, Sir, he's not speaking in sentences, and the words for the most part are a mixture of two different languages."

"Paul, can you understand any of it? You've been with him a lot of years so maybe you had the same experiences and the same chance to learn the languages he is using. There's something about James that has sparked a change in this man so I'd like to know what that is," JW finished in frustration.

Paul squatted down and listened to the mumbling for a moment. When Paul stood up he said, "He's saying something like, 'sister', 'mom' or 'mother', 'small steps', and I think something like 'turn quick, turn little' and 'paper'. But I can't be sure because he's slurring his words, and the mumbling doesn't help at all. But earlier, about an hour or so, he said, 'Die no, live me'. He said that while you both were down below."

JW patted Paul on the shoulder and thanked him for trying, "Now we know about as much as we did ten minutes ago, which was nothing."

Paul walked away and continued helping with the fueling of the boat. JW looked at James. He could see that James was deep in thought, as he looked down at the man holding his feet.

Reb walked up and asked JW if he could give him a hand with wrapping the wire around what looked like an old broomstick.

"Why sure, since James is lost in his own world right now. What do you need me to do?"

"I need you to turn this antenna as I put the wire on it."

"Ok, but why this long loop?"

"Well, this long loop, as you call it, is the part that sends out the signal you or James will be sending out. As you can see, I've removed the protective covering on this loop part. That will allow the signal to escape out into the atmosphere," Reb carefully explained.

"Reb, what kind of range might this have?"

"Well, JW, again I just don't know. However, the longer the piece of wire I use, the longer the staff, and the higher up the antenna. Hopefully, that means the farther it will transmit. Seems to me that's the way it works from what I remember of the lesson in that class a few years back."

While JW and Reb were still working on the antenna, James walked up. He stood watching, as Reb wrapped the wire around the wooden staff and then he asked, "Where did you find such a long wire?"

Reb replied, "I think it was part of the running light at one time. I had to fish it out from around the enter edges of the boat. That's what took me so long to get this far. With a little luck, it might be close to one hundred and forty feet long. And I'm thinking with that kind of length, I can control the wavelength from long to short wave. You've heard of short wave radio haven't you?"

"Uh, yes, I'm sure I have at some time in my life."

"Well, James, I also hope to control the channel, and yes, James, again I'm not sure I have it right or if it will even work," Reb answered before he could be asked.

189

"Reb, you and JW keep up the work. I'm going to check on the fueling of the boat. Oh JW, we need to think about feeding the men. I know I could use something. As high as the sun is getting, we might need to get these men below deck for a rest."

"I understand, James. Reb and I will finish with this antenna, and then we can all take a break and eat," JW answered.

About thirty minutes later, James returned and said, "JW, the refueling is coming along just fine. In the last four hours, approximately three hundred gallons of gas has been transferred into the main tanks. I've instructed the men to take a break below deck and out of the sun."

JW replied, "Very good. Reb and I are done with the antenna for now. As soon as we can make sure it is secured to the boat, we will join you and the other men below deck. Oh James, don't forget your foot hugger." James just shook his head and smiled at JW's last comment.

Twenty minutes later, Reb and JW joined the rest of the men below deck to take a badly needed break and eat a very meager portion of their strictly rationed food and water. Most of the men didn't say anything. However, the ones who were talking were reminiscing about home and what it would be like when they got there. JW spoke of his two boys and how they must be grown men by now.

As the conversation quieted down, JW turned to James and asked, "You said some three hundred gallons had been transferred to the main tanks, is that not so?"

James responded, "Yes, and I don't see why we can't restart the engines and get underway. That will smooth out the ride on this boat and make it easier to complete the fueling."

JW told the two cousins, "When you are done resting, please restart the engines." Before JW could say anything else, the two cousins stood up and headed for the engine room.

The other men got up and returned to the upper deck and continued fueling the boat. JW asked James to try and get his foot hugger to remain below deck, as he felt it would be safer for both him and James without the two of them tripping over the man. James agreed.

About fifteen minutes later, James returned topside and assisted with the fueling. After several attempts, the engines finally restarted and the old PT boat was once again under way. This made the boat ride a lot smoother as it was no longer drifting at the mercy of the ocean waves.

One of the two cousins came topside and asked if James and JW thought the engine settings were ok?

JW asked if they were checking the fuel flow gauges when setting the engine speed. The cousin answered, "Yes, as per the flow gauges, this was about the optimum setting. If the setting were moved up, more fuel would be used. If less throttle were used, the same amount of fuel would be used. So this is the fastest the engines can run without wasting any fuel."

JW's response was, "Very good but please keep a close eye on the gauges. One of you can take a nap while the other stays awake. Does that sound fair?"

The cousin replied, "Yes, Sir, I will relay this to my cousin." The man then returned to the engine room.

James walked up to JW and said, "I think the message we send should read, 'Twelve alive escaped POW camp'. Like you said, JW, don't give a location but let who ever might be listening try and do a triangulation on us."

JW nodded his head yes, but didn't say anything for a long time as he thought things over. He finally said, "James, I think you're right. I was considering putting in the word 'Vietnam' but what you said I think is better. I'm thinking if we put in the word 'Vietnam' it might have people looking in the wrong place. I'm sure we were somewhere in the area of the Chinese and Russian border. However, we might add 'west Pacific' making our message read 'twelve alive escaped POW camp west pacific'."

"JW, don't you think we should mention we're in a small boat?"

"I suppose we could, James, but don't you think whomever might be listening would think we're in a small boat or a raft of some kind anyway?"

"Well, I guess you're right about that, JW," James answered with a smile. "We can think about it for a while, besides Reb doesn't have the radio ready yet anyway. And JW, why don't you go below and get some rest? I will keep us on our present heading, as best I can. It's late and the sun is starting to go down anyway."

"Ok, James, I could use some rest but don't let the men throw the drums over the side. I'm thinking we can drain the small amount of fuel from each drum into one drum and have ten or twenty gallons more for the fuel tanks."

"Don't worry, JW, I will make sure no one throws any of the drums over the side. Go get some sleep," James encouraged JW.

JW went below deck and fell asleep almost the second his head hit the deck. Some of the men finished the fueling, some went below deck to join JW in much needed sleep, and some just lay on the upper deck.

James kept the boat on course like he said he would. He looked around at the miles and miles of open water while keeping an eye on the horizon for any ships that might appear. James also could see on the upper deck where some of the men had been using some spots for a bathroom. The smell was atrocious but where else could the men go to relieve themselves? A bucket would be nice, but there wasn't any bucket on board. Being men, they could piss over the side of the boat so at least that was easily taken care of even if the rest was still a problem. James knew he needed to keep his mind busy to keep himself awake and this problem might just do the trick.

Meanwhile, Reb returned from the lower deck with the rest of the components for the transmitter. As Reb assembled the last of the components, he and James talked. James asked Reb what he thought about the message that he and JW had come up with.

Reb responded with his own question, "Are you two sure about not giving any kind of location is the best thing?"

"Yes, Reb, if you think about it, giving degrees of latitude and longitude could throw people way off, possibly having someone looking in the wrong place. And like I told JW, just one degree can be as much as two hundred miles. Then given the fact we're in a small boat anyway, we are already going to be hard to find."

"But James, this transmitter may not transmit very far, so any chances of triangulation would mean whomever might be listening would have to be right on top of us!"

"Reb, I think JW will try and transmit at night. I'm not sure why, but signals travel better at night. I guess it's because there's less interference from the sun."

"Well, James, I know you and JW have a lot of naval training, and I'm sure the two of you are doing the best you can with what you have to work with. I just wish I could build you a better transmitter so you had one that receives as well as transmits. But I'm afraid all the salt air has eaten up the old radio in this boat. I can't even get any power up here because of all the salt corrosion. I'm afraid I might start a fire, and I'm sure we don't need that," Reb explained as he let some of his frustrations show in his voice and on his face. He knew he was doing the best he could and just hoped that would be enough.

Reb was ready to turn the transmitter over to his friends. He looked back at James and said, "This transmitter is ready for use. And so you know, you take this small wire and touch it to this copper strip stuck in this smaller fruit. The power will travel from the larger piece of fruit to the smaller. Watch this. As I touch this small wire to this piece of copper, we get a spark. Now when it sparks like that, the loop up there at the top of this pole sends out a signal in the form of a dot or a dash. Morse code, if you will."

"Ok, Reb, I think I understand that part, but where does the power come from?"

"The acid in the fruit is dissolving the copper strip and the zinc strip. And as these two pieces of metal dissolve, it creates electrical power."

"Very good, Reb, but how long will it last?"

"It will last until the copper or zinc dissolve or the fruit dries out. James, I expect the fruit will dry out long before the metal dissolves," Reb explained.

"Reb, would you take over the controls for a bit? I need to relieve myself and wake JW. He's been asleep for about four hours now and I'm damn tired myself."

"Sure I will do that. Hey, how do I know if we're on course?"

"Well, Reb, as per the Russian, we need to keep the moon over our right shoulder."

"And you guys believe him, James?"

"Reb, it's like this. We don't know exactly where we were when we got in this boat but we had some ideas. If we were right about that location, then the Russian telling us to keep the moon over our right shoulder should put us on a straight course for the Hawaiian Islands. Right now, I'd sure like to think that is where we are heading. Either way, that's about all we have going for us right now," James answered.

"Ok, James, you do what you need to do. I will keep the moon over my right shoulder until I'm relieved by JW and then I'll join you below deck."

About thirty minutes later JW made his way to the controls. He asked Reb to hold on for a minute or two before he went below to get some sleep. JW explained he had found a led pencil and wanted to write out the message he would be sending. As JW wrote out the message on the shelf of the control panel, James arrived.

"JW, I thought you could use some help in making sure all the dots and dashes are correct," James told him.

"Good thinking. James, take a look at this. 'Twelve alive escape POW camp small boat west pacific west of Hawaii'."

"Take out 'west Pacific' since I'm thinking most people know Hawaii is in the Pacific Ocean. The letter 'I' only has two dots, the letter 'S' has three, and the letter 'A' is dot dash, not dash dot."

"Are you sure, James?"

James said, "I'm quite sure JW."

"Ok, James, how about this, 'twelve alive escape POW camp small boat west of Hawaii'?"

"That's good, JW. What do you think, Reb?"

"What I think is I don't know Morse code so I have no idea what you two are doing. Besides, isn't there two 'E's' in Hawaii instead of two 'I's?"

"No, Reb, there's two 'I's in Hawaii."

"Well I never said I could spell anyway."

James and JW spoke at the same time and said the same thing to Reb, " Hell, Reb you never were able to spell!" The three men laughed together for a minute. It felt good to be able to laugh again. As they thought about how long it had been since it had been safe to laugh out loud, their faces grew somber again. They were still a long way from home.

Reb turned and walked away. He went below deck to get some badly needed sleep, as James and JW prepared to send the first message.

"Well, JW, I think this is the best we can do. Are we ready to transmit?"

"Yes, James I believe we are."

JW started tapping out the message in Morse code:

He said quietly as he tapped, "Twelve alive escape POW camp small boat west of Hawaii." When he was finished, he turned to his old friend, "James, I wish we could hear some kind of response, at least we would know someone could hear us."

"JW, we just have to do the best we can and hope. I'm going below and get some sleep."

"Ok, James, I'm going to transmit about every five to ten minutes for the first hour or two. Then change to every 15 or so minutes. What do you think?"

"Sounds good to me, JW, sounds good to me."

JW sent the message approximately every five to ten minutes during the first hour as planned and then changed to approximately every fifteen to twenty minutes. JW was thinking if someone thought the message was some kind of child's prank, then they would change their minds if the same messaged were being transmitted so frequently. He also figured the only chance for the signal to reach someone would be if they were passing close to a ship. The more frequently the messages were sent, the more likely someone would receive one of them.

What James, JW, and even Reb didn't know was just how well the transmitter was working. Although the signal was weak and not on the right channel, Reb had come so close to the emergency channel that a number of ham radios could be adjusted to pick up the off channel signal with almost no problems other than the signal being weak. There were actually quite a few radios picking up the signals, as JW continued through the night. There were Boy-Scouts in Montana, a ham radio in New Zealand, another in Australia, some radios in Japan, and a group of explorers at the South Pole who were all getting parts of the signal. Ham radios up and down the western coast of California and South America were getting more of the signal. On two different transmissions JW added, "Can transmit only can't receive." That added part and the repeating of the message is what caught the ears of a number of ham radio operators.

After four or five hours of transmitting the same message over and over and keeping an eye on the horizon for possible rescue ships, JW was sure that anyone who might have heard the message would not think some kid was playing a joke on everyone with his or her new radio set. Only a desperate man would continue for so many hours. With no way to receive a transmission back to let him know for sure, JW could only pray that someone was acting now to find them. Between sending messages and checking the horizon, JW pondered the thought of how long before someone came looking and worse yet, he wondered how long before someone found them.

JW knew that by going out to sea, their chances of survival were greatly diminished by the fact that food and water was limited. They had no way of catching any fish, and there was no wild game to trap. Fresh water enough to last them very long was also a problem. JW didn't want to think about what would happen to them when they ran out. None of them had started the journey well fed or very healthy. He knew it wouldn't take much to be the end for at least some of them. He wondered how long they could stay twelve alive.

If they had stayed on land, they might have been able to catch a field mouse or a rat. With a little luck they might have found a rabbit or two. Most likely water would not have been problem either. However, had they stayed on land, the Russian would have been forced to track them down. The Russian already had orders to destroy them along with the camp. Though none of them had even considered it at the time, JW realized that all of them probably would already be dead if they had tried to make a run in the truck.

JW thought the time must be around 12:30 to 1:00am. He was getting tired but felt he needed to transmit the message two or three more times before waking James. JW continued transmitting and checking the horizon.

It was just after sunrise when James came topside and was sure he would find JW asleep. James was shocked to see JW was still transmitting. It was obvious his friend was dead on his feet as he mechanically tapped out the message. James turned as he heard Reb come up beside him and asked Reb to help him get JW below deck. James and Reb tried talking to JW, but JW kept on trying to transmit even as the two men carried him below deck and gently placed him on an old cot.

As James started back up the ladder, he thought he heard someone say, "James, me Larry." He shook his head as if he had imagined it and didn't stop. He needed to get topside so he could align the boat to what was left of the moon. James knew if he could align with the moon before it disappeared, he could determine the angle of the sun and that would keep them on course or close to it.

When Reb came topside again, he told James, "I checked with the engine room. The flow gauges show we're doing just fine and the engines seem to be running ok. However, the two cousins think that with our present rate of fuel consumption, we will be out of fuel some time after sundown today. So what do you want to do?"

"Reb, JW is asleep so I can't leave the helm at this time and its imperative we stay on course as long as possible. I need you to do whatever you can to squeeze all the mileage out of the fuel we have left. And Reb, JW and I never thought we could make it to the Hawaiian Islands with the fuel we had onboard. We did think we could make it to the shipping lanes and hopefully be rescued by a ship passing. We just need to make it that far. Since none of us really know how far that is, I guess we just have to keep going as long as we can." As Reb turned to walk away, James called to him one more time, "Reb, is it possible to run on one engine?"

Reb paused for a moment and then answered, "I don't know, James. I'm not sure if the transmission is geared that way. I will see what I can do."

After a short time the RPMs of the engines rose up. The boat slowed way down and it sounded like someone trying to put a transmission in reverse while it was running forward. Then the RPMs dropped and the boat started moving forward again. After about the third or fourth time of this happening and the boat was moving forward again, Reb came topside.

"James, I don't think this old girl will run on one engine. Now she may have at one time but she's not going to do it this time. I'm going back down there. The two cousins and I will see if we can trim the engines a bit more. Oh, by the way James, are you sure you don't know that guy down there? He keeps calling your name and he's getting louder and louder."

"Reb, I don't know him as far as I can recall, I know when I was coming topside earlier he said 'Larry; but that doesn't ring any bells with me. It could be I met him on a ship or in some port of call. I just don't know, Reb, I just don't know."

Reb returned to the engine room. And after about two hours, Reb and one of the other men from the engine room came topside to take a break and get some fresh air. James called to Reb, as Reb walked up, "What's going on, Reb?"

"We're taking a break, James. The air down there is getting a bit thick with some of the guys shitting all over down there. And that head-case, well he's crawling and rolling around in it."

"Reb, the next time you go below, ask everyone but JW to come topside. I guess I will have a talk with them. Reb, JW's not laying in any of it is he?"

"No, JW's in a safe place."

"That's good, Reb."

Reb and the other man returned to the lower deck, and all the other men came topside. As all the men gathered around James, he did a head count. Satisfied that he had everyone with him who needed to be there, he took a deep breath and spoke in the voice of a commander, "Ok, listen up Men. It seems someone is taking a shit in the lower deck and that has got to stop. If you need to relieve yourself, then you need to get your ass topside and try to do it as far back towards the stern as possible. The spray we get back there will wash some of it away. The lower deck is for sleeping, and it's the only place we have to get out of the sun. Does anyone not understand what I just said?" James looked around. "Ok then, carry on."

An hour later Reb came topside. "James, we've done all we can with the engines. The flow gauges indicate a very slight drop in the flow, and we are running just about the same speed. And James, we're going to run out of fuel sometime around or just after sundown like the cousins thought."

"Thanks, Reb, after you take a rest, get some of the men and start dumping the small amount of fuel from each drum into one drum and then we can pump that fuel into the main tanks. Be sure and put the lids back on the drums, and then put the empty drums back towards the stern. I know what you're going to ask, and I don't know the answer. It's something JW wanted done."

About an hour and a half later, Reb and two other men completed the fuel exchange and Reb reported to James. "James, we are completed with the fueling. I think we got about forty five gallons from all the drums, and that might buy us about thirty or so more minutes of running time. Now, James, explain to me about the course and how to stay on it, because you look to me like someone who needs a break out of this sun."

After James explained how to stay on course and Reb seemed comfortable with it, James headed for the lower deck. He stopped and turned back to Reb, "I might go to sleep, Reb. I don't know that I can stay awake once I put my head down."

Reb looked at James with a smile on his face and with his hand he motioned for James to go on as he said, "We could all use some sleep, and I will be ok up here for now."

James found a relatively clean place to lie down. As he lay there, his thoughts were of home and how nice it would be to be on a clean bed. With the throbbing of the engines, James went to sleep. When James woke, he found he couldn't see as he was in total darkness. James realized that meant the sun was down, and Reb should have wakened him up long before now. He realized another thing--the boat was quiet. There were no vibrations or throbbing from the engines, and the boat was rocking like it did two days ago. James rushed as fast as he could to the upper deck only to find JW at the helm, tapping out the message "twelve alive escapes POW camp small boat west of Hawaii".

"JW, where's Reb? He was supposed to wake me."

"He's on the foredeck asleep. James, I told him to let you sleep. You were sawing logs pretty good when I woke up, so I thought you should sleep."

"Well thank you, JW, I think that's about the best sleep I've had in a long time. It might have been even better if I wasn't so hungry and thirsty!"

"I've given the other men their rationing of food, and your share is right here. I hope you like beans and fried potatoes, I'm afraid the biscuits are cold, and we only had margarine not butter. I hope that is that ok with you."

"Well JW, I hope we have salt and pepper and a cold glass of milk to wash it all down!"

JW and James started laughing. The laugh came all the way from their shrunken bellies, until the two men fell to their knees and then down to the deck. These two men laughed until they both cried as they rolled on the deck.

"James, you best eat, and I want you to know I'm sorry for talking you and the other men into coming out here. I guess, I dreamed too high and expected too much from chance. But I want you to know, when you told me what you heard the Russian and the Vietnamese guards talking about destroying the camp and us as well, I grabbed the first thing that came along. And that just happened to be this boat. James, you know as well as I do what our chances of surviving are without food or water. And James, just so you know, this is the last of the food and water."

"JW, please don't talk like that. Hell we might all be dead by now if I hadn't learned about this old boat. This old boat is our lifeboat, and lifeboats save lives and the last time I checked, we were all still alive. And besides JW, God is watching over us. That's why we've made it this far. And we are going to make it home."

"James, did you not hear me when I said this was the last of the food and water?"

"Yes, I heard you JW! Have you forgotten all you and I learned in church?"

"No, James, I guess I haven't. I guess I just lost myself for a while. I'm sorry James."

After a few minutes that JW took to calm down, he said, "James, take one of the lids off of the drums. I think you will find the drums will have a hissing sound to them. The lids were put on in the heat of the day and now that it is kind of cool, the pressure in the drums will change. We need them to have cooler air in them."

"Ok, JW, but what do you have in mind for the drums?"

"Well James, I'm thinking we can put one drum over the side. One every two hours or so. I'm hoping this will work like a trail of breadcrumbs."

"Not a bad idea, JW, but what's with the air inside them? I don't understand that at all."

"Let me see if I can explain it the way I see it in my mind. If you take the lids off, the air from the daytime will have condensed, lowering the pressure inside. This will allow the air pressure to equalize to the cooler temperatures of the evening like now. By putting the lids back on and tithing them down, we will trap the cooler air inside. Then when we put one over the side, the water temperature will not have as much affect on the air pressure inside. Then when the sun is shining on the drum while it's in the water, the sun will heat up the air inside causing the drum to float higher in the water and making the drum more visible to anyone who might be looking for us."

"Sounds good to me, JW. When do you want to put the first drum over the side?"

"Let's put the first one over the side when you get them all done."

"Not a problem, JW, not a problem."

A short time passed and then James walked back to JW, "I've completed taking the lids off. Should I put the lids on as we put them over the side or not?"

"No, James, go ahead and put the lids back on now and make sure you get them tight. Then I will come help put the first one over the side."

"I got you, JW," James replied and then hurried back to the drums. A few minutes later he said, "JW, I've got them all back on and tight. You want to come and give a hand?"

"On my way, James, I just need to finish this transmission."

"James, I'm thinking after we put one over the side, I want to make sure it's not going to follow us. We need it to guide the way, not sit on our tail. We should know by morning. When we complete this one, we can sit down and relax for a bit."

James replied with, "Whatever you say, JW." After they got the drum over the side, he spoke again, "JW, at least we have a bright moon out tonight. The drum is about twenty feet away and I can still see it."

JW had returned to transmitting the message when James asked, "JW, do you think we should say in the message that we're releasing fifty-five gallon drums?"

"Yes I do, James. And that's what I'm doing now."

Two days came and went with no sightings of any kind of possible rescue. The men were totally out of food and water. The only sign of anything onboard to eat was the two pieces of fruit being used as a battery for the transmitter. Even though the fruit was getting dried out, it would be better than nothing to a starving man. This meant that JW or James would have to remain awake and alert to ensure that no one ate the fruit, as this was the only form of communication or link they had to the world.

By the third day of no food and water, the men lay on the deck or below without moving or talking. They were too weak to even get up to relieve themselves and lay in their own feces as they waited to die. These brave men who had answered the call of America to fight for freedom, to fight for free speech, to fight for the right to assemble peacefully, to fight for the right to protest, to fight for freedom of the press, and maybe the most important of all to fight for the freedom of religion were worn down and had no strength left to fight for their own lives. Those who had strength left to think, felt the weight of knowing they would not make it to their home shores once again.

What none of them could know was that a shortwave radio (Ham) operator located in a fishing village in New

Zealand had been receiving their transmissions from day one. Knowing he could not transmit back to the sender, he began contacting anyone he thought might be able to help. There were others who had received the transmissions but this man spoke up the loudest and kept speaking up. He called Pearl Harbor Naval command more than once a day. After the first day, he was placed on hold time and time again. This old man could see he was trying to go through the wrong door. He had a feeling that time was running out for the "twelve alive" he had heard about in the transmissions.

As he sat talking to his wife of sixty years, the two of them came up with the idea of asking all the fishing boats in the target area to keep a close look out. He would put a call in to a California to senator he knew from his past. Although the man hadn't talk to the senator in ten years, he would ask this man for help.

The old man turned his radio on, changed the direction of the antennas to the target area, and called out to any boats and ships in that general area that could hear him, "Look for a small boat or raft with twelve men alive and leaving fuel drums like bread crumbs, save these men, one of them could be my son."

While he was on the radio, his wife was on the phone. She called California, Senator Mendoza's office.

Senator Mendoza's secretary took the call. She was trying to put the woman off but after a bit of explaining, the secretary buzzed the senator and asked, "Do you want to take a call from Mr. and Mrs. Sylvan of New Zealand?"

"You said Sylvan of New Zealand?" the Senator asked.

"Yes, Sir."

"Why hell, yes, I'll talk to them, put it through right away!" The Senator shouted. When he heard the click of the transfer, he said, "This is Senator Mendoza, to whom am I speaking?"

"Senator, this is Betty Sylvan, Carl needs to talk to you, please just one moment. Carl, Mr. Mendoza is on the phone, and you know he's a busy man."

"Mr. Mendoza, this is Carl. How are you doing? Just so you know, this is not a social call. I need your help. Are you there?"

"Yes, yes, I'm here. What can I do for the man who saved my brown ass twice in the same week?"

"Well Sir, it's like this."

As Carl explained the radio transmissions, the Senator listened very intently. When Carl was completed, the Senator spoke, "Carl, you know I'm a small senator, and I'm busier than a cat covering shit on a hot tin roof. But for what you've done for me in the past and I know your one and only son disappeared in Vietnam, Carl, I will make a call. I have a friend in Washington and I'm sure she knows someone who can help."

"Senator, I will keep sending out messages to the boats in my target area, getting them to look for that boat."

"Very good, Carl. I should be getting back to you in twenty-four to forty-eight hours. And Carl, I'm giving you a special number to call me back on. Don't give it out to anyone, please."

"I thank you, Senator, and I will be in touch soon I hope. Unless I have something very important, I will not use this number you just gave me so until later my friend."

"Yes, until later my friend."

The old man went back to his radio just in time to catch another transmission, "Out of water, food and now out of fuel. Adrift at sea, twelve alive small boat west of Hawaii." Carl called out to his wife to call the special number they were just given. Senator Mendoza needed the new message right away. She made the call and set the wheels in motion.

Two more days passed for the twelve men on the boat. The only two men left moving, and not much moving at that, were JW and James. By this time, even James and JW were at the ends of their strength. These two men had once been strong and righteous. They would never take anything that did not belong to them. They would never take anything that was needed for the survival of others. These two men had been forced to eat food that had human feces mixed in and water that someone had pissed in. Along with the other men, they had been beaten and forced to work long, hard hours. They knew they had very little time left and were openly considering eating the last two pieces of fruit that were all but dried out. The spark created by the fruit for transmitting was intermittent at best. It took both James and JW with their combined strength to squeeze the fruit enough to create the power to make a small spark, that by now wasn't lasting long enough to complete one transmission at a time.

James lay down on the deck in a stream of human feces and urine that was coming from the men lying on the fore deck. At this point it no longer mattered, as James just didn't have the strength to move or even relieve himself other than in the rags he wore for cloths. JW was in the same condition.

James dreamed of going to Heaven again and seeing his father and his grandmother. He pleaded with them to let him stay, that he had done all he could to save the others, but he was starved to death and there was nothing more he could do.

James' grandmother took him by the ear like she had done in times past. She turned him around and started him walking back to the boat as she explained that his work was not yet completed. She told him that many people were depending on him. When his work was completed, then and only then could he join them in Heaven.

James called to his father and asked him to save him. He explained again that he had starved to death. His father told him he needed to return. He told James that his grandmother was right. He then reminded James that he was not to back talk his elders.

When James awoke, he thought he could see a very large ship of some kind. In his mind the ship was very close, but he was unable to call out or signal in any way. James watched the ship disappear off in the distance, and he felt the PT boat rock from the wake of this large ship.

James tried to think of something he could do. He had tried to leave all this behind and had failed. Both his father and his grandmother had told him that he wasn't done on this earth. In his weakened condition, the only thing that came to mind that he could still do was to pray to his God. God Almighty.

James looked around for the best place to pray. He struggled to his feet and staggered towards the stern of the boat. James stood on the stern of the old P.T. boat with all the strength he could muster just to continue to stand. The boat was rocking with the motion of the

Pacific Ocean in a continuation of endless water and waves.

James looked towards Heaven, his arms out stretched, his palms turned up and fingers spread apart. From his sun and wind burnt face with sunken eyes came tears as he prayed to God.

"Dearest almighty God,

Before you stands an imperfect man. O Lord, I beseech thee to be merciful. Oh God, hear the cries of our hearts' needs. Lord, if it be your will, I ask of thee these things.

I ask thee for rain that thou would quench our thirst. I also desire for a fish, that thou would meet our hunger. I lastly desire that thou would guide the men and women who might be looking for us. Oh Lord, help them to help us.

Oh God, we trust you to rescue us. And Lord if your wish is for us not to be rescued, please Oh God, I beg of you to be swift and merciful by sending your angel of death and ending our suffering.

My dearest and most beloved God, in payment for all I've ask of thee, God, all I have to offer you is me.

Amen"

James staggered back to the helm area where he could hear his friend, JW, talking in his sleep. He had listened to this sleep-talk so many times before, but this time he thought he could hear the voice of Karen. James heard JW ask, "Who is this young lady I see you with? Have you forgotten me? Have you remarried and this a child by someone else?"

James thought he heard Karen answer, "Oh no, my love, I've never forgotten you and I never will. The boys are grown and the young lady you see with me is . . ."

At that point, JW jumped to his feet. JW started screaming as loud as he could, "Karen, who is this young woman? Why have you forsaken me? I'm here! I'm not dead! Oh God help me, God! For God's sake help me!"

James had never seen his friend like this. JW stood with his fists clinched. JW was crying but no tears came out, as he looked toward Heaven and screamed for God's help.

JW reached down suddenly and grabbed James by the arm as he said, "James, I need your help to squeeze this fruit so I can send a message." Together the two men squeezed as hard as they could but again the signal was intermittent at best because of the fruit being so dried out.

JW said, "James, I think that might be the last transmission we can make. God help us all!"

James lay back on the deck. He had used his last ounce of strength to help his friend and no longer had the strength to do anything more. He mumbled about seeing a large ship. Just as his eyes closed, James saw the best friend he had ever had clasped to the deck in a heap of skinny arms and legs.

The Aircraft carrier

The ship that James thought he had seen was in fact an aircraft carrier and this aircraft carrier had seen them as well. However, this old PT boat looked like a dead whale on the radarscope. The sighting was reported to the shift commander. The commander asked if they were absolutely sure that the sighting on the radarscope was that of a dead whale.

About an hour later, a young Lieutenant returned to Lieutenant Commander Walker and reported, "Sir, we've rechecked the radar readings against any known small ship and boat readings. Sir, per the computer, it was a dead whale with very small chance of it being a boat."

"Very good, Lieutenant, please keep a sharp eye out and report any and all sightings. All the information we have is telling me we should be close if not on top of them. And Lieutenant, I have a strong feeling that these men haven't much if any time left."

"Commander, there has been another messaged received. I'm told it was the strongest one yet."

"Is this message the same as the rest?"

"Yes, Sir, but this one is much more intermittent. Whatever they are using to transmit is breaking up."

"Copy that, Lieutenant, please carry on."

"Yes, Sir."

Approximately two hours after sunrise, the flight deck of the carrier was buzzing with the activity of preparing six rescue helicopters for flight. Each helicopter was being fueled and was loaded with special provisions in case it might be the one to locate the survivors. The provisions in part would consist of water and a very bland tasting mush-like food. This special food was fortified with vitamins and proteins, just what a human body would need after being starved for a long time. Also included were some sugar pills, which could be placed under the tongue. This would give the person some instant energy and was included in case the survivor could not get the mush down or keep it down. The sugar pills could also be dissolved in water the survivors could then drink.

Approximately three hours after sunrise, the pilots and flight crew received their briefing on what to look for, which included fifty-five gallon drums and some kind of small boat. The best description they had of the boat was that it might be an old WW2 P.T. boat but for the most part, the type of small boat was unclear at best.

A commercial vessel had reported seeing two drums in the area two days ago. Given the currents in this area of the ocean, the survivors should be within a five hundred mile range. The six rescue flights would be able to cover two thousand miles.

A medical officer then addressed the pilots and flight crews as to what to do if the survivors were found. He then asked if there were any questions. There were none.

Less than an hour later, all six-rescue flights were off the deck, doing what they were well trained to do, which was search and rescue. Their call signs would be Strawberry one through six.

Lt. Commander Walker returned to the radar and communications center. He asked for the printout of the sighting from the night before. This was the one described as a dead whale.

The technician now at the radar and communications center pulled the records for the time and location in question. He then ran a profile of the sighting and explained that, per the computer, the density of the object in question was consistent with that of a dead whale. In addition, the profile had seemed to be that of a dead whale. The technician then stated, "However, Sir, the infra red profile wasn't running on the screen."

Lt. Commander Walker asked, "Just what does that mean?"

"Well, Sir. That means it wasn't turned on to this screen, and it should have been. Now let me see if I can still bring it up? Ok, here we go, Sir. Sir, I've only seen a few profiles of whales with infra red, and this doesn't look like anything I recall."

"What are you saying?"

"Well, Sir, the center should look red and the outer edges would be paler yellowish-green."

"Ok, but again what does this mean?"

"This has a black center and no yellowish-green anywhere. And then there are three, maybe four red splotches. And one splotch right there, this one comes and goes like its maybe under water or under a water line. I can't be sure, as the system wasn't turned on like it should have been."

"Ensign, give me your best guess."

"Sir, my best guess is, I don't know, I just don't know, Sir! But if I were you, I believe I would have it checked out if for no other reason than to eliminate it as a possible target. That is, if I were you, Sir."

As the Lt. Commander turned to walk away, he told the ensign, "I think that's the best advice I have gotten all day, thanks."

The Lt. Commander returned to the air boss of the carrier. He requested another helicopter with a flight crew. The air boss asked, "Just what do you need another flight with crew for?"

Lt. Commander Walker explained the radar setting to the air boss. The air boss said, "I'm not sure but I think the only thing I have ready for flight at this time is a helicopter that would be at its maximum range by the time you would reach that target point. Commander, you would only have time to take a quick look and then return to base. Now what do you want to do?"

"Is it an amphibious aircraft?"

"Commander, this is your lucky day, because it is amphibious. I will have it fueled and ready for flight in twenty minutes. Will that work for you?"

"Hell yes! I'll get the medical officer and supplies."

Lt. Commander Walker returned to the flight deck a short time later with the medical officer and supplies. After placing the supplies on board and ensuring all was secure, the helicopter lifted off the deck of the carrier and headed northwest.

While in flight, Lt. Commander Walker discussed the target coordinates with the pilot. The pilot explained there was not enough fuel to remain on target for more than five or so minutes.

Lt. Commander Walker looked at the pilot and crew members for a moment before speaking. He then said, "The best guess of the condition of the survivors is that this might be the last chance for these men to make it if they are not recovered today."

Very little talking went on after that until the helicopter reached its target coordinates. The men kept a sharp eye out for anything in the water.

Back on the PT boat, JW awakened, only to discover he was all but blind. Although he had slept, he still felt very tired. He rubbed his dry and sunken eyes trying to clear his vision. As he looked down at the deck, he could see a blurry figure of a man lying at his feet. He knew it was his life long friend, James West.

JW was able to get up on his feet. The thought of all the men dying around him started to flood his mind. He knew they were dying because he had convinced them all to follow him out to the open sea on this ship of death. There were miles and miles of water around them but not a drop to drink. Within this water was an abundance of fish but no way to catch them. It was too late to do anything for his friend and the men who lay motionless around him.

Then there was a spark of hope, as he heard a sound somewhere off the stern of the boat. It was not close yet but it was moving closer. As JW listened, he knew it was the sound of a helicopter.

JW tried to wake his friend, but the seemingly lifeless body of James West did not respond. He stopped trying for a minute as he thought the sound of the helicopter was fading into the distance. JW started screaming as loud as he possibly could, "O no, no, my God please no. God tell me what to do, O God please help me!"

Then the idea came to him. If he could rehydrate the two pieces of fruit, maybe he could get one more message out. But rehydrate the fruit with what? JW couldn't even spit. The boat rocked from a wave and a small spray of water came across the gunwales and landed on JW.

JW staggered and stumbled to the side of the boat. Looking over the side, he could see the water was about three to four feet below the gunwales. A wave ever so often came to within about a foot below the tops of the gunwales.

JW stumbled back to the helm, grabbed the two pieces of fruit, and returned to the side of the boat. He got down on his knees and held one piece of fruit in his hand over the side of the boat. JW waited for a wave to come up high enough to wet the fruit. When the fruit had been soaked with waves, JW returned to the helm as quickly as he could. He reconnected the fruit to the transmitter. Knowing he was facing the stern of the boat and the sound of the helicopter moved from left to right, JW sent this message, "Search aircraft turn starboard."

JW attempted to send the message a second time but collapsed to the deck into a state of unconsciousness.

The aircraft carrier received the one time message, but this is how it read, " earch air aft urn arboard."

Two captains and two lieutenants were looking at the message. One of the captains said, "What the hell is this?"

The young ensign overheard the officers talking. He knew something about what was going on and asked if he could take a look at the message.

One captain looked at the other three officers and said, "Why not, we sure as the hell don't understand it." And the message was handed to the ensign.

After a moment or two, the ensign jumped to his feet saying, "O my God, O my God! Captain, it reads, 'search aircraft turn starboard'!"

The four officers yelled at the same time, "Send out this message now! All search aircraft are to focus on this area. Send it!"

The technician quickly sent out the message, "All search aircraft, turn ninety degrees starboard. Execute, Execute. Repeating all search aircraft turn ninety degrees starboard Execute, Execute"

"Captain, we're getting messages from Strawberry 1 through 6 reporting low fuel. What do you want me to tell them?"

"Tell them we don't know whom, but someone is on top of the survivors. They need to keep a sharp eye out. Keep them out about other fifteen or so minutes. If no boat is reported, tell them to mark their location and heading and then return for refueling. They will be going back out immediately. We're trying to rescue some men, but we don't need to add to the list of men to be rescued. And I'm not interested in buying any aircraft today."

Lt. Commander Walker's flight (Strawberry-7) on board communications was silent except for the pilot informing Lt. Commander Walker of the order to turn ninety degrees starboard and low fuel. Lt. Commander Walker was also informed that the radar contact that had appeared to be a dead whale was in that same area.

Lt. Commander Walker said, "That's our target, head for it. What kind of range to target?"

"Sir, just over thirty-five miles and closing."

"Very good, advise the carrier."

"Copy that, Sir."

A few minutes later, the pilot called to the commander, "The reading is changing. I'm starting to read some metal content." After another few minutes, the pilot informed the commander, "Sir, it's not a dead whale. It's a boat! We're thirty miles to target and closing."

"Copy that. Inform the carrier."

Back on board the carrier, the order was given for all search aircraft except Strawberry Seven to return and change to standard frequency. Strawberry Seven would remain the only aircraft using the emergency channel.

Back on Strawberry Seven, the pilot called out five miles to target, three miles, and one mile. Then the helicopter started to slow. The helicopter performed a three hundred sixty degree spin, while announcing the target was directly below.

Directly over the top of the old boat, the crew counted nine bodies. Even with the strong wind caused by the blade of the helicopter (prop wash), none of the survivors moved. This raised grave concerns with the rescue crew.

Lt. Commander Walker instructed the pilot to inform the carrier, "Believe we've located the POWs and boat in question, no sign of movement at this time."

"Copy that, Sir, sending video as well."

As the crew prepared to kick the supplies out the open door, the pilot dropped a line with a grappling hook to the deck of the old boat. Lt. Commander Walker had a surprised look on his face. Before he could ask what was going on, the helicopter moved over about seventy feet and gently set down in the water.

The pilot told Lt. Commander Walker, "Sir, we don't have the fuel for a safe return to the carrier, and it looks like these men need our help. I don't know that any of them would be able to retrieve the supplies and make use of them without us."

Lt. Commander Walker looked the pilot straight in the eye for a moment and then smiled as he shook the pilot's hand.

The crew loaded the supplies into the raft and headed for the old boat. Lt. Commander Walker was the first to board the old PT boat and found the smell to be almost overwhelming. Some of the other rescuers started vomiting over the side of their raft.

Twenty to thirty minutes later, the medical officer informed Lt. Commander Walker that all twelve survivors were indeed alive, "But so you know, Sir, there are some of these men who might not make it. Even if we had them on the carrier right now, their chances of survival would improve only slightly. All the men are in bad shape but four of them are worse off than the others."

Lt. Commander Walker communicated all the information to the carrier that was about two hundred fifty miles away. Lt. Commander Walker was informed by the carrier, "As soon as the other search aircrafts are recovered, the carrier will be heading their way at top speed. However, it will be approximately five and a half to six hours before the carrier will reach them."

With help from the medical officer, Lt. Commander Walker worked on JW and tried to get some water in him. It was slow going as JW was able to swallow small amounts of water and then gradually small spoons of the mush. After an hour or so, JW consumed eight ounces of water mixed with sugar and six spoons of food. The medical officer and Lt. Commander Walker kept telling JW to just sip the water.

JW asked about his friend, James.

Lt. Commander Walker pointed to the man near them on the deck and said, "If that is James, he is still alive. Sir, in fact, all twelve of you are still alive," Lt. Commander Walker added. Now that JW had started talking, Lt. Commander Walker wanted to keep him talking, "Sir I'm Lt. Commander Walker of the United States Navy. Can you tell me your name, Sir?"

Before JW could answer, his eyes rolled back in his head and he passed out once again.

Lt. Commander Walker asked the medical officer, "Well, what can you tell me about the condition of the survivors?"

"Well, Sir, I'm most surprised that these men are still alive. I've never seen anyone so depleted and emaciated in my life. The last time I heard of anyone being this bad was the Holocaust survivors of WW2. Hell, Commander, we don't even train for this kind of shit any more. As far as their chances for full recovery, that's something I just don't know and only time will tell. However, these two and the one and only black guy up front seem to be doing the best out of the twelve. Commander, what we need to do is to get these men on the carrier as soon as possible. In sickbay we could do so much more for them than we can here. It would be even better yet if we could get them intensive care in a hospital. There are also three men below deck that I'm not so sure will live to see the light of day come tomorrow."

Lt. Commander Walker contacted the carrier and asked for the ETA. He also asked if there was any chance of sending three or four helicopters to transport the survivors to the carrier. If that was not a possibility, then they needed to send at least one helicopter with additional medical staff, supplies, and equipment.

The response from the carrier was, "ETA approximately three hours making all possible speed, four helicopters being fueled and will launch in thirty minutes. Will advise as soon as the last helicopter lifts off the deck."

Lt. Commander Walker advised the medical officer and the other men, "The helicopters should be here in approximately one and a half hours."

The next hour and forty-five minutes seemed like an eternity until some one called out, "Incoming helicopters!"

All the survivors had been moved to the upper deck awaiting pickup. Lt. Commander Walker worked as hard as anyone helping load the survivors on the helicopters. James and JW were the last two survivors to be loaded aboard the helicopters. Lt. Commander Walker reached down, picked JW up from the deck, and placed him aboard the helicopter. Lt. Commander Walker then climbed aboard next to JW and closed the door.

CHAPTER TEN

THE RESCUE

After being rescued, plucked from the sea, and safely on board the helicopter in route back to the carrier Kitty Hawk, JW kept asking about the condition of the other men. He also wanted to know if they could save the old PT boat, as it had saved the lives of twelve men.

A young lieutenant commander assured JW that he and the other eleven men were doing fine and the best of care would be given to all of them. Unfortunately, he didn't know if anything could be done about the boat, but he would check with shipboard command.

Approximately thirty-five minutes later, the helicopter touched down on the air flight deck of the Kitty Hawk. A large number of various personnel had gathered to try to get a glimpse of these twelve survivors. The crowd didn't need anyone asking them to stay back, as the sheer smell kept them back. Even with the wind blowing away from the crowd, the smell permeated the air.

The on lookers could see the men were mere skeletons with badly tattered clothing, long stringy hair, long beards, and open sores. They were covered with what looked and smelled like excrement all over their bodies and even in their hair.

All twelve survivors were rushed to the main sickbay on "D" deck. As soon as the survivors entered the corridors of the ship, the ventilation system started carrying the strong aroma throughout the rest of the ship. Men and woman in other parts of the ship started choking and gagging from the smell. Some young sailor made the remark, "Damn! Did someone shit in the vent system again?"

After the survivors arrived in sickbay, the doctors and other medical staff had trouble breathing at first due to the smell. While checking the survivors, one of the staff expressed how it seemed like something out of a bad horror show. The men's hair was long and springy and as dirty as could be. Their scalps had sores and scabs. Even their ears were full of dirt and covered in small sores. More sores covered their backs, sides, armpits, arms and legs. Some of the sores had become infected and it seemed there was no spot free from bruises. Human excrement had caked to their butts and legs.

After checking the survivors, a preliminary report was given to the admiral stating that all twelve survivors were still alive but in poor condition. At least two or three might not live to see the light of day again. The rest were not much better. All of the survivors suffered from dehydration, malnutrition, gout and rickets caused by starvation. They needed to be in a hospital as soon as possible.

The admiral directed the doctor and his staff to do whatever it would take to ensure the survival of the twelve. The men were to be cared for by the most qualified staff around the clock. The doctor assured the admiral that he and his staff would do the best they could.

After being in sick bay only twelve hours, JW started feeling better and was the first to try to get up out of bed.

He asked the closest medical staff member if he could have something to eat.

The doctors and medical staff were surprised at JW's rate of recovery. Soon after he had been given food and water, he was asking for bath soap, a washcloth, a towel, a toothbrush, and a pair of boxer shorts. The nurse assigned to him explained that he had been sponge-bathed upon arrival but agreed to help him with the items he was requesting.

The other men were starting to recover as well. JW was glad to see this included his best friend, James West. They were slowly gaining strength to sit on their own and look around their new surroundings. It looked like even the men who had been in the worst condition were going to survive.

JW had identified all eleven men as his fellow prisoners. Each man had given his name, rank, and serial number to the doctors. However, there was one exception as one man's identity was still unknown. This was the man who did not speak except for strange mumblings when he was near James. Identification of this man would not be completed until fingerprints could be run at Pearl Harbor.

JW requested to take a shower. The doctor told him, "No, Sir, you need to rest."

JW turned his sunken eyes to the doctor and said, "I can rest when I take the big dirt nap. Now I want a damn shower!"

The medical staff was totally astounded by JW's rate of recovery and his determination to take a shower. They finally relented and approved the shower. The doctor told JW, "I will arrange for an escort. In your condition I don't want you going anywhere by yourself."

JW argued, "I'm a big boy and I don't need someone to hold my hand."

The doctor turned to one of the male nurses and said, "Give this man a bath here in his bed."

JW conceded the argument to the doctor and said, "All right, all right. Get someone to hold my fucking hand so I can take a shower!"

The escort assignment was given to a male nurse who helped JW move to the shower that was only thirty feet down the hall. JW was given a special bar of soap and was asked to use it all over his body, including his scalp. A bottle of shampoo and a change of cloths would be delivered to him before he finished his shower.

After walking to the head (shower), JW could feel the strain on his body due to his depleted condition. He wanted a shower so badly that he wasn't letting anything stop him. It had been too many years since he had enjoyed a good, hot shower. The nurse said, "I will wait here in the hallway. If you need anything, just give a shout."

JW stepped into the shower. He carefully placed his towel on a hook and cast the open-back gown towards the door. Now was the moment he had been waiting for, and he turned the water on. The water was clean and clear as it cascaded down over him. Raising the temperature to as hot as he could stand brought back memories of long ago when he was home with his wife and young sons. He remembered taking showers with his wife and how wonderful she felt in his arms, as he held her ever so close to him in the shower. It was such a long time ago and so much had happened since they had last been together.

As he started to wash himself, tears came to his eyes and a big lump formed in his throat, as he remembered the dreams he had of his wife while he was in the POW camp. The dreams had been so real that he felt he could reach out and touch Karen, but JW knew these were only dreams manifested in the mind of a man deprived of food and the love of his wife. JW had also seen a young girl in his dreams. The girl had been with his wife, but JW knew he and Karen only had two boys. He didn't understand who the girl was and it upset him to think about her.

JW crumpled onto the floor of the shower. He knew he must have cried out because the nurse came in to check on him. JW looked at him and said, "I'm ok now please go!" The nurse stepped out of the shower and returned to the hall.

JW stood up. The doctors and nurses had washed most of the excrement that had been stuck to his body away. What was left was starting to soften and come off. JW fought back the tears, and the lump in his throat went away as he continued to wash. JW thought about how good it felt to be clean once again. Then a knock came from the door. It was the nurse with the shampoo and clean cloths. JW thanked him.

After taking his shower, JW was tired and returned to his bed in sickbay. The bed now had clean sheets on it as a nurse had changed sheets while JW was in the shower. As he passed James West, who was feeling better by the hour and asking for food, JW told him how good it felt to take a shower.

Other survivors were also starting to come around and asking for food. JW ate the soft food left for him next to his bed, and then fell asleep for about three hours. When JW woke up, he told the doctor, "I need a hair cut and shave, and where is the mess hall?"

The doctor thought for a minute and not wanting to hear about a dirt nap again, told him, "Mr. Walker, I will get you an escort."

About an hour later a young ensign arrived in sickbay and asked, "Who needs an escort?" One of the medical staff directed the ensign to JW and told the ensign to keep a close eye on him. The ensign walked up to JW and said, "I'm Ensign Farmer. I will be your escort, Sir."

JW stood up and said, "Young man, I'm Lt. Walker and I am proud to meet you."

The young ensign snapped to attention while presenting a smart salute.

JW returned the salute and then said, "Lead on young man, I need a haircut."

CHAPTER ELEVEN
THE HAIR CUT

Leading the way down the corridor, the ensign was thinking how the name Walker seemed strangely familiar, but ensigns don't ask lieutenants personal questions. The longer they walked, the more the ensign thought about the name Walker. After stopping a couple of times, Ensign Farmer and JW arrived at the enlisted men's barbershop. JW walked in and sat down.

The ensign said in a low voice, "Sir, this is for enlisted personnel."

JW told him, "This will do, Ensign, besides I need to sit for a while."

The only thing the ensign could say was, "As you wish, Sir."

It wasn't long before a young sailor asked JW, "Sir, are you one of the twelve survivors we've been hearing about."

JW replied, "Yes, yes, I am and I need a haircut."

Another sailor asked, "How long were you a POW? The scuttlebutt is you were a POW for a long time. What war would that be, Sir?"

JW looked slowly around the room. He could see the faces of the young sailors and the face of the barber, as all eyes and ears were on him. Their rapt attention reminded JW of his two boys when he would be home either on leave or for the weekend. They always wanted to hear what was going on and what had happened to their dad since the last time they had been together. He smiled at the memory and turned back to the grown men now wanting to hear what had happened to him for so many years, "Yes, I was a POW probably longer than most of you have lived. I was held for about twenty years, I think. By the way, just exactly what the hell year is it anyway?"

"It's 1998, mid-November! What year did you become a POW, Sir?"

JW responded, "It was April 1973!" He then leaned forward and placed his elbows on his knees and his face in his hands. With a low and barely audible voice he said, "Oh my God." JW shook his head slightly as if to clear his thoughts and said again a bit slower, "Oh my God." Then opening his fingers like a comb, JW combed his long, thin hair back and over the tops of his ears.

As JW sat up right, he again looked around the room. This time his expression was blank, as he found it hard to believe how long it has been. He was thinking to himself that his wife and boys might have forgotten about him. Twenty-five years would be a long time to live without hearing anything from him. They would have had nothing to hold onto but hope and prayer. Although JW's belief in God was still strong, twenty-five years was a very long time. Suddenly, JW could picture his wife on her way to church with a young lady he didn't know.

Then JW asked, "What day is this?"

Someone said, "It's Saturday."

"Well, that means in Illinois it would be Sunday."

JW then started telling his story to the young sailors. While the ensign listened, it clicked in his head why the name Walker was somewhat familiar. The ensign stepped out into the corridor still pondering the name Walker. He knew that Lt. Commander Walker was part of the rescue team that brought the survivors aboard. There was also a Lt. J. G. Walker in aircraft maintenance. So the name Walker could just be a common name.

However, as fate would have it, Lt. Commander Walker was coming down the corridor.

Ensign Farmer asked the lieutenant if he could ask a question.

Lt. Commander Walker stopped at a point where he could see in the barbershop and hear what was being said. He could see only a side view of the former POW. As he heard the voice of the man talking to the sailors about his experiences, a slight chill came over the lieutenant. The ensign then asked, "Wasn't your father a POW?"

"Yes, we think he was, but we haven't heard anything of him in some twenty-five or twenty-six years. Aren't you escorting one of the survivors?"

"Yes, Sir, I am."

"What's his name?"

Just as the ensign stated the name, "Lt. Walker," a million thoughts went through the Lt. Commander's mind. He thought about the voice, the side view of the man's face, the words being spoken. He heard one of the sailors ask, what year the survivors had become a POW?

When the former POW's answered, "April 1973" the ensign could see a tremendous change come over the face of Lt. Commander Walker.

The Lt. Commander stepped in to the barbershop and asked, "What time of the year did you become a POW?"

JW replied, "It was the spring of 73. I was shot down while trying to evacuate other military personnel." A strange feeling came over JW, as he looked up at the big man now standing in front of him. He could see tears in the big man's eyes a crying quiver on his lips.

As the big man knelt down to his knees in front of him, JW was asked these questions, "What was the name of your duty station? What ship were you on? Are you John Fredrick Walker of Carlinville Illinois?"

"Yes I'm John Fredric Walker! I was born and raised in Carlinville Illinois. The name of my duty station was Yankee Station. I was on the USS Ranger (cv61)."

As JW spoke those words, he could see a change coming over the face of this man who was on his knees before him. He could feel a tremendous amount of emotions welling up inside.

Lt. Commander Walker was almost unable to properly speak these next words, "What is my mother's maiden name?" Now trembling uncontrollably with tears streaming down his face, he said, "I mean, did you marry Karen Macintosh in 1967?"

JW, now with tears in his eyes and a lump the size of Texas in his throat, managed to mutter these words, "Are you John boy, my son?" Both men now wrapped in each other's arms began to sob out loud, as twenty-five years of praying and searching came to an end.

The other young sailors cleared out of the barbershop like it was on fire, but none spoke a word. A few minutes later, Lt. Commander Walker stepped into the corridor asking for the barber. Lt. Commander Walker said, "I would like you to meet my father, Lt. Walker, and he needs a haircut."

The barber expressed, "Sir, I would consider it to be an honor to cut your father's hair and give him a shave as well."

Sunday morning in Illinois, Kathryn was doing the breakfast dishes while her

mother read the morning paper. This had become the routine for Sunday morning before the two of them left for church. Paddy-boy was tending the livestock and would join them in church, if at all.

Karen said, "Look at this. It's a Hawaiian vacation ad about a place called the 'Pink Palace of the pacific'."

"Well, read it to me, Mother, while I finish the dishes."

"It says, 'elegance of a bygone era the pearl of Oahu, the pearl of Pearl Harbor. A place to rekindle old flames and find new love'. It sounds so romantic, doesn't it?"

Kathryn said, "Well there you go, Mother. Maybe its time for you to get out and spread your wings once again. I'm sure it would do you some good to get away for a time."

Karen responded somewhat harshly to her daughter, "Kathryn, that is quite enough. You know your father is the only man I want and we will be together again one day soon. Now don't speak like that again. You know I don't like it!"

Kathryn accidentally broke a plate while saying, "Mother, enough! You keep going on about someone I've never known or even met."

Kathryn then changed her tone, "Oh Mother, I'm so sorry. I so much want to see my dad. I want to be held in his arms so I can tell him how much I love him, even though I've never meet him. I've seen all the pictures, spoke to all the people who've known him, been to all the places you and he were at. I've been told all the stories about him. Mother, what if he doesn't like me? What if he thinks you did something wrong?"

Karen's response was very simple and to the point, "Kathryn, the second your dad lays eyes on you, he will know you're his daughter without a doubt. Now let's go to church. There's something different about today. I'm not real sure just what, but something's different about this day."

CHAPTER TWELVE
REUNION AT PEARL HARBOR

Lt. Commander Walker was called to the office of the Admiral. Without knowing the nature of this summons, Lt. Commander Walker reported as ordered without hesitation. A lower ranking officer who worked as the admiral's aid announced Walker's arrival to the admiral. The aide then asked Walker to please be seated and informed him that the admiral would be with him in a minute or so.

After about five minutes, the phone on the aide's desk rang. The aide stood up and announced, "Lt. Commander Walker, the admiral will see you now."

The aide opened the door to the admiral's office for Lt. Walker. After Lt. Commander Walker entered the office, the aide closed the door while Walker stood at attention three feet from the admiral's desk.

The admiral asked, "Are you Walker?"

"Yes, Sir, I am Lt. Commander Walker."

"Very good, you're just the man I want to speak with. Have a seat. Walker, I have some questions to ask you, for which I hope you will have very good answers. Do you understand?"

"Yes, Sir. I will do my best."

"Very good, Walker, I expect no less from any officer under my command. It is my understanding you were part of the team that found and rescued the twelve survivors and transported them to this carrier?"

"That's correct, Sir."

"It has come to my attention that you've been spending a great deal of time in and around sickbay, while getting other officers to cover your post and duties, thusly, neglecting your responsibilities," then speaking in a bit higher voice, "Is that correct, Mr. Walker?"

Lt. Commander Walker eagerly began to respond, "Yes, Sir, but you see, Sir, you may not quite understand the situation, Sir."

The admiral slammed his hand on top of his desk quite abruptly and quickly interceded, "Mr. Walker, let me be the judge as too what I understand or what I don't understand! Just so you know, Mr. Walker, that is why I am asking questions in order to better understand why one of my officers is derelict in the performance of his duties. Now, is that okay with you, Mr. Walker?"

In a lower voice and not sure how much trouble he might be in, he took a deep breath. As he let his breath out slowly, the lieutenant answered, "Yes, Sir."

"Excellent answer, Mr. Walker! Now seems you've identified one of the survivors as one Lt. John Walker, someone who clams to have been a POW for some twenty plus years and you claim is your father. Is that correct, Mr. Walker?"

In a more positive upbeat tone, Lt. Commander Walker responded quite briskly with, "Yes, Sir."

"Mr. Walker, are you comfortable with your identification of this person?"

In a voice barely containing his excitement, Lt. Commander Walker responded, "Oh yes, Sir!"

"I understand your mother is still alive. Have you informed her of this matter?"

"Yes, Sir, she is still alive. No, I haven't informed her of this as yet."

"Well, Mr. Walker, I can understand your interest in this matter, but you leave me no choice but to relieve you of your duties and responsibilities till further notice. Be advised, identification will not be completed until all twelve have been fingerprinted and checked out at Pearl Harbor."

"Sir, fingerprinting has been completed and faxed off to Pearl. It is my understanding that all but one of the twelve has been positively identified. My father is one of them who had been identified."

"Thank you, Mr. Walker. I wasn't aware the fingerprinting had been completed. Mr. Walker, I have authorized full phone access to the phone in your quarters. I thought you might want some privacy."

Thank you, Admiral, that is greatly appreciated. I will get my father from sickbay, return to my quarters, and call my mother.

After being dismissed, Lt. Commander Walker went directly to sickbay. After checking his father out, the two Walkers returned to the lieutenant's quarters and began making phone calls.

The first call was to Karen. As the phone rang, JW pondered what he should say to his wife after twenty-five years. JW's mind raced back through time to the sixth grade when he fought for the chance to sit next to Karen in the school cafeteria. He thought again of all the times they had studied and completed homework together. He thought about their trips fishing, swimming, and riding bikes. He remembered the talk he had with Karen's father on the morning he asked Karen to marry him. Then he pictured their wedding day, the honeymoon, and the birth of his two sons.

Finally, someone on the other end picked up the phone. The voice that answered was that of a seemingly very excited young man, "Hello, hello, please speak fast. I'm in a hurry!"

"Paddy, this is your brother, John."

"John! Thank God you called. I have the most wonderful news! I just had a call from Scott Air Base asking for directions to Mom. They're sending a helicopter to pick us up! John, Dad has been found, John, Dad is alive! I'm getting some clothes together for Mom, Kathryn and myself."

John had to raise his voice to be heard over his brother's excited rambling, "Paddy, are you sitting down?"

"Oh John, come on. I've got to hurry!"

Still in a louder voice John said, "Little big man sit down! I have someone who wants to talk to you!"

"Okay John, I'm sitting down. What have you got that could be more important than what I just told you? Why don't you seem interested in what I just told you anyway?"

Paddy listened intently as someone other than his brother began speaking to him, "Paddy boy, is that you? Hello, hello? Are you there, Son?"

After a long pause, the young man on the other end of the phone responded in a voice that was clearly crying and almost inaudible, "Dad, is this you? Oh Father, I've waited so long just to hear your voice. Oh Dad, I've missed you so much, please tell me this is you!"

"Yes, Son, it's me. I'm safe and with your brother John. I too have waited a long time to hear your voice. I can't wait to see you and your mother!"

After talking for about ten minutes Paddy told his dad, "I hate to cut you short, but I've got to get to the church. Scott Air Base is sending a helicopter to pick us all up and Mother doesn't know you've been found yet."

"Ok Son, give your mother a hug and a kiss for me, and I will see you all soon!"

Paddy hung up the phone, grabbed the two suitcases and his sea bag, and ran out the door. He piled the luggage in the trunk and ran around to the driver's side of the car. After getting in and placing the key in the ignition, he turned the key and said to the car, "Come on old girl, I know you're old and tired, but now I need you to run like a big dog." The old Mercedes screamed to life one more time.

Putting the old car in reverse, Paddy pressed the accelerator to the floor. The car moved backward. The rear wheels spun and grabbed for all the traction possible, as plenty of dirt flew in the air. Paddy let off the accelerator and cranked the steering wheel to the right. The front of the car swung rapidly to the left. Paddy turned the steering wheel back to the left and dropped the car into drive as he once again pressed the accelerator to the floor and held it there.

As the old car sped down the dirt driveway, Paddy was sure he caught a glimpse of a helicopter in flight. Paddy had close to eighteen miles to travel before arriving at the church where his mother and sister were attending service. Paddy wanted to be the first one to give his mother the great news. As the old Mercedes hit the blacktop, the rear tires started smoking. The engine labored hard to achieve the request for full acceleration.

In the past thirty years, the Mercedes had been driven very carefully. It was never driven over the speed of fifty-five miles per hour and only in and out of Carlinville to attend church or do grocery shopping and visit relatives. Paddy pushed it to sixty-five MPH, and the engine acted like it wanted to quit running. As Paddy looked in the rearview mirror, he could see a large black cloud forming behind the car. There was something that looked like small black chunks landing on the road. Then the engine seemed to clear and accelerated to just over seventy-five. After a mile or so, the engine spit and sputtered. It then coughed a couple of times and again kicked out a large black cloud with black chunks landing on the road. The engine smoothed out and accelerated to over ninety and gave no further indications of wanting to quit. Paddy didn't slowdown till he entered the city limits of Carlinville.

When Paddy turned the Mercedes right on to the main street of Carlinville, he could tell the old car seemed to have more power and accelerated much quicker than it ever had before. Although he was in a hurry, he didn't exceed the speed limit too much. As Paddy was passing by the old two story stone jail, he saw his grandmother and grandfather McIntosh going the other way.

Paddy put his head out the window and honked the horn twice, as he yelled to his grandparents, "They found him! They found him! He's alive!"

As Mary Beth and William looked at each other, William said, " Now what's up with that boy driving like a bat out of hell and yelling they found him? Found who?"

Mary Beth thought for a moment then said, "My God, William! Turn around and head for Karen's church!"

"Why? What's up?"

"William, just do it, and I will explain as you drive."

William turned the Cadillac around in front of one of Carlinville's finest and accelerated. Then said, "Mary Beth, this better be good because now I've got a city cop on my ass."

"William, you remember just before Karen and John were married, she ran out into the field next to the church?"

"Come on, Mary Beth, that was premarital jitters and you know it."

"No, William, Karen told John's mother and me all about it later on. She told us she didn't know when it would happen but a helicopter would land next to the church and it would all have something to do with John! William, five minutes ago, you said how strange it was to see a military helicopter flying around town and how it seemed to be looking for something."

"Yes, I remember saying that."

"And what direction was it going?"

"It was going southeast towards Gillespie. Why?"

"And from here, what direction is Gillespie and Karen's church?"

"That would be southeast."

"Now William, if Paddy were going to his grandparent's house, he would've turned two streets back. As he passed us, he yelled out, 'They found him, he's alive!' and he's headed towards the church at a high rate of speed."

William accelerated the caddy to sixty as he said, "I guess all the things Karen has been telling us over the years are not nightmares after all."

William and Mary Beth passed the Deep Rock gas station and the motel and turned right onto state route four heading for Gillespie and Karen's church. William again accelerated the caddy while one of Carlinville's finest was still on his tail like stink on a skunk. No matter how hard William accelerated the caddy, all they saw were taillights of the old Mercedes-Benz.

Paddy knew the helicopter had been out of sight for at least a minute or so and someone by now was surely informing his mother of the great news. With that thought in mind, Paddy accelerated the old Mercedes to maximum. Holding the gas pedal to the floor, he said to the car, "Come on old girl, please give me all you got left and just get me there." The old car's speed steadily increased as the engine ground laboring hard under the acceleration to achieve a top speed just over one hundred and twenty five miles per hour, a speed the old car had never been at before.

Finally within a half mile of the church, Paddy could see the helicopter in the field next to the church. He could see the figure of a man walking from the helicopter towards the church. From this distance, Paddy was unable to tell the rank of the man in uniform. About a quarter of a mile away, Paddy started decelerating the old Mercedes and was still doing at least twenty-five when he turned into the driveway of the church.

Paddy pressed hard on the brakes. At the same time, he put the old car into park. Before the car came to a complete stop, Paddy opened the door, jumped out, and ran for the church door, which had just closed after the officer had entered. Paddy opened the door and rushed in. He ran past the Air Force officer while saying, "By your leave, Sir."

Captain Johnson observed the condition of the uniform this young man was wearing as he rushed past him. His boots were unlaced, the pant legs of the uniform were bunched atop his unlaced boots, his belt was in its belt loops but unfastened, and his uniform shirt was not buttoned or tucked in. Paddy couldn't have been more out of uniform if he had walked in naked.

The minister had stopped talking and the congregation started to turn to look at who had just come in and caused the interruption to the service. Paddy took the opportunity to call for his mother, "Mom, Mom! They found him. Mom they found him. Dad is alive. And he's safe onboard the Kitty Hawk with John!"

Karen stood up and turned towards her hysterical son. Kathryn stood beside her mother and faced her brother.

Paddy approached his mother slowly with his arms outstretched. Big tears ran down his face as he told his mother, "Mother, Dad's alive. I spoke to him on the phone, and he's with my brother John on board the Kitty Hawk. Mom, I want to see my dad so bad!"

As Paddy embraced his mother, she said, "I know my son, so do I!"

Kathryn joined in hugging her mother and brother and all three of them were crying. While other members of the congregation were saying, "Thank God, praise God, praise the Almighty."

After a couple of minutes, Karen looked at the Air force officer who was still standing just inside the door and said, "I'm Mrs. John Fredrick Walker. Are you looking for me?"

"Yes Ma'am, I'm Captain Johnson of the United States Air Force out of Scott Air Base. I have a helicopter just outside to transport you to Scott where you will be placed on a fixed wing aircraft and transported to Denver. Will you come with me, please?"

"What about my two children?"

"Yes Ma'am, this transport includes them as well."

Karen's mom and dad were standing behind the captain. Karen walked up to them. Her dad gave Karen a big Irish hug and a kiss on the forehead then said, "Karen, if there's anything you need, Honey, I mean anything at all, you give your mother and me a call any time day or night. Karen, your mother and I love you very much, and we want you to be happy." Then in a voice almost crying, Karen's dad told her, "Now Honey, you go to your husband and please tell him we love him. Then bring that big bastard home, so I can kick his ass!"

"Dad, John told Paddy boy that he only weighs about ninety-four pounds!"

"Karen, you tell him we all love him, and we want him to come home. Honey, you can leave out the part about me wanting to kick his ass. Honey, just bring him home. Just bring him home please. Because Honey, I'm so tired of seeing you with tears in your eyes and the look of a lost puppy on your face. My little girl deserves better than what you've been though these last twenty or so years."

Karen said, "Why thank you, Dad. I always thought you liked my husband and it makes me so proud for you to tell me."

Karen was surprised when she and her two kids walked outside and saw the Mercedes parked in the driveway with the driver's door open and the helicopter in the wheat field next to the church. It was all just as she had seen in her vision so many years before.

As Karen climbed aboard the helicopter, again she was surprised as her eyes fell upon Reb's mother, Mrs. Benjamin. Sitting with her was a young black lady that Karen wasn't familiar with. There were two more women in the helicopter and both were named Mrs. West. One was James's mother Mary Ann and the other was his wife Sara Beth. After everyone greeted and hugged each other, Karen and her two children were seated and strapped in. The helicopter lifted off the ground and headed for Scott Air Base.

All the passengers found it had to talk during the flight due to the noise of the helicopter. Before the flight was over, Karen was crying quite uncontrollably while her daughter tried to comfort her. Kathryn had placed her arm around her mother and her head on her mother's shoulder.

The forty-five minute flight back to Scott Air Base seemed to take forever. When it finally landed, they all disembarked the helicopter and headed for a waiting bus. Captain Johnson turned to Paddy, "Mr. Walker, I can understand the circumstances, but Mr. Walker you need to square away your uniform or put your civvies on."

Paddy responded with, "Yes, Sir." Paddy quickly straightened his uniform and climbed on the bus with the other family members.

The bus took them to another part of the air base. The time was just after the noon meal, and the family members were taken to the mess hall where they could eat and talk. They did far more talking than eating. Paddy and Kathryn listened to every word their mother spoke about their father. Paddy was so very young when his father became a POW, and Kathryn wasn't born until after.

As Kathryn and Paddy sat listening to the stories being told, the two of them were very surprised to learn how Mary Ann and Sara Beth West had dreams so similar to the ones their mother had been having. Sara Beth had a piece of cloth she claimed to have torn from the rags James was wearing while he was being beat to death. Mrs. Benjamin recounted when her son, Reb, almost drowned when his helicopter crashed into a river. She said she knew Reb had been saved by his best friend, John.

Kathryn asked Paddy, "As long as we have known all these people, how is it we have never been told these stories about our father and his friends?"

Paddy replied, "Kathryn, I don't know. I do know this, though, our dad is alive and well and now safely with our big brother John. John is a good size man, and he won't let anything hurt our father anymore.

While sobbing slightly Kathryn said, "But Paddy, Father doesn't even know about me. What if he thinks Mother did something wrong and then I was born? What if he doesn't like me?" She sobbed harder even harder as big tears ran down her face and cried, "Oh Paddy, what if Father doesn't like me?"

Paddy reached for a tissue the sergeant had brought. After gently wiping the tears away and placing a kiss on her forehead, Paddy told Kathryn, "Like our grandparents have told you in the past, the second Dad sees you he will know whose daughter you are without a doubt."

About an hour and a half later all the family members were returned to the bus and taken to the east side flight line where they all boarded an aircraft used for VIPs. They were very surprised how spacious it was for a military aircraft. They found stereo headphones and a dropdown screen for a projection TV. Not only did the seats recline but they would swivel as well.

With the exception of Kathryn and Paddy, none of the family members had ever flown before. After the sergeant made sure everyone was seated and strapped in for takeoff, the pilot announced that the flight to Denver would take just over three and a half hours. It would include a short stop in Des Moines, Iowa to take on more family members. The pilot informed his guests with a laugh, "If there is anything you need, please ask the go-for sergeant. Feel free to eat and drink but no smoking. This is all courtesy of the United States Government. As the pilot of this aircraft, I would like to thank you for all you have been through."

After the aircraft was in the air, the sergeant informed the family members they could get up and move around if they were so inclined. He indicated where the restrooms were located. He then repeated the pilot's offer if any of them wanted anything to eat or drink to let him know, as he would be more than glad to get it for them.

Reb's mother Ruth turned to the young lady next to her and said, "Brenda, I want you to meet some very dear friends of mine." The young lady followed Ruth without question.

Ruth walked over to Karen and asked if she would mind if the two of them sat down. She explained that she wanted Karen to meet the young lady with her.

Karen said, "Please be seated, and who might this be?"

"Karen, this is my granddaughter and she's just over twenty-five."

"Ruth, I thought you only had one son, that being Reb, and I didn't know he was married. We didn't get an invitation to a wedding as I recall."

"Well, Karen, I didn't either. It would seem Reb took a couple of extra days of leave in Texas with one of his Marine buddies, who had a sister, Brenda's mother. I guess Reb didn't have time to tell me anything before becoming a POW."

"Ruth, I know we have lost some contact over the last five or so years. But I heard a couple of years ago you had a young lady come stay with you. I thought she was someone to help you after your health problems. And how is your health now?"

"Well, Karen, I'm doing much better now and the doctor said the tingling in my left arm and leg will be with me for the rest of my life. So I thank God it's not any worse," Ruth answered and then continued, "But Karen, it would seem the information Reb left with Brenda's mother was somehow lost over the years and only the general area of where Reb was from remained. It was just by chance that Brenda stopped into the Granite City airport asking questions about Roscoe Benjamin."

"Ruth, I don't mean to sound suspicious or be cold, but can you be sure? What assurances do you have that this young lady indeed belongs to Reb even though she does resemble him?"

Brenda then pulled some old pictures from her purse and displayed them to Karen. Karen took the pictures in hand while looking them over very carefully, and then said, "Well that certainly is Reb." Then a smile came over her face as Karen took Brenda's hands in hers and said, "Brenda, please forgive me for being suspicious. And please allow me to welcome you to our family."

Karen watched as Brenda put her head on Ruth's shoulder and started to cry. Karen again took hold of Brenda's hands and asked, "Why are you crying? You have every right to be proud of your dad. Your dad was second best man at my wedding when John and I were married. My husband and your dad and I have been best of friends for many years."

As Brenda was crying she said, "Except for pictures, I've never seen my dad and I'm not sure he even knows I exist."

"Brenda, my daughter has never seen her father except for pictures. And the letter I sent letting him know I was pregnant was returned with his personal effects unopened. Brenda, where is your mother?"

Brenda took a deep breath then looked up to the ceiling. After a long moment she said, "It was my sixteenth birthday. My mother was on her way home from work when she stopped at a stop sign. A drunk driver slammed into the back of her, shoving her into the path of an oncoming eighteen wheeler." Brenda was crying while tears streamed down her face. In a voice that was almost inaudible she said, "She didn't have a snowball's chance in hell" and continued to cry even harder.

Kathryn, hearing Brenda's story, started crying as well and tried to comfort Brenda.

The sergeant over-hearing what Brenda had said, came over and asked, "Are you Brenda Benjamin of Raymondville Texas?"

"Yes, yes I am!"

"Is your father Roscoe Ethane Benjamin from the state of Illinois?"

"Yes," Brenda and Ruth answered in unison.

"You're on a list of people the government has been trying to find for quite sometime. You may very well have a lot of back pay coming to you."

"My dad knew about me?"

"I believe he did, young lady, I believe he did."

Brenda's spirits were lifted to say the least just knowing her father knew she existed.

It seemed to be no time at all when the plane touched down in Des Moines, Iowa and started taking on more family members from New York, Ohio, Pennsylvania, North and South Carolina, Georgia and Mississippi. It seemed the military's plan for gathering the family members was well orchestrated.

The new family members said they had only been on the ground for twenty minutes when they were told the flight was on the ground. After the plane was refueled and all the family members seated and strapped in, the plane took off for a non-stop flight to Denver.

All the family members started introducing themselves. Two of the newer family members were sisters from Georgia and Mississippi and seemed to be the only ones uncomfortable with Ruth and her granddaughter Brenda.

When Karen and her kids noticed this, they stayed close to Ruth and Brenda. Although they had just met Brenda this day, their mother had welcomed her to the family and that made it okay with them. As for Ruth, well she had done diaper duty on Kathryn and Paddy boy.

The rest of the flight into Denver went well and the time passed quickly with everyone talking about what their sons had done while growing up. They shared how proud their sons were when they first put on their uniforms.

Once the aircraft landed in Denver, the family members were told they could leave their things on the seats but would need their boarding passes. They would be taken to the officer's mess and could order anything they might want to eat. Then the sergeant said, "Oh yes, please remember Uncle Sam is footing the bill, so please eat like kings. You deserve it."

All the family members the government could find had gathered in the mess hall. They had come from all over the United States. It seemed like one big family reunion. Everyone greeted each other like long lost friends. After a little over an hour an Air Force captain walked in and called for everyone's attention. He then said, "I have great news for all of you. This includes the family members and any military personnel who can hear me. At approximately fifteen minutes ago at 1200 hours Hawaiian time with brass bands playing and fireboats spraying water as high as possible, the USS Kitty Hawk entered Pearl Harbor with twelve survivors of a war that ended over twenty-five years ago. All are alive. The radio message transmitted by the Kitty Hawk reads: 'Entering Pearl Harbor with all Twelve Alive'."

The captain's voice quivered slightly as he continued, "If there is anything within my authority that I can do for you, please ask!" The captain then snapped to attention and gave a salute to the family members. Seeing this, other officers and enlisted men did the same.

A very old and frail looking lady dressed in what looked like well-used secondhand cloths stood up. She returned the salute to the captain and then turned slowly while holding the salute, gave this same salute to all the officers and enlisted men. When she had turned back to the captain, she dropped the salute and said, "I'm not sure if I can talk for all the family members, but I would like you to tell the president thanks. Thanks for all that has been done to bring my son home and for taking me to my son."

All the family members stood up and started applauding. They then began shaking hands with each other and with any military person they could reach. Smiles and tears of joy were seen on all their faces.

When the family members left the mess hall, a brass band was outside and started playing as they boarded the bus. When they reached the flight line, another band was playing while they boarded the plane. They were touched to receive a military honor guard and a twenty one-gun salute. By this time all of Denver had learned what was going on and had lined the fence. Some were shouting while others were honking their horns.

After taking off, the family members were informed that they would land at Wright Field in approximately three and a half hours. Further instructions would be forthcoming. Within fifteen minutes, the intercom came on. It was the president speaking to all the family members, "To all the family members, this is President Bush. I received your message. I thank you for that, but I'm afraid it is we Americans who need to say thanks to you. Our thanks go to you for all the time you've lost not being with your loved ones, for all the nights you've prayed and waited so patiently for this very day, and for all the family time that has been lost and can never be reclaimed. Our debt is to you for your government not doing its absolute best to account for your sons, husbands, brothers, and fathers; for all the sleepless nights, all the dreams and plans that never had a chance to come true. As the President of the United States and as a fellow American I want to thank you, because you are what continues to make America strong. I am proud of your loved ones who are coming home for all they have endured. I'm very proud of you for sticking to your guns and to your belief in your loved ones."

After the president's announcement and with the plane well underway to Pearl Harbor, the two sisters were talking by themselves. As they talked they would ever so often look over towards Ruth and Brenda.

Kathryn and Paddy noticed this and informed their mother and Ruth. All became concerned due to all the racial problems in the states of Mississippi and Georgia in the last few years.

Brenda asked her grandmother, "What should we do if any problems arise because on this air craft we've no place to go?"

Ruth responded, "Just stay calm. Let them make the first move. That will show their true intentions. Do you understand? Try not to look at them."

After about twenty minutes, it seemed the two sisters were agreeing with each other about something. They then seemed to be crying and praying. Other family members stopped by and spoke with them. After a few minutes, the two sisters stood up and walked towards Ruth and Brenda, while still talking to each other.

When the two sisters reached Ruth, they introduced themselves. They asked if they might sit and talk with her and what seemed to be her group.

Ruth replied with, "Yes, you may."

The one sister started off with an apology for her and her sister's attitudes towards Ruth and the young lady, who must be her granddaughter.

Ruth then said, "Yes, this is my granddaughter, Brenda. The others here are some of my best friends. This is Mrs. John Walker and two of her three children Kathryn and Paddy. Over here is Mrs. West, Mary Ann, and Sara Beth, the mother and wife of survivor James West."

"Well, if you don't mind me asking, how did you all come to know each other?"

Ruth replied, "I've done a lot of diaper duty over the years."

"Oh, I see. You worked for all these people you've called your best friends!"

Ruth got a very surprised look on her face, as did everyone else.

Sara Beth started to speak, when Karen interrupted her, "Let me answer her question before you say something God might not like! In the state of Illinois, we have a place we call 'The Rope'. It is a state park, if you will. As kids, our mothers and fathers took all of us to this park to swim and have picnics. Now the Benjamin family owns some farmland directly adjacent to this park. So Roscoe, who is better known as 'Reb' to all of his friends, would be helping his dad with plowing and planting. His dad would let Reb come over and swim to cool off. This is how James, John and I got to know Reb. I think we were all about ten or twelve when we first met."

"When John turned sixteen and got his license to drive, we all went to St. Louis to watch the St. Louis Cardinal's baseball games. Not always did Reb have the dollar twenty-five cents to get in, but my parents and John's were a little better off. So John and I would pay Reb's way in. James would meet us at the front entrance and the four of us would have a great time together."

"When we were still in our teen years, Mr. Benjamin died from a farming accident. At the time of his death, he owed John's dad a large amount of money. Now I wasn't there, but from what I understood, John got down on his knees and asked his dad to forgive the money owed to him by the Benjamin's and that he would find a way to repay it himself."

"When we were grown up, Reb and James attended John and my wedding. When John and James were away attending the Academy of Annapolis, Reb would come over and help with the yard work and take care of the garden when I was too far along with my first pregnancy to do those things myself."

"Although I've never asked my children to refer to Ruth as 'Aunt', all three of my children refer to Ruth Benjamin as Aunt Ruth. So you see you're not just looking at people who are white or black. You're looking at God-fearing people, who've been best of friends through good times and bad and who have been there for each other almost all our lives."

Karen paused after her long speech and looked at the two sisters. Everyone waited in silence as the sisters looked from Karen to Ruth and then to each of the group standing together. The sister who had first talked with them said, "Ruth, Karen, we had no idea of the history of your two families. We do sincerely apologize for our ignorance and hope you might find it in your hearts to understand and maybe forgive us. You see, we were told a little bit about a report our sons gave to the military about what took place on the boat. We were told that a black man called Reb helped our sons keep the engines running. They said he built a radio and that this black man worked as hard, if not harder, then anyone on the boat. As we looked around, you're the only person of color we have seen on this plane."

The two sisters started crying, as one of the sisters took hold of Ruth's hand and said,

"We would consider it an honor to meet your son. We are hoping that you would please consider our request."

Ruth and Karen took hold of the two sisters' hands. Mary Ann, Sara Beth, Brenda, Kathryn, and Paddy gathered around. They joined their hands together. Ruth looked at Karen, and Karen gave a slight nod. Ruth then said," Welcome to the family."

All went on talking, as other members joined in from time to time. Then the Air Force sergeant arrived and asked them all to return to their seats, as the plane would be landing at Wright Field within twenty minutes.

When the aircraft landed at Wright field, all the family members started asking about the location of the hospital. They wanted to know how soon they could see their loved ones.

The Air Force sergeant responded, "All in good time. Right now we need to get all of you to your quarters for the night." The sergeant directed the family members towards the bus.

Everyone found a place on the bus and waited until the bus was in route before again asking where the hospital was and when they would see their loved ones. Again were told, "All in good time."

As the family members were looking out the windows of the bus, they could see people lining the streets, waving American flags, and cheering. The closer the bus came to the Royal Hawaiian Hotel, the more people who lined the street. Soon the bus pulled up and stopped in front of the Royal Hawaiian, as limousines and other fancy luxury cars gave way to the military escort bus. All the residents of Oahu knew about the impending arrival of the family members of the twelve survivors.

As the family members disembarked the bus, the staff of the Royal Hawaiian greeted each member as though each were a king or a queen. Other patrons of the Royal Hawaiian had purchased roses and gave them to the family members as they entered the hotel.

The manager of the Royal Hawaiian gave the mothers and wives of the survivors each a dozen long steam roses. Then assured them that if there was anything they might need day or night, all they needed to do was ask.

A Navy lieutenant had joined the Air Force sergeant. The lieutenant assembled all the family members in an area where he could talk to just the family members without the public. The lieutenant informed the family members that the survivors were undergoing multiple, extensive medical tests and should be available for visitation the next day at approximately 0900. He then stated, "If you will all please be patient a little while longer, it should only be another twelve to sixteen hours. Then you all can see your loved ones."

One of the family members stood up and announced he was a doctor. He wanted to know more about the condition of the survivors.

The lieutenant responded, "I'm glad for you, Sir. However, I'm not a doctor. I can only relay the information I've been given to give to all of you. Let me ask you this, Sir. Have you ever dealt with severe dehydration and starvation?"

"Well, yes I have. As a doctor, I've dealt with patients with diarrhea, which will cause dehydration. I have had patients with severe stomach problems that can lead to starvation. So yes, I have dealt with the two problems of dehydration and starvation."

"Well, Doctor, have you read about the Holocaust or seen any documentary of the Holocaust of World War Two? Are you familiar with the death camps of that time?"

Suddenly, the room became quiet as a mummy's tomb. The realization of what the lieutenant was discussing was coming to each of them, one at a time.

The doctor replied, "Well, yes I have. I'm sure most everyone has seen documentaries about World War Two and the Holocaust, but the world has changed. I sincerely doubt the world will ever see such a travesty like that again!"

"Doctor, I don't wish to impugn your intelligence in any way. However, just five miles from here in a military hospital, are twelve men who can prove you wrong. It is my understanding that if the search and rescue had taken another twenty-four hours, four of the twelve survivors wouldn't be with us now! So you see, Doctor, although you may have dealt with dehydration and starvation, you haven't come close to dealing with starvation and dehydration of this magnitude!"

With a look of total surprise and disbelief on his face, the doctor sat down. The group sat huddled together for comfort. The joy in learning their loved ones had survived was joined by the thoughts of the horrors these men had lived through.

The families were then taken to their rooms. Later on that evening, the group was taken to the dining room. After eating, some of the family members talked to the local press. Others went back to their rooms and watched some traditional Hawaiian shows. Others sat talking to each other. Regardless of the variety of activities, each and every one of them was doing the best they could to get through the long hours before they would finally be reunited with the men who had been missing for so many years.

The next day most of the family members were up really early compared to Hawaiian time. This was partly due to the time difference from where they came. A few had stayed up most of the night and were slower to wake.

Around 0615 (Hawaiian time), the phone rang in Karen's room. Karen said, "Go on and get your shower, Kathryn. I will get the phone. Hello!"

"Hi, Mom. This is John, how are you? I didn't think you would be in till today."

"Oh, I'm fine son, but I can't wait to see your dad! Can you tell me how he's doing? How does he look?"

"Well, he looks much better than he did when he was rescued from that old P.T. boat. He was up till after eleven last night. The doctors were doing all kinds of tests to make sure he was strong enough to have visitors."

"Dad, Uncle James, and Uncle Reb are all doing really well. I spoke to Uncle James. He keeps asking about this one survivor wanting to know if he has been identified. I told him about twenty minutes ago that the military is still working on it. Uncle Reb wants to see his mother and Brenda. Mom, who's Brenda?"

"Well John, Brenda is Reb's daughter. I've had the pleasure of meeting her on the flight over here. She is very concerned about meeting her father. She has only seen him in pictures."

"I don't think she needs to be worried. Uncle Reb is very excited about seeing her. I bet it will be some meeting. Mom, Uncle Reb also wants to see his girlfriend. I hope she made the trip as well. I'm guessing she is the mother of his daughter but was never married."

"Yes John, Reb's girlfriend is Brenda's mother, but no she didn't make the trip. You see, John, through no fault of her own, she now sleeps in the arms of the Lord."

"Mom, I'm sorry to hear that. I won't say anything to Uncle Reb. I will let Aunt Ruth tell him. Can you tell me Aunt Ruth's room number?"

"John, she and Brenda are in room 108. Mary Ann and Sara Beth are in 112. Are you going to call them?"

"Thanks, Mom. Yes, I will give them a call. I know they have a lot of questions, too."

"John, where are you staying?" his mother asked.

"I'm staying on board the Kitty Hawk," John replied.

"Ok, are you going to come over to this hotel?"

"Yes, I will try and arrange for a room now that I know you're all here. I will talk to you later. Oh Mom, have you had any breakfast yet?" John asked.

"No son, not yet."

"Mother, give me about one and a half hours, and I will meet all of you in the restaurant. Is that Ok?"

"John, I think that would be just great. Then we can all go to the hospital together."

"Ok, Mom, see you then. I love you, bye."

After hanging up the phone, Karen told Kathryn, "That was your brother John. He's going to meet us in the restaurant for breakfast. I'm going down and try to get a good table. When you're ready, come on down."

After completing her shower, Kathryn dressed for breakfast and started to leave. Just as she reached for the doorknob, the phone rang. Kathryn answered, "Hello?"

The voice on the other end sounded gravely and was a bit slurred, "May I speak to Karen Walker? This is Lieutenant . . . "

Hearing "this is Lieutenant," Kathryn interrupted before allowing the person to finish. She said, "Karen Walker is out to breakfast. Can you please call back later?"

The voice hesitantly replied, "Uh, Uh, ok."

Kathryn hung up the phone and left the room to join her mother in the restaurant. After sitting down, Kathryn told her mother some lieutenant had called and would call back. While Karen wondered what the call was about, she knew if it had been anything important, the man would have told her daughter.

About an hour later, Mary Ann and Sara Beth West arrived. Both of them were talking about a phone call they had received from James. They thought he sounded like he was drunk, as he had been slurring his words a bit. They were excited and wanted to share what all they talked about.

Twenty minutes or so later Ruth and Brenda arrived. Ruth and Brenda talked about Roscoe calling them. They too stated that he sounded like he was drunk. Of course, Brenda was in seventh heaven. After all these years, she finally had spoken to her father.

Brenda said, "I don't care what he sounded like. To me, he sounded like an angel. Now there is no doubt that he knows about me, and he can't wait to see me. I want to see my father. I want to put my arms around him and hold him so tight forever!"

While Brenda was still talking, Paddy arrived. Paddy was elated as he told his mother and sister, "I just talked to Dad on the phone. His voice sounded gravely and was slurring a bit. It sounded like he was a little drunk. Dad said it was the medications the doctors gave him and should wear off by the time we see him. Mom, Dad said he called your room and the maid told him you were out to breakfast."

Kathryn cried out, "Oh my God!" Placing her hands over her face, she started crying uncontrollably as she stomped her feet on the floor and twisted her upper body back and forth. Kathryn tried talking while crying, but her words were totally inaudible.

Karen and Paddy looked at Kathryn in total surprise. Other family members in the restaurant started looking towards Kathryn and Ruth. Brenda and both Wests, who had been in the height of their glory, sat looking at Kathryn in shock!

Karen and Paddy tried calming Kathryn. Ruth came around the table and tried to assist in calming Kathryn. It was all to no avail.

Karen said, "Kathryn, Kathryn, what's wrong? What's wrong honey?"

Ruth placed her arms around Kathryn and pleaded, "Talk to me my child! You can talk to me about anything. I don't care what it is! Now please calm down and tell us what's wrong!"

After a few minutes, Kathryn calmed down only a little. With her hands still covering her face, with tears running all the way down her arms, and dripping off her elbows, she held onto Ruth as though she would fall apart if she lost contact.

When John walked into the restaurant of the Royal Hawaiian, he didn't have any trouble locating his family. Everyone was looking towards a table where a young lady was crying quite loudly. As John walked up to the table, Ruth stood up. Kathryn looked up, saw her oldest brother, jumped up, and placed her arms around John's neck. Kathryn put her tear soaked face against John's right cheek while still crying. John placed his arms around his sister and asked, "Now what's wrong with my little sister?"

After a minute or so, Kathryn tried to speak but her words were still inaudible. After a few minutes had passed, John was able to get Kathryn to sit down and start to calm down a little more. One of the waiters of the Royal Hawaiian brought John a chair without being asked. John sat himself between his mother and sister. Kathryn put her face into John's neck and shoulder and continued crying. John asked, "Now can you tell me what's wrong?"

Kathryn was considerably calmer than she had previously been and spoke in a very broken voice,

"When Mom left the room, the phone rang. Oh John, I didn't know it was Dad! John, I've never heard his voice. Mom, I didn't know it was Dad!"

Ruth was standing behind Kathryn and was rubbing her shoulders. She asked, "Are you ok now?"

Kathryn stood up and put her arms around Ruth, "Thank you Aunt Ruth, I'm so lucky to have such a loving family during this very stressful time in my life." The rest of the family did their best to let Kathryn know it was not her fault that she did not recognize a voice she had never heard.

All the family members were almost completed with breakfast when the Air Force sergeant and the Naval lieutenant entered the restaurant. The two were seated and had coffee until 0850. At 0850 hours, the sergeant started directing the family members towards the bus. The two officers found to their surprise that the movement towards the bus was more like a well-orchestrated stampede.

Once all the family members were on board the bus, a head count was conducted and completed. The bus pulled away from the Royal Hawaiian and was led by a military escort. Some of the family members were crying out loud, and some had tears running down their faces. None of the tears being shed were tears of sorrow. Quite the contrary, as these were tears of joy. This would be the first time any of them would have seen their loved ones in over twenty-five years.

The naval base informed the local media that they would not be allowed on site for at least the first four days. Any contact with the survivors would be strictly limited at that time.

After the bus stopped in front of the hospital, the family members were assembled in the main lobby. One of the doctors caring for the survivors addressed the family members and told them what to expect when they first saw their loved one.

Next to speak was the Naval lieutenant. He said, "Please make sure you stay together in your personal family group." He then called out the name of each survivor one at a time and gave the room number.

When the name Lieutenant John Fredrick Walker was called out, Karen, Kathryn and Paddy all started crying. All three clung to Lieutenant Commander John Fredrick Walker III, the oldest son for support. As the Walker family started for the elevator, they could hear the names of Sergeant Roscoe Ethane Benjamin and Lieutenant James West. All three families were together on the elevator to the third floor as John explained, "We will be passing the room of a yet unidentified survivor. He cries out, but no one seems to be able to understand what he is saying. So please, pay him no mind. It would seem he's been a POW for a very long time. There is one of the survivors who was with him longer than the others. He said this man has been this way as long as he has known him."

After the door opened, John directed them down the hall. He turned to the West family, "James is the fourth door down. Aunt Ruth, Uncle Reb is in the second room next to my dad who is in the third."

As Mrs. West walked past the first room, she heard the man call out. She stopped in her tracks, and she turned her head to the right in a jerking motion. She was looking at the door that was only opened about a quarter of the way. She could hear what the man inside was saying.

John placed his hands on Mrs. West's shoulders and whispered to her, "I told you what it might be like when you walked past this room. Please move along and pay him no mind. Please Aunt West, James is waiting."

As Ruth and Brenda walked into Reb's room, everyone in the hall could hear Brenda cry out "Oh, Daddy I love you! I've waited all my life for this moment!"

The Walkers waited in the hall for the Wests to enter James's room. All four of the Walkers could hear the one unidentified survivor calling out. This is what they thought he said, "Mudth-er, me here. I no died, I me hear. Me airey, me Mary. Mother, Aims me elp. Larry me."

Karen then said, "John, who is that poor man and why does he call out so?"

"I don't know, Mom. Dad told us that he has been that way ever since he arrived in the POW camp. Seems he was attracted to Uncle James for no apparent reason."

Then the Walkers saw two nurses enter the room. A moment later, the unidentified survivor became quiet.

Before the Walkers entered the room of their husband and father, John reminded all of them not to expect him to look like he did twenty-five years ago. The Walkers then entered the hospital room of Lieutenant John Fredrick Walker II.

When Karen saw her husband for the first time after all these years, she started crying. Huge tears ran down her face. Taking her husband's hands in hers, she placed a kiss on the lips of the man she had loved with all her heart.

Karen then told her husband, "I love you, John," as she cradled her face on John's shoulder and neck. A thousand thoughts went through her mind. She thought of when she first became aware of John in school, how he fought for the right to sit with her in the school lunchroom, riding their bikes, doing homework together the day at the rope, when John asked her to marry him, which was a situation so very cleverly engineered that John thought it was his idea. She thought about their wedding day and honeymoon in St. Louis and then the birth of their three children. All the lonely days and nights of the last twenty-five years had finally come to an end.

Karen again gave John a kiss on his lips, as she looked into his sunken eyes now filled with tears. When she tried to stand up straight, she found John held on to her. He pleaded, "No Karen, don't leave me. Oh honey, please don't leave me. I have waited so long for this day. I don't ever want to be apart from you ever again!"

"John, I won't ever leave you. I too have waited so long for this day. But you have a son who wants to see you." As Karen looked at Paddy, she said, "Paddy, this is your father."

With trembling hands, Paddy took hold of his father's hands. Placing a kiss on his father's cheek, he said, "Daddy, I love you. I want you to come home and show me how to throw and catch a baseball. I want you to look at my coloring books and all the letters I have written you over the years. I may no longer be a child, but I want you to know that I never forgot you all those years. I want you to see you were always a part of my life. Oh Dad, I don't ever want to be away from you again!"

When JW spoke, it was in a voice broken by crying. He said, "I guess we have a life time to catch up on," and then asked, "Do I hear someone crying in the hall?"

John Jr. said, "Oh my God, its Kathryn, we forgot her again!"

Karen said, "John fetch your sister while I tell your dad about her!" John left the room to get his sister while his mother informed their father about his daughter, Kathryn.

As John entered the hallway, he looked around. At first he didn't see his sister. Then as John looked down, he could see his sister sitting on the floor. She was sitting with her knees pulled up against her chest. Her arms were around the tops of her legs, and her hands were on her forehead while she cried. John knelt down in front of Kathryn, placed his hands on her shoulders, and spoke to her in a low voice, "Kathryn, that's our father in there and he's waiting to see you."

Kathryn looked at John and replied, "What if he doesn't like me? What if he thinks Mother did something wrong? Oh John, I'm so scared! What if Dad doesn't like me?"

All in the room could hear what was being said in the hall. Before John could say anything else, a gravely voice came from within the room, "John if my daughter Kathryn is out there with you, tell her that her father wants to see her."

John helped his sister to her feet. Kathryn was still trembling and crying even with assistance from her brother John. Kathryn turned and stepped into the room. She stopped at the foot of the bed that contained her father. This was a man she has never seen except in pictures. She remembered that her grandparents had always told her, "He will know who you are as soon as he lays eyes on you!"

Always trusting what her grandparents and mother told her, she knew now was a test of all her trust and faith. With her head tilted slightly down to hide her tear soaked face, Kathryn spoke, "Father I'm Kathryn, and I'm so scared you won't like me."

When John started to speak, Kathryn tightly closed her eyes expecting the worst. Then to her ears came the following words, "Kathryn, there is not a whisper of doubt in my mind that you are my daughter. Kathryn, please come here, so that I may put my arms around my daughter for the first time."

Kathryn moved quickly to the side of the bed and placing her arms around the man she had waited all her life to meet. The very second she touched her father, it was like the weight of the world was removed from her shoulders. All the times she had wished her father was home and wondered what it would be like to be held by him and to hold him had just been answered.

The rest of the four hours allotted for the primary meeting of the survivors and family members passed quickly. Kathryn rarely lost physical contact with her father. Kathryn, like her mother and brothers, could see her father was showing signs of tiring. Soon a nurse came by and announced it was time for all the visitors to leave.

Kathryn hugged and kissed her father. Her brothers did the same and then Karen hugged and kissed her husband. Ever knowing he was now safe, they still didn't want to leave him. Karen told her husband, "I know we must go for now, but Honey, I don't want to ever be without you ever again for as long as we live."

"Karen, as soon as I'm released from this hospital I will be going home with you and our kids. I hope we will never be separated like this again. When you are walking down the hall, please pay no attention to that person down the hall. I don't know who he is. He came to the POW camp shortly before we escaped. He calls out like he does but none of us understand why."

As Karen and her children entered the hall, Mrs. West met them. They all walked together down towards the elevators. The man in the first room had been quiet for some time.

As Mrs. West came close to the door of the first room, she took a quick glance at the door and then walked on by. The door was only opened about a quarter of the way. Anyone the man inside could see walking by would be for the briefest of time.

As soon as Mrs. West passed in front of the narrowly opened door, the man inside started calling out again, "Me arry, I not died. Amma, momer, I me arry."

The group had reached the elevators and entered. As the doors to the elevators started to close, Mrs. West reached over and pushed the button to reopen the doors. She then stepped out. John stepped out with her and said," Aunt Mary, what's wrong?"

Mrs. West started walking towards the room where the man was calling out. John placed his hand on Mrs. West's shoulder while stepping in front of her. John then said, "Aunt Mary, please don't go in there. Please let's get back on the elevator."

Mrs. West looked at John with a look that John had never seen from her before. The man in the first room was still calling out. Mrs. West then told John, "That's my son, Jerry, in there. And I haven't seen him in about thirty-two years."

John replied, "Jerry? I thought Uncle James was your oldest son!" John turned to his mother and in a voice full of concern asked, "What should I do?"

Karen asked, "Mary Ann, after all these years, how can you be so sure?"

Mrs. West responded, "Because I'm his mother." She then stepped in front of the door and pushed it open. The man inside calmed down. Mrs. West entered the room, and the other family members followed her. Two nurses entered just behind them.

The man was strapped to his bed but clearly never took his eyes off of Mrs. West. She moved over to him and had just put her hands on the man when James entered the room. The man made eye contact with James as he entered the room. Then the man in a very clear voice said something, which shook James to his very core, "James, I'm Jerry your brother."

JW and Reb entered the room after hearing all the commotion. They were totally surprised to say the least, when they were told who the man was. James untied his brother's hands. Then he gave his brother a hug and told him, "I'm so sorry, Jerry, I didn't know."

Mrs. West put her arms around her oldest son and cried uncontrollably. The rest of the group stared in amazement and joy. This is how two military officers found them a short time later. One of the officers was carrying a small folder in his hand. He said, "This is the proof of identity. However, I think he's already been identified from the looks of things!" Everyone responded with nods and smiles through their tears.

A doctor entered the room and the officer handed the folder to him. The two officers then left. The doctor told the two nurses that they could leave but the others could stay for a while to visit. With a smile on his face, he reminded them, "Please keep in mind the patients need to get some rest."

James asked the doctor, "Can my brother and I be placed in the same room?"

The doctor replied, "I will have that taken care of right away."

About two hours later, the family members left for the hotel. Mrs. West was in the height of her glory and couldn't wait to get to the hotel and call her other children with the good news about their oldest brother.

EPILOGUE:

PAUL A. RED BEAR   (SGT. U.S.M.C.)

After being in the hospital all this time and no one had came to see him, Paul became depressed. Other survivors' families had arrived and had been visiting for the last two days. Paul wondered why his mother and father had not arrived with the others. Had his government again forgotten an American Indian? Then through the door walked an officer dressed in a United States Marine Corp uniform. Although Paul's vision still was not what it used to be, it was getting better by the day.

As the man stepped closer, Paul could tell he was not only a Marine, but also a general at that. As Paul ran a million thoughts through his mind as to whom this might be, the one thought came to him, a thought that was so well ingrained, even Paul was surprised it took so long for him to come up with it. He was not just a marine. He was a lifetime member of a very elite brotherhood. It was the best brotherhood of all. It was the band of brothers called the United States Marine Corps. When all else failed, a fellow marine would always come to your aid!

Paul tried to sit up and salute this general. As this big marine placed his arms around Paul, Paul realized this was one of his best non-Indian friends. It was Sergeant Galvan, now General Galvan. Paul felt his spirit and soul soar higher than it had in many years.

Paul had tears in his eyes, as he held onto his friend. Somewhere deep inside, Paul was afraid to turn loose of this man. He was afraid if he released him and opened his eyes, this might all have been a dream. It was a dream he didn't want to lose or ever wakeup from. Paul said this to his friend, in a low voice.

General Galvan whispered in his ear, "Be not afraid my friend, this is not a dream. You are safe and in a military hospital in Pearl Harbor."

Paul asked, "Where are my mother and father? Why have they not arrived? With all I've been through, with all I've done for my country why is the American Indian the one who is forsaken and forgotten by the very government I've pledged to defend?"

"Paul, it's my understanding the FBI agents have tried to locate your parents! It seems FBI agents aren't trusted really well by the people of your tribe. We know they're alive and well, but they're just hard to locate. I assure you that the government is doing what it can to locate and get them here as quickly as possible!

As Paul started to reiterate about how the American Indian has been forsaken, the sound of a language Paul hadn't heard in so very long arrived in Paul's ears. The general could see a great change come over his friend. The look on his face changed, and there was a change of sensation within his body, as the sound of this language came to the general's ears as well. The sound of this language became louder and louder. It was hard to tell how many were speaking, but for sure, there was more than one speaking this strange language.

As General Galvan stood up, the door of the hospital room swung open widely. Standing in the doorway was a seemingly very old and round woman with long gray hair, braided on both sides. An old and slightly taller man aided her. Four obviously younger people, two women and two men, followed the two of them. Almost simultaneously, the older couple spoke calling out a name in the Cheyenne language that General Galvan couldn't understand.

Paul rose up while speaking the Cheyenne language. General Galvan barely had time to move out of the way, as this older woman rushed in and put her arms around Paul. Without asking or being told, General Galvan understood who these people were. He quietly slipped out of the room.

After two weeks all the survivors were released to return home with their family members. The old PT boat was recovered by the U S navy and placed in a museum. The museum was located four blocks from the Royal Hawaiian Hotel.